Last True Hero

ALSO BY DIANA GARDIN

The Nelson Island Series

Falling Deep
Ever Always (novella)
Wanting Forever

Last True Hero

Honor & Valor

DIANA GARDIN

FOREVER
YOURS

New York

Forever Yours
Hachette Book Group
1290 Avenue of the Americas
New York, NY 10104

www.HachetteBookGroup.com

First edition: November 2015

Forever Yours is an imprint of Grand Central Publishing.

The Forever Yours name and logo are trademarks of Hachette Book Group, Inc.

The Hachette Speakers Bureau provides a wide range of authors for speaking events. To find out more, go to www.hachettespeakersbureau.com or call (866) 376-6591.

The publisher is not responsible for websites (or their content) that are not owned by the publisher.

ISBN 978-1-4555-9470-2 (pbk.)

For Carrington and Raleigh: Mommies are supposed to be the heroes. But instead, I was given two little heroes who inspire me every single day. I love you to pieces.

Acknowledgments

Thank you to my Lord and Savior first and foremost. I am so blessed to be able to do this wonderful thing called a writing career, and it's through You that I can.

To my superman, Tyson. Thank you for showing me what true love is. It's because of you that I can write love stories.

To my busy bees, Carrington and Raleigh. Thank you for being patient with Mommy when I am just letting you run around like maniacs while I type away on this computer. You're always in my thoughts, and I do it all for you.

To my mama, Inez. Thank you so much for passing on your love of books. It meant everything.

To my crew, the Fab Five: Crystal, Emilee, Beth, Christy, and Maria. Without you hot mamas and our girls' nights, our girls' trips, and our group texts, I would go stark raving mad. I'm infinitely blessed to have you in my life, and I hope Dare keeps your hubbies happy for a while! Love and kisses, Kitty.

To my BFF of the South, Natalee, you are truly one of my favorite people on this planet. Thank you so much for being the first one in line to buy each and every book, and for your unwavering love and support. With each new hero I write, I can't wait to see what you'll think of him. I heart you.

To Stacey Donaghy. What a lucky day it was when you agreed to be my agent. I'm still not sure how it happened, but I'm so thankful it did! Your hard work and positive words, especially about this book, are incomparable. I would not want to navigate this publishing world without you, because what I've learned with you by my side can't be traded. Every time I write something new, I can't wait until you read it, because you're my biggest cheerleader. Thank you!

To my editor, Dana. Thank you for falling in love with Dare and Berkeley! Your input is awesome, and I can already tell this will be a wonderful relationship.

To my Forever publicist, Fareeda. Thanks for helping to get the word out about my books. You are an excellent guide through this process, and your quick responses feed my type A complexes. Thank you!

To the entire team at Grand Central Publishing's Forever Romance. You all work so hard, and it makes me look good. I can't thank you enough for your exceptional diligence on each one of my books.

To Autumn Hull, I'm still so thankful I reached out to you to help market *Ever Always*. Our relationship is growing and changing, and because of your attentiveness and industry knowledge I'm reaching even more readers with *Last True Hero*. Thank you for all you do behind the scenes! I wouldn't trade you for the world now that I've found you.

To the authors who read *Last True Hero* first: Rachel van Dyken, Chelsea Fine, Lia Riley, and Megan Erickson. I look up to all of you ladies so much, and I'm honored that you read my little story. Thank you for your support and loving words! You all rock the Romance world, and I'm lucky to have you on my side.

To the CPs who helped me perfect Dare and Berkeley's story: Kate L. Mary and Jamie Shaw. You guys helped me turn this couple into what they are today, and your input was invaluable. Thank you for being amazing!

To my warm and fuzzy writing group, the NAC. Kate, Ara, Marie, Sribindu, Meredith, Jamie, Jessica, Sophia, Marnie, Missy, Laura, and Amanda. I found you guys when I was already well into this biz, and now I don't know what I ever did without you. I wouldn't trade any of you, and I can't wait for the day when we can all have dinner together. See you in Vegas? Remember, I would cut a bitch for any one of you.

To the bloggers and readers who find this book: *thank you*. Thank you so much for reading, purchasing, reviewing, and spreading the word about the Battle Scars series. Without you, what would I be? You make all of this possible, and I want to hear from each and every one of you soon!

Last True Hero

Being alone was something I had always excelled at. As a kid, I kept to myself from the time I started school. I noticed how the other kids seemed to crave company, how they sought out a pack of friends to roll through life with. That wasn't me; I never needed anyone. Or anything. As I grew up, that feeling of everything being better if I didn't have to share it followed me wherever I went. I got strong, and smart, and completely self-sufficient. That was the way I liked it.

That was the way it had always been.

Then, one day, I met the pin in the grenade that blew my entire world apart.

And she obliterated my desire for a simple, solitary life. She destroyed my existence, as I knew it.

I was slain by her; where years in the army had failed to demolish my lone spirit, she blew it to smithereens. She owns me.

And I will walk through fire to protect her.

1

Dare

Welcome to Lone Sands, North Carolina. Where lonely hearts find a home in the sun and the sand.

Seriously? This postage-stamp-size town off the coast thinks that their best feature is that it's full of lonely people?

This is probably the point when I should turn around, drive pell-mell in the opposite direction of Lone Sands. But I don't. I keep plugging. The love of my life, my Ford F-250, has made it this far from Fort Benning. I'm tired of driving, tired of pulling through fast-food drive-throughs. I just want to stop.

I just want to live.

That sounds so simple, just live. But how am I supposed to do that, now? I have no idea what the hell I'm supposed to do with my life from this point forward.

But according to my buddy Drake, this quiet little town is the place to be if you're looking for some peace and quiet after the army sends you packing.

I observe as I drive. That's something I've always been good at. Observing. Reading people. Taking mental notes.

Each new road I turn on is picturesque, dusted with sand. Charming shops and restaurants in bright colors adorn the quaint little streets. The ocean is visible sometimes when I glance down a side street, shining and winking with the afternoon sunlight. Cottages are scattered in clusters, tall sea grass intermixed with small dunes for yards.

I'm going to be living in a town that doubles as the cover of some damn girly book.

When I pull up to the address I'd put in my GPS back in Georgia, Drake strides out of the unpretentious bungalow. The front garden beds are alive with the leafy fronds of palm bushes, waving at me as if in welcome.

"Man, you made it!" Drake is pulling open my truck door and dragging me onto my feet. He proceeds to squeeze me in a bear hug so tight I think a few of my ribs are left cracked in his wake.

"Yeah." I rub my sides as he releases me, wincing. "I made it."

He's already standing beside the extended truck bed, reaching to grab my suitcase, pulling it up and out. "This all you brought?"

"That's all I've got."

Drake nods his blocky, shaved head. It sits atop his neck like a boulder perched on a stump. Every inch of him is like that: big and steady. The dude is as solid as a mountain.

He disappears through the heavy oak front door, and then pokes his head back outside to peer at me. "Get in here!"

When I enter, I look around, my eyes drinking in the living room. Whistling, I nod my head in appreciation. "This is nice, Drake. Real nice."

The floors are some sort of dark hardwood, and although the living area we've just entered is a little tight, the ceilings are high and decorated with exposed beams. The fireplace takes up the entire far wall, made of some kind of natural stone that makes me stupid with envy. I walk over and reach out a hand, feeling the rough texture beneath my fingers.

"This is amazing."

"Yeah." Drake shrugs. "I knew that would speak to you. I worked on all of this myself. Place was a wreck when I bought it. But I can see the water from here, and I wanted the beach in walking distance. It was worth it to fix this old dump up."

I can tell from the loving way he talks about his house that he doesn't really think it's a dump. Whatever the opposite of a dump is, that's how my friend feels about this house.

"You did good, man. It's beautiful."

He grins his trademark, full-on cheesefest of a grin. "Thanks. Let me show you your room."

The house has two bedrooms; Drake leads the way to the smaller of the two and sets my bag down on a queen-size bed. The room is sparse: a bed, a dresser, and an en suite bathroom off to one side. But the ceilings are high here, too, and there's a sliding glass door that leads out to the sand beyond.

"Drake," I begin. "I don't know how to thank you for this."

He shakes his head and lifts a hand, cutting me off. "Don't. We're brothers. Maybe we don't have the same blood running through our veins, but you'll always be my family, Dare. I look out for my own. And I know what it's like when you first get out. You'll come work with me at the garage tomorrow, and we'll take it from there. You hungry?"

I nod, gratitude filling my chest. The feeling steals my words away; all I can do is nod. "Starving."

"Let's go to a little place I know. Crab legs and shrimp. We can eat till we're stuffed, drink a few, and then come home and crash. Sound like a night?"

"Sounds like the best damn night I've had in a while."

He grins ear to ear and slaps me on the back so hard I'm forced to take a lurching step forward.

A few minutes later, we are rocketing down the town's main drag and my long legs feel like they're wrapped in a burrito.

"I'm used to more legroom than this," I groan. "How do you drive this thing? Your ass is like five hundred pounds bigger than I am."

Drake cuts his eyes at me. "Don't. Talk. Shit. About. The. Challenger."

I roll my eyes so hard my forehead aches. Drake's always had a thing for fast cars, especially if they're packing extra heat under the hood. "Next time, we take the truck." My gorgeous, black, four-door, extended-cab, extended-bed demon.

We pull up in front of the restaurant, and I just sit in the car and study it a moment while Drake lugs himself out of the driver's seat. It's tiny, like everything else seems to be in Lone Sands. It's definitely a hole in the wall, with its gravel parking lot and creaky old sign hanging on rusty chains above the door. Written on it is the name of the place, SEE FOOD.

"Clever," I mutter as I exit the Challenger. Drake's breath hitches as my belt buckle scratches against the side of the car. I wince, checking the dark gray paint to make sure it's intact.

"My bad." I shoot him a chagrined smile. "All good."

When we're seated at a tiny booth inside the restaurant, I've already changed my mind about the sketchy vibes I was getting on the outside. In here, it smells like coastal heaven. My mouth is watering as I gaze hungrily at the menu, and I'm ignoring Drake completely, which is okay because he's ignoring me, too.

"What can I get for you boys today?"

I keep staring at the menu while Drake begins rattling off his food order for the waitress. I can imagine her eyes growing rounder and larger as he keeps going, because Drake normally eats enough for three men. Finally, I zero in on what I want and glance up at her to relay my wishes.

Now is a good time to point this out: I've been in the army for seven years. I've lived all over the United States. I've traveled plenty outside of it, too. I'm not a saint; I've met women all over the place that made my time in their native lands worthwhile. I'm only a man, and I've always enjoyed a woman's company.

But I've never in my twenty-five years seen a woman like *this*.

At first, as I stare, I'm not sure what exactly it is that sets her worlds apart. Her face is gorgeous, yeah. It's the kind of face that keeps men alive in a desert far, far away. The warm, whiskey-colored eyes that pierce me straight through my heart are Disney-princess big, and when she blinks something in my chest explodes. Or maybe it's her hair. All those light-colored curls piled high on top of her head, one wavy tendril hanging into her eyes.

Damn. I physically have to restrain my hand from reaching up to brush it away.

But it can't be any of those things, can it? I'm no stranger to meeting beautiful women in all shapes and sizes.

Maybe it's her body. Which, even covered up in a tight restaurant

T-shirt and short-enough-to-peek denim cutoffs, is luring me dangerously closer to those legs that seem to go on for days.

Fucking. Days.

But, as I continue to embarrass myself because I can't pull my eyes away and force my mouth to work, I realize it's her total aloofness that has me salivating at the mouth. She could give two shits about who I am or what I've done. She's barely even looking at me. Wait, she really *isn't* looking at me. She's looking at a spot just above my left ear.

So, I'll make her look at me. I clear my throat and ask, "What's good here?"

Finally, *finally*, her gaze slides to mine, and whatever exploded in my chest earlier detonates once again, only about a million times harder.

"Everything's good here," she replies. Her tone is cool and cautious, as if she thinks I'm hitting on her. Huh. That must happen a lot.

"Okay." I shoot her what I hope is a winning smile. "Then get me one of everything."

Her mouth drops open slightly, and I enjoy watching her tongue play across her top teeth. "What?"

My grin grows as wide as one of Drake's kooky ones. "Just give me whatever you usually eat. I'm sure I'll love it."

She frowns, and a tiny crease forms in the center of her forehead that draws something inside of me up, out, and into the open. Looking at her is causing me to feel too exposed, too out in the open and unprotected. I glance back down at my menu, but the smile doesn't fade from my face.

"All right," she finally says. "I'll bring you a few of my favorites. But don't blame me if you hate them."

Her voice is a little haughty, and so soft and feminine that an extra surge of testosterone races through me. All those hormones centered in one particular place in my body, and I shift in my seat as I feel my jeans shrinking.

When I look up again, she's gone. But Drake is now staring openly in my direction, his grin as wide as I've ever seen it.

"You just fell in love a little bit, didn't you?"

"Shut the hell up."

He laughs. "I don't blame you. She's definitely hot."

"I don't want to talk about it."

"Okay, Romeo, we won't. I just want to watch you make an idiot of yourself for the rest of the night."

I'm halfway through my second bottle of Killian's when she returns, laden down with two trays of food. She sets them down on the table opposite us, and I watch closely as she first lays three platters in front of Drake.

"Thanks, sweetheart." His whole face lights up with his trademark smile, and it appears it's contagious, because she smiles right back at him.

When I see it, I suck in a breath and bite down hard on my tongue.

She has *dimples*.

"You're so welcome," she answers.

I like the slight twang in her tone. I like it a whole damn lot.

"And for *you*," she continues, aiming that gaze, the one that stabbed me earlier, in my direction. "I have a little selection."

She rattles off the name of each item as she sets it down: crab cakes, calamari, mushrooms stuffed with succulent lobster meat, and a metal bucket of buttered corn on the cob.

I'm still starving, and somehow the fact that this food is brought to me by someone who looks like her is making me so much hungrier.

"Thank you. You have amazing taste. Everything looks delicious."
Including you.

"It will be," she assures me, leveling her gaze at mine for another second. When she turns away, she leaves the sweet scent of roses in her wake. I inhale deeply, receiving the blend of seafood and flowers and mentally adding the mixture to the list of things I can't resist.

"Y'all let me know if you need anything else." She flounces away.

"So." Drake begins tentatively, and I know I'm not going to like the turn our conversation is about to take.

I stuff my mouth full of lobster-infused mushrooms and have to close my eyes because they taste fucking incredible.

"Your physical therapy is done, right?"

Drake doesn't waste time; he gets directly to the point. It's one of the reasons he's one of few friends I have in civilian life. I hate bullshit.

"Yeah. It's done, Drake. I'm clear."

"But you weren't cleared for duty. So how much are you going to be able to handle in the shop? I'm serious, dude. I don't want you getting hurt on my watch."

"I'm a grown-ass man, Drake, and an ex-Army Ranger. I can handle getting under some cars and getting shit done. You don't have to worry about me."

Drake continues to chew a mouthful of food while he studies me, and then washes it down with a gulp from his own bottle of beer.

"I know you're tough. But you've gone through a lot, Dare. I wouldn't blame you if you just wanted to take it easy for a while."

"I live at the beach now, right? I *am* taking it easy. But I'm going to earn my keep. Conversation over?"

He nods, not taking his eyes off of me. "Roger that."

I nod, allowing my eyes to wander around the restaurant. I spot Legs over by the computer on the back wall, checking her cell phone. I keep track of her as she busies herself with bringing food and refills to her tables. Other than ours, she has only two others. I've arrived in Lone Sands in April, a good month before the tourists will surge in, searching for summer fun.

Finally, she returns to us, holding our check.

"How was it?" she asks me. The wariness in her voice bothers me. She doesn't seem as cautious with Drake, and I want to know why.

"Drake," I say suddenly. "It's on me tonight. Want to head out to the Challenger while I finish up?"

Chucking, he salutes and heaves himself out of the booth. "Yes, Sergeant."

The waitress—how do I not yet know her name?—glances sharply at him as he speaks, and then aims her steadfast gaze at me while I take the check gently from her fingers.

"Berkeley," I read aloud. Damn, even her name strikes an image of perfect beauty.

"That's me. Did you like everything?" She's asking me as if she doesn't *want* to ask, but she *needs* to know.

"Best meal I've had in a long time," I answer honestly. "Thank you for that."

"I didn't cook it." She finally reaches up to pull that curly tendril off her face. My fingers curl on the table in response.

"I know that. But you chose it. I appreciate that."

She nods. "Anything else?"

"Yes." She waits, and I toy with my empty beer bottle as I talk myself into what I'm about to do. "I'm new in town, and—"

"No."

"What?" I haven't even asked her yet, so I'm more than a little confused about her refusal.

"No. I'm not going out with you."

"I haven't even asked you yet!" I know my mouth is agape, but I'm unable to force it closed. This is new territory for me. I'm drowning in uncertainty.

"Doesn't matter. I get a lot of guys like you in here. Can you understand that? I don't date customers."

I begin to nod. She takes the crisp bill hanging out of my outstretched hand. "Especially not *military* customers."

She walks away quickly before I can tell her to keep the change, disappearing behind a door leading to the kitchen and the back of the restaurant.

I let my head fall back against the booth, muttering a curse and closing my eyes. Somehow, that had gone so much more smoothly in my mind. Not that I'd thought it through well enough.

"Idiot," I whisper as I slide out of the booth and head for the door with my proverbial tail between my legs.

Lone Sands, 1. Dare Conners, 0.

2

Berkeley

The last two weeks of my college career fly by in a whirlwind of final exams, tearful exchanges with friends, and extra-special pressure from my parents to "get serious" with Grisham.

That would be Grisham Abbot, the man, according to my parents, I'm going to marry.

Grisham, quite honestly, is a great guy. He's the son of a navy admiral, a man who serves just under my father at the base he commands. Grisham's father and mine go way back to their days at the Naval Academy, where they both emerged as officers. Both men met their wives shortly thereafter, and the four of them have been an unstoppable team ever since. It's only natural, at least in their minds, that Grisham and I live happily ever after as a product of their lifelong friendship.

But Grisham's just not *my* guy. He just graduated from the Naval Academy, exactly like our fathers. I don't want to marry a younger version of my dad. I don't want to become the new and improved carbon copy of my mom. That's so not the life I've planned for myself.

What kind of life do I have planned for myself?

Ain't that the question of the century?

I have no clue. Trained chimps have a better grasp on their future than I do. I graduated with a major in interior design. My mother thinks that's perfect, because I'm going to be planning and designing navy events for the rest of my life. Sigh.

My welcome home begins with a bang.

My parents have thrown me a graduation extravaganza. Because my mother can't just call it a party. That would be ludicrous.

It's also, in a sense, my "coming out" party with Grisham. My reflection in the full-length mirror in my bedroom at my parents' house mocks me. The girl staring back at me looks as though she was made for this life. She was made to belong to affluent parents, her father one of the most powerful men in the United States military. Her mother is a flawless version of herself, always on top of her game, always the picture of class and authority. The girl staring back at me looks like she belongs on the arm of a handsome, clean-cut man of privilege who will work his way quickly through the ranks of the navy.

But inside that girl, another is fighting to claw her way to the surface. The real me, just waiting for a chance to spread her wings. The me who loves to run around in funny T-shirts and cutoffs. The me who spends hours in her room drawing beautiful spaces and painting canvases to hang on the walls inside of them. The me who is most at home in a seafood restaurant with old wooden floors and down-to-earth people who love me for me. Not for the future me who will make them proud, just the me I already am.

I leave the room, shutting the door a little too loudly behind me, and crash directly into my mother.

"Honey," she coos. "You look beautiful. Here, let me fix your hair. This piece is falling down again. I wish you'd grow out these layers. And flatiron it. It really would become you so much better."

I puff my lips out and blow, allowing the strand of hair in question to flutter flippantly around my face. "Better?"

She frowns, an expression her face doesn't handle very well due to the monthly Botox injections.

"Don't be smart. Get downstairs. Grisham's been waiting on you for thirty minutes, at least."

"Grish knows me well enough to know he could be waiting all night."

My mother's eyes roll skyward and I can almost hear her counting to ten.

I hold up my hands in surrender. "All right, Momma. I'm going."

The pins holding my hair up are already giving me a headache as I reach the bottom of our grand dual staircase, but I plaster a giant, fake smile on my face and begin to greet guests as they hover near me. Just dying to offer me their sincere congratulations on my completion of four years in college.

The University of North Carolina at Wilmington wasn't at all where my parents envisioned me earning my four-year degree. Since I was born a daughter and not a son, a military academy was out of the question. At least for my father. But they just knew I'd be headed to an Ivy League school after I graduated high school in Brunswick County, North Carolina. The last place my father was stationed when he earned admiral quickly became my home. Even though I've lived in many places before this town, I feel like I belong here. The Carolina coast is in my blood, and leaving it, even for four years, would have completely shattered my heart. So I fought hard, and won.

The faces around me are a blur as I head for the dining room table, which was nearly sagging under the weight of all the food littering the top of it.

"I swear to God, Berk, if you hadn't shown up in the next five minutes I was going to either shoot myself, or just straight-up leave this party and hit the bars."

I whirl around, and the sight of the caramel-brown skin, long, spiraled hair, and chocolate eyes of my friend Mea is so healing that instant tears spring to my eyes. Wiping them away, I slam myself into her arms.

"Mea! Ohmygod, they invited you? There *is* a God!"

"Of course they didn't," she scoffs, cheerful as ever. "I crashed. Just got back into town. I missed you, Berk!"

I just sigh and squeeze her tighter. After high school, Mea and I went to separate colleges, and a friendship with her didn't really fit into my parents' plan, anyway. She comes from blue-collar parents, and our families never ran in the same circles. But we were inseparable as teenagers for a reason. Mea just gets me, and I get her. We know who the other is, and she knows who everyone in my life expects me to be. She doesn't judge, she just loves me unconditionally. The same way I do for her.

"Please tell me you're here to stay." My words are lost in her bare shoulder, and she laughs and pushes me back so that she can look into my eyes.

"You look like you need rescuing. Here, you take this and chug, and I'll keep watch. Do it!"

I grab the silver flask from her hand like a lifeline and let the liquid inside burn my throat. If Mea is going to be in Lone Sands this summer, I can make it.

I will make it.

"Berkeley."

I freeze, but only for a second. Grisham's voice is full of disapproval. But we've known each other for so long, I just don't care. And he knows it. I down about a third of the liquid in the flask before turning around to face him. The grin on Mea's face is so wide, I'm scared that her face is going to crack from the extra pressure.

A not-so-delicate snort escapes me, and I wipe my mouth. Good thing I didn't apply the sensible pink lipstick my mother left on my dresser.

"Grish? You want a sip?"

His thick, blond brow furrows, and I can see the internal battle going on behind his gorgeous, perfectly sculpted features.

Grisham's dirty blond hair is so thick shampoo models everywhere are screaming with jealousy, and it's expertly styled into an array of spikes. His skin is tan and smooth, and his eyes are a green so deep a girl could see the rain forest if she stared into them long enough. There's no denying that his tall, muscular body, the one that helped him earn Navy its first football win over Army in twenty-three years, is every woman's fantasy.

He just isn't *my* fantasy.

But he's my friend, and I love him because he doesn't hold me to the high standard our parents do. I know he wishes things could be different. But he's very aware that they aren't.

"Give me the flask." He sighs after a minute's hesitation.

I grin and hand it over. "Atta boy, Grish."

Grinning at him as he swallows, I chuckle. "Remember the first time we got drunk? We went to Manny Reyes's party sophomore year of high school, and I forced you to play that stupid drinking game with me? We both ended up throwing up in the bushes."

"Uh-huh," he replies with a wry grin. "You were always getting me into trouble." He leans closer and whispers in my ear. "Still are."

"Can we get out of here?" Mea's impatient. She hates being in my parents' house, she always has. I can't blame her. I feel the exact same way.

"Can't." My tone is mournful. "I haven't seen the Admiral yet."

So we stay, and we eat. The three of us stick close together, but each time my mother sends me a death glare fit for the Queen of the Damned, I make a round of my guests. I shake hands and smile, tilt my head and laugh. It's all so empty I'm afraid if I huff out a breath too hard, everything will just blow away. Somehow, hidden in her tank top and short skirt, Mea has managed to sneak *two* tiny flasks of vodka into a party that's only serving champagne.

When the Admiral finally makes his entrance, I'm more than a little tipsy. Mea is flat-out drunk, and Grisham has his large, strong hands full, trying to contain the two of us. His parents are here, and he doesn't want to disappoint them any more than I do mine. Only my back is so hunched from the load of expectations that I'm sinking, and I'm tired of trying to hold it all up.

"Berkeley." The Admiral states my name with a punctuation point at the end. The sound of his voice sends three different emotions coursing through my body all at once: anxiety, exhaustion, and affection.

Affection because I love my father. He's a good dad. He's been my dad in the only way he knew how. He was forceful at times, and gruff at others. He's firm and immovable in his opinions, and the sky-high standards for his only child are probably just as difficult for him to uphold as they are for me.

Anxiety because every time I see my father, I know that something is going to happen that will inevitably take me farther away from where I actually want to be. Like when I came home at Christmas of my sophomore year, I was excitedly bringing brochures for a spring break trip that all of my friends had been planning since the dawn of time. Only my father preempted me, and informed me that I'd be taking a tour of navy bases overseas with him and my mother for the week of spring break instead. It was like he could feel it when I was finally going to do something for myself, and was compelled to drive me off my course and back onto his.

Exhaustion because the person I am around my father is not the person I really am inside. I've been putting on an act with him for as long as I can remember, and the sand in that giant invisible timer is just about out. I can't pretend anymore. And when the real me finally emerges, it's going to either break his heart or flat out kill him.

I don't want to marry the man he's chosen for me. I don't want a life as a navy wife like he always wanted. I want to be free and independent. And I've never had the courage to tell him, or my mother, how I really feel.

As a twenty-two-year-old college graduate, I'm aware that this makes me a giant wuss.

"Admiral," I say just before pulling myself carefully into his embrace. He's in dress whites, of course, and all of his decorations are badged on his uniform proudly for all to see. He should be proud of everything he's accomplished; I understand that. But to a normal person, all that metal glinting on his shoulders is like a warning.

Bright flashing lights that say STAY THE FUCK AWAY FROM ME AND ALL THAT I LOVE.

"Welcome home, sweetheart. Tomorrow we begin planning your future, yes?"

I nod numbly. "Sure."

His eyes zero in on Grisham and he smiles warmly, and then they slide to Mea, and that smile falters slightly. "Grisham, my boy. I've been hearing great things about everything you've accomplished during your time at the academy. You're prepared for your move to San Diego?"

My eyes travel back and forth between the two of them. "San Diego? Grish…you didn't tell me you've been stationed! Congratulations!"

"Got my orders yesterday," he whispered into my ear. "I hadn't had time to talk to you about it yet. Apparently, we've been summoned to brunch with our parents in the morning."

Sunday brunch has always been my mother's *thing*. Even while I was away at college, I was still expected to attend at least once a month. Grisham's family is always there, and our mothers love to *ooo* and *ahh* about how cute we look sitting next to each other at their tables. It irritates the heck out of me.

My father leans closer, eyeing first me, and then Grisham. "No more vodka this evening, understood? You're not in college anymore, Berkeley."

Don't I know it.

My father forgets to greet Mea before my mother pulls him in another direction. I watch him go, my eyes narrowed and the vodka swimming in my veins contributing to the feeling of nausea in my belly.

"Now? Now can we leave?" Mea tugs on my hand.

"Yeah," I mutter. "Now they won't notice I'm gone. Grish, you coming?"

He shakes his head. His mouth turns down on one side in a frown. "If I go, who's going to cover for you?"

I reach up on my tiptoes and wrap my arms around his neck. "You're the best."

He leans into the kiss I plant on his cheek, and the look in his eyes is full of understanding and melancholy. "Be safe. Call me if you want me to come get you."

I don't have time to think about how Mea and I are going to get our drunken asses out to a bar as she pulls me outside into the salty night air. My parents' house is located in the most affluent portion of Lone Sands. They consider this residence their beach house, because my father also occupies admiral's quarters on the base. He stays there most of the time.

The slightly broken look in my mother's eyes when he leaves to go "home" is another reason I have no desire to become a military wife.

There's a car idling at the end of our long driveway, far enough away from the house to be inconspicuous. When Mea opens the door to the backseat, I'm greeted by her brother, Mikah, who is a couple of years younger than us, and one of his friends.

"Hell, yes." Mikah grins over the driver's seat at me as I climb in. "Welcome home, Berk baby."

Mea slams the door behind me and sends me a smug smile as we buckle up.

"Have they been waiting out here the whole time?" I'm already feeling bad for Mikah and his bleary-eyed friend.

"Mikah has been on text alert all night," she answers. "I sent him a message when the Admiral came in."

I nod. "Get me the hell out of here, Mikah."

Chuckling, he takes off, and the large muffler on the little beater he's driving revs loudly. "I'm glad you're home, Berk."

I smile at him. But the jury is still out on whether or not I'm happy about being back in Lone Sands. If it's up to my parents, I won't be staying long.

3

Dare

I slide back underneath the little Honda Civic, feeling more at home than I have in a long time. Since I left the army. There's still a twinge of pain in my back when I bend or lean the wrong way, but it's only enough to remind me that I'm no longer whole enough to serve my country.

I love cars. I love everything about motors, the inner workings of a vehicle. I know most cars inside and out. Working here, at Drake's automotive shop, is satisfying in a way that nothing has been since I was discharged, following the closest months to hell I've ever endured, with a stack of paperwork and a "thank you for your service."

My true passion is for rebuilding cars. Taking something old and mangled, pulling it apart piece by piece, and then lovingly putting it all back together again like a three-dimensional puzzle. But working here at Drake's Automotive is close enough for me, and I'm so thankful to him for the job I want to kiss him right now.

"I wanna kiss you right now, Drake," I announce.

"Please don't," he replies from somewhere close by. "I don't swing that way, and you know it."

"Save it for later?"

"No."

The large glass garage door next to me opens, signaling that one of Drake's two other employees is bringing in another car to be serviced. I glance over, and all I can see is shiny, high-quality tires. Big ones. Must be a truck or an SUV. The owner might be talking my language.

I slide out from under the Civic and raise an eyebrow at Will, the twenty-year-old kid learning the ropes around here.

"Escalade. Nice."

He nods. "That's what I said. Custom interior, too. The girl who brought it…" He whistles. "I'd kill to rework her motor. You know?"

I smile wryly. The kid has some work to do where the ladies are concerned. "I know. What's she need done?"

"Just an oil change."

I glance at the wall of glass separating our work area from the waiting room, and I'm floored.

I haven't seen her since the first night I arrived in town. See Food. I've actually been in there a couple of times a week since, just hoping to catch a glimpse of her again. I figured she just didn't work there anymore, or I was very unlucky.

But my luck has obviously changed, because here she is. Standing in Drake's shop. Her heart-stopping side profile is exposed to me as she stares at the mounted television. Her long, tan legs are visible again, covered only by tiny, white shorts. God, those legs. They go on for days, weeks, months.

Years.

A peek of her flat belly is visible beneath a short, loose-fitting pink tank top with the words LIVING FOR SUMMER written across her perfect, perky breasts.

Her curly hair is free and wild, the honey-blond strands in beautiful, sexy-as-fuck disarray around her shoulders.

I know my mouth is hanging open, but I can't manage to get my wits about me long enough to pull it closed. This girl did something to me the first night I saw her, and seeing her here in my own element is doing it again.

Fuck. She's perfect.

I glance down at myself, and groan. I'm filthy, my coveralls are smattered with oil and grime. I look like…well, I look like a damn auto mechanic. I've struggled a lot in my life with feeling inferior. Growing up in the system will do that to a kid. Joining the army and working my way up to Ranger and sergeant helped that tendency a lot, but it still comes back in flashes in situations like this one. The girl is drop-dead gorgeous, but hell, the first time I saw her at See Food I thought she *needed* to work. She was waiting tables at a seafood restaurant by the beach, for shit's sake.

But now she rolls into the shop in a custom black Escalade, and she looks like she just walked out of an American Apparel ad.

My inferiority complex is definitely rearing its ugly head.

A chuckle beside me snaps me out of my inner rant, and I glance over to see Will standing there with his arms crossed, staring at me with a stupid smirk on his face.

"See. Told you."

"Yeah, yeah. Get out of my face." I wipe my hands on a rag and look across the room to where Drake is standing at the garage door. He's grinning so hugely I know he's landed a look at Berkeley, too.

Berkeley. I want to know her.

I decide. Right then and there, inferiority complex or not, that I'm going to. Know her, that is.

I sure as hell hope she's on board with that.

I roll myself under her car and get to work. It's obvious she's had her oil changed like clockwork, and none of her other fluids are low. The vehicle is in perfect working order. I wonder if she's the one who keeps it that way. Or if maybe her father brings it in for her.

Or…her boyfriend.

That thought has my face burning with angry heat. More than anything in the entire world right now, I don't want her to have a boyfriend. I don't want to be cut off from this mission before it's even begun.

When I roll out again, I smooth my longish dark hair down to make sure it's not sticking up, and I run a clean rag over my face and neck. I clean my hands meticulously, but I know there's nothing I can do about my coveralls. I send up a silent prayer, and shoot Drake a nod. He looks back at me with a knowing gleam in his eyes, and salutes me.

When I open the glass doors, those deep, liquid-amber eyes set so deep in her face find me, and I'm lost.

Like I said, my mission is set. No aborts, no retreats. This is do or die.

I walk over to the counter and begin typing up her receipt. I haven't found any words yet, and I decide to wait and see what she'll do.

She walks slowly over to the counter, her eyes never leaving me as she moves. When she arrives, she sets both elbows on top and leans forward. I will my eyes to meet her gaze, and swear I will scratch them out if they dare to glance down to the cleavage I'm sure is revealing itself from the top of her shirt.

"Hey." That slow drawl is going to get me every time, I know that already.

"Hey," I reply. I hope my cool attitude is coming across, and that the sweat beginning to dampen my hands isn't also affecting my brow.

"I know you." Her tone is casual, but not as cautious as the first night I saw her. Is that curiosity ringing through?

I'm going to take that as a good sign.

"I know you, too, Berkeley."

She draws back, surprise crossing her face. "You remember my name."

"I do. Couldn't forget it. Not with a face like yours."

She smiles, as if she can't help herself. Thank God I found my charm somewhere among the bag of nerves opening up in my insides.

"Well, you can't hold it against me that I don't know yours. You never told me."

"Huh," I say as I thoughtfully scratch my rough chin. "If I recall correctly, I didn't have a chance to tell you my name. I believe you wrote me off as army trash on sight, and asked me never to disgrace you with my presence again."

She gasps. "I did *not!* I would never do that…"

When she trails off, I shoot her a grin. "Didn't you?"

The tiny wrinkles are back in her forehead, and my lips practically twitch with an unexplainable need to allow them to meet her skin. I finally let my eyes leave her face, and rake them across her body as quickly as I can so as not to appear like a sleaze. Which I might be, because every inch of her just calls out to me like a siren. She's invit-ing, she emanates warmth and sultriness, and my nerves are standing at attention just being this close to her.

"Okay, maybe I did." Her admission of guilt comes complete with one corner of her plump bottom lip being pulled into her mouth. I think I manage to contain the groan that forms in my chest.

I think.

I suck in a breath and refocus on her eyes. "What do you have against guys in the military, Berkeley?"

I use her name because it feels fucking delicious in my mouth.

She studies me and there is a question in her eyes. I want her to ask it. Badly.

"I don't have anything against guys in the military. My dad…"

Her hesitation fuels my curiosity. "Your dad…what?"

Suddenly, she changes the subject. "What's the damage on my car, uh…"

"Dare. I'm Dare." I tell her the total while I wait for her to com-ment on my name.

She doesn't.

She hands me her card, and I scan it before I run it. I stare at her face as I wait for the receipt to print, memorizing each minute de-tail. Sprinkle of light freckles on the bridge of her nose. Lashes long enough to brush her cheeks. Natural-looking makeup, not pasted on like a lot of other girls our age. Her eyes seem darker at this distance, the most satiny brown I can imagine, and it is such a contrast with her hair color that I can't pull my gaze away.

"Thank you, Dare."

Fuck me. I want her to say it again. And again.

And again.

"You're welcome Ms. Holtz. You seem like you keep a good regular upkeep on your vehicle. Keep that up. The sticker on your windshield will tell you when you're due back."

She nods, and turns and heads for the door. Before she reaches it, she whirls around.

"Will I see you back at See Food?"

"I've been at that restaurant a few times a week for the past three weeks. Do you still work there?"

Her dimples deepen in her cheeks as she smiles, and my heart flutters.

Yeah. Like a bitch, my heart flutters.

"I do. Were you looking for me?"

"Maybe." I shrug.

"Well, if you were, keep looking. You might just get what you came for. I finished my senior year of college last week. Back home in Lone Sands...until."

"Until?"

She walks back toward the door.

"Just until," she tosses over her shoulder on her way out.

And then, she's gone.

I hope to hell she's telling me the truth about going back to work at See Food. Because I'm about to buy stock in the place.

My body is cold and clammy, a thin sheen of sweat covering every inch of me as I wrestle ferociously with my bedsheets. When my wild thrashing finally wakes me out of the shitty excuse for sleep, I discover I've been shouting. Drake is standing over me, his voice cool and placid as he instructs me to calm down. He tells me that I'm home, I'm not *there*, and I'm safe.

I'm safe. I'm safe...

My hair sticks to the back of my slick neck. I've been here so long it's grown longer than the army standard. I slap at it as I hustle in the darkness.

The subtropical African climate fucks with my head, my body. I'm a Ranger, so I've been trained to fight in all climates, but I've been here too long. My hamstring convulses in a heat cramp, and I clutch it as I go down.

Crawling, flies buzz around my face in the long savanna grass, and I'm thankful for the camouflage, even if I have no way of knowing what else hides in these grasses.

My head snaps up, whips around. My night vision goggles are long gone, just like my battalion. My breath catches, and my stomach heaves as I think of them. God, *help me. Their voices are getting closer, my escape has been broadcast across the radios, and if they find me, they'll kill me. I gotta move.*

Army crawl is how I travel the mile between the jungle camp where I've been kept and the village nearby. I don't want to bring the hell I've been experiencing to the innocent people in the village, but I have to get out of here.

The blood cakes my elbows as the sun rises behind me, a brilliant burst of color and light that I can't believe exists in a place like this. At one point, I thought I'd never see the sunrise again. Tears cover the cheeks I'm sure are the same color as the mud covering my ripped fatigues, and I can see the first hut of the village not far in front of me.

I made it. I'm safe...I'm safe...

And then I lose consciousness.

I start back to complete consciousness and focus on Drake's huge form standing beside me.

Gasping for air, I raise both hands to my head. My hair is sticking to the back of my neck just like it did back then, but as I take in my surroundings I can see that I'm not there. I'm not in that jungle anymore. That was months ago, although sometimes it seems like it couldn't have really happened in this lifetime.

"Shit," I mutter. "I did it again?"

Drake nods. "You talk to anyone about this PTSD?"

I nod. "Yeah. Did some therapy after I got back. Didn't stop the dreams. Fucking jungle creeps in at night, only at night."

Nodding again, Drake thumps me on the back. "I'm here, man. If you want to talk about it…I'm here. I still feel all kinds of guilt that I got out before…before it happened. I should have been with you."

I shake my head, looking him full on in the eyes. "No, you shouldn't. You might have died like the rest of them. You're here for me now. Now get the hell outta here. I'm gonna try to get a little more sleep."

One side of his mouth turns up, nowhere near his normal grin, and nods again. "See you in the morning."

I lay in the dark, just staring up at my ceiling, trying as hard as I can to claw my way back from the memories. I pull a pillow into my chest, clutching it as tightly as I can. I want to scream into it, but I don't want Drake to have to come running back to my rescue.

I save myself. I always have.

These nightmares will not break me.

My thoughts are just turning to wild, straw-colored curls and a goddess's face when my phone jangles on the nightstand.

I check the screen; a Florida number.

"Hello?"

Chase's voice is strained. "Dare."

I sigh. I've known Chase since we were eleven and living in the same foster home. Other than Drake, he's the closest thing I will ever have to a real brother.

"What's wrong, Chase?" I'm instantly alert and wary.

Trouble has a way of finding Chase, and Chase has a way of finding me to help get him out of it.

"Look, Dare, I swear to God I'll pay you back. I need a little green to pay back these dudes I got in with. If I don't pay 'em...I gotta pay 'em. You got me?"

An angry, frustrated growl leaves me as I stare at my phone. I want to hurl it across the room, but again, Drake.

"You've gotta be fucking kidding me, Chase! I can't keep doing this shit. At some point, you gotta grow up. Get your shit together, man."

I can picture him nodding his head. "Yeah, man. I know. Spot me this, I swear I won't ask again. I'll get it together."

I don't believe him for a second. I give him this, and he'll ask again and again. But he's my brother. And I love him. He's had my back in some tough times as well, so our relationship goes two ways. But since I entered the army at eighteen, I haven't needed to ask Chase for help once.

I scrub my hands over my hair and then across my face. Sighing, I try to hold him off.

"Let me move some shit around, Chase. I'll get back to you."

"Don't take too long, Dare. You gotta come through for me."

I end the call, and roll over in my bed. It's only four in the morning, but this is already turning out to be a shit day.

4

Berkeley

Berkeley Jane Holtz." My mother's voice sounds too weary to yell. So she just states my name, like she's rattling off the wine selection at dinner.

"Momma, I'm going to work."

"But *why*? Your father and I enjoy paying for everything you may need. And one day, you'll be married, and then your husband—"

I throw up a hand in aggravated frustration. Is that really all my mother thinks life is about? Having your parents pay for everything, and then moving right along to having your husband pay for everything?

I'm a woman who needs a sense of accomplishment in my life. She's never understood it. She doesn't even bother to pretend.

The door slams shut behind me, and I know I'll hear a lecture about respect from the Admiral at some point in the near future.

My bosses at work are an enormously generous and giving middle-aged couple that treat me like I share their blood. It amazes me every day. The moment I turned up in their lobby as a lost and confused seventeen-year-old, they took me in as more than just an employee, and I'll never be able to repay them.

"You're late," says Lenny as she breezes by me on her way into the kitchen.

"I'm never late," I protest.

It's not true. I'm nearly always late. I always have the best intentions, thinking I'm leaving myself plenty of time to get ready for an event or appointment. But then when I check the clock, hours have slipped away as if they were mere minutes, and I'm left scrambling to arrive with some semblance of respect for the other person's time. I can't seem to help it.

It's a thing.

Lenny ties on her apron as she prepares for the first tables of the evening shift, grinning at me from the drink machine.

"But I made you check the time, didn't I?"

I throw a lemon wedge at her.

"Leave her alone, babe!" Boozer, her husband, ambles over to squeeze me in a one-armed hug. His other hand is wielding a butcher knife that he's using to chop off the tails and heads of pounds and pounds of fish.

Our evening begins in something of a whirlwind. It's the first packed Friday night of the season, really, and the beach crowd is flocking to Lone Sands's well-known eatery. The dinner rush won't slow down until after nine on a night like this, so I'm too busy to pay much attention to anything but the diners seated at my tables.

That's why I notice when Mea and Mikah roll in with a small posse, because they've demanded to be seated at one of my tables.

That's why, around eight, I notice when Dare and his friend are seated at a table just behind them only a minute later.

The sight of Mea brings a genuinely happy smile to my face. I know she'll want to make plans for when I get off around eleven. To me, hanging out with Mea until the sun comes up is the symbol of summer.

The sight of Dare sends a hot flush creeping up to my face and a flutter of nerves coursing through my stomach.

I'm aware of the danger the second emotion signifies. Being attracted to a military guy has never been in the cards for me. In fact, I've been fighting against my parents for years on the very subject. If I'm not going to end up with Grisham, I'm not going to end up with any man in uniform.

But something about Dare, from that very first night I met him, has had his stupidly rugged face creeping into my thoughts just before I fall asleep at night. And even though I turned him down that night, it didn't help matters that I ran into him again at the auto mechanic's shop. Since then, and since I actually had the nerve to flirt back with him, I've been wondering how his very large hands would feel wrapped around my waist. Or grasping the back of my neck. Or…other things.

"Berkeley!" Mea is flagging me down from her table, waving her napkin like a white flag.

I roll my eyes and head that way. I grab her and Mikah's glasses without asking them what they want, and hurry back to them with a Coke and a Sprite. Neither of them is holding menus, which would be unnecessary, since I already know what they want to eat. I throw them a quick smile and hold up a finger before scooting over to Dare's table.

"Hi." The cleverness of my greeting sends a jolt of embarrassment flaming straight to my cheeks.

"Hi, yourself," he answers. "Berkeley, this is my friend, Drake. Drake, this is Berkeley."

His friend is huge, and sexy, and all smiles. I shake his beefy hand and return his grin, then turn my attention back to Dare.

"Should I bring you boys a beer?"

He nods, one corner of his mouth turning up in a lopsided smile. *God, that's hot.* His face is lacking nothing, in my opinion. His sort-of-long dark brown hair is just the right length to tug at if my fingers happen to find themselves running along the nape of his neck. It curls slightly at the ends, disappearing under his collar. His face is so ruggedly handsome, I finally understand what they mean in books when they say ruggedly handsome. There's a thin coating of scruff along his strong, square jawline, and his skin is tan underneath. His eyes are a green so light I'd call it sea-foam, and clear as the Caribbean Sea. They're set under heavy brows that move when he's feeling something. Right now, they're furrowed as he looks back at me, and I know he's wondering what I'm thinking as I stare at him a beat too long.

I might be in trouble. Focusing on those obscenely gorgeous eyes is causing my skin to heat and my toes to curl in my boots.

I refuse to let my eyes travel to the rest of his seated body until I'm safely beside the kitchen door, and then I peek. I lean against the wall and leisurely take him in. Snug gray T-shirt with the word ARMY printed on the front. Tattoos peeking out from underneath the sleeves at both biceps. Another runs the length of his inner forearm, script that I'm aching to read.

I've never, ever dated a guy with tattoos. And this guy has three. That I can see.

My assessment continues. Dare isn't nearly as beefy as his friend

Drake, but his size is formidable to a normal guy my age. He's tall, at least six foot two if I'm guessing correctly from his seated position, and his muscles are…profound. They leave me breathless as I inspect them. He has sinewy cords rippling in his forearms as he studies his menu.

"Why don't you just go take a bite?"

Lenny's voice startles me, and I crash backward into the kitchen door. The noise alone is enough to have me hiding beneath the little window once I'm inside.

"Lenny!" I hiss.

"Sorry!" She's laughing, her face reddening as her giggles erupt from her petite body. "I've never seen you stare so hard. Army's a hottie. He a friend of yours?"

"God, I wish!" I moan as I prepare to walk back through the doors.

I head to the bar to grab Dare's and Drake's beers, and then march back to their table. By this time, Mea is watching me with narrowed eyes, scrutinizing my face and glancing at the table where Dare sits. I'm so busted.

I set down the Killian's in front of Dare. He eyes it appreciatively, and then turned his gaze back to me as I set down Drake's bottle of Bud.

"You remember all of your customer's drink orders, Berkeley?"

Oh. When my name falls off of his lips like that, I have a hard time finding enough saliva to make my mouth function correctly. But I try, anyway.

"Not all of them." *Good girl!* My answer is as cool as a fall evening. Somehow, I'm managing to keep up the appearance that this guy's incredible looks and infallible charm haven't affected me.

He nods, and a slow grin spreads across his face. "Busy night?"

I nod. "Want me to bring you the same thing you had last time?"

Drake nods. I smile at him, and then look at Dare. Dare studies me a moment before answering.

"I want the same thing you brought me last time, plus something extra."

I wait. He doesn't name the something extra.

With my heart beating just a little faster, I force my lips to turn upward as I nod and walk away.

When I get back to Mea and Mikah, I send her a pleading glance. She knows I'm silently asking her to wait until we're alone to bombard me with questions, and she obliges.

"But, later?" One finely shaped eyebrow arches. "I'm all over this."

"I know. I'm simultaneously dreading it and can't wait to tell you."

I spend the next hour serving the tables holding my friends and my newfound acquaintances, building up my courage. When Mea, her brother, and their friends exit the restaurant, leaving me a generous tip, she sends me a meaningful glance before vanishing out the front door.

I peek toward Dare and Drake, who have just requested their check. I suck in a breath, because Dare's intense eyes are locked on mine. One corner of his mouth tugs upward in his smile, and the butterflies currently making a home in my gut take flight.

That's what I needed. That tiny confirmation from him gives me the gumption to scribble my cell number down on the bottom of their check with a note.

See? I told you I have nothing against the army. I Dare you to use this.

I wear a special little smile of my own as I drop off their bill.

"Have a nice night, boys," I advise them over my shoulder as I escape.

The next morning, all I can do is analyze my decision to give Dare my phone number. Had he really been flirting, or was it all in my mind? I know military men like I know the formula for scale when designing a room. Army may be a different breed from navy, but they're all members of the same species.

A major element in any military guy's life is his love of women. It's like they all crave the nurturing and attention that only a woman can bring to their lives. A lot of them end up settling down pretty young and starting families to care for. But for many, the desire for freedom wins out, and they spend their free time with as many different women as they can handle.

Which of those men is Dare? I have a pretty good idea, because he doesn't appear to be very settled down.

And what is he doing here? There isn't an army base in Brunswick County. Maybe he's just on leave, and visiting his friend?

I can handle a summer fling. After this summer ends, I have some major life decisions to make. The pressure from my parents to start a life with Grisham isn't going anywhere, and now that I'm done with college it's only going to intensify. I don't feel any pushing from Grish, but I know where he stands. If I want him, he'll be happy to want me back. He's a great guy, he'd take good care of me. I just don't know if I can ever learn to love him that way. No matter how much my parents want it.

I interned at an interior design firm in town last summer, and absolutely adored it. I loved how the owner used her creativity every day to make people feel good inside their own spaces. I loved meeting new people and clients, and being exposed to different environments. It was everything I'd ever wanted for myself. And I know that one day, if I want to, I can make that happen.

I so badly want to.

The internal conflict that comes with this decision is suffocating sometimes. I just want to live my life, without having to worry about crushing my parents' hearts into dust.

I'm broken from my thoughts by a pillow being thrown over my face.

"Hey!"

"Get up, get up!" Mea is bouncing so merrily on my bed, my whole body is thrown up and down each time her ass hits the mattress.

"Get off of my bed!"

"No." She pouts. "And I don't like your tone."

"My tone! It's ass o'clock in the morning!" I can't help my grumbly morning voice. Mornings have never, ever been my friend.

Mea, on the other hand, has been. We met in high school, when I finally began to notice that not everyone's parents planned their children's lives out like a thoroughly detailed treasure map. Thinking back to when we first met in the hallway after school, I smile.

I'd been rushing toward my second activity meeting of the afternoon when my hugely heavy backpack slipped off my shoulder and spilled out all of its contents. I was crouching, trying to stuff everything in as quickly as possible when two tiny hands appeared beside mine, picking up my stuff.

"Need some help?" asked Mea's chipper voice.

She was dressed in our school's cheerleading uniform, with bands of black and gold swirling around her petite, lithe body. A huge ribbon held back her bouncing curls, and she looked…happy. Not frazzled, like me. Not like she had a million too many things on her plate, like me. Just happy.

"Thanks," I'd said.

When we stood, she scrutinized me, and then asked where I was headed.

I told her that I was on my way to debate club, and had a mini-freakout when I glanced up at the clock on the wall.

"Oh, no," she tsked. "If you're reacting like that to being a few minutes late to debate club, you've got some problems you need to share. Come on."

She firmly grabbed my elbow with the strength of a football player and towed me along toward the exit.

"I can't miss it!" I exclaimed. "My parents will kill me."

"Honey," she said, slowing down and facing me solemnly. "Keep going at the pace you are, and I'll be watching you die of a heart attack by the end of senior year. Blow off debate and come hang with me and my friends. We're having a study date, but there will be actual *fun* there. And I won't take no for an answer."

Smiling, I was filled with a warmth that I hadn't experienced before. This girl, in just a few minutes, had managed to make me feel like she wanted me around. Not for what I could do for her or give her, but just because she liked me and wanted to help me.

"I'm Berkeley," I'd said, sticking out my hand.

"Mea." She grinned back.

And that was the beginning of a seriously beautiful friendship.

"No, it's not, Berk. It's almost lunchtime. Why are you so lazy?" Mea's curls shake as she shoots me a stern look of disappointment.

Ugh. I really do hate mornings. And if I'm not out of bed yet, it's morning. No matter what time the clock says.

"Fine." I groan as I sit up and stretch my arms high above my head. "I'm up."

"That's my girl. Now, on to more important topics. If you don't tell me right the hell now who that delicious specimen of a man was last night, I'm going to start screaming bloody murder until your momma comes to check on us."

"Oh, no! Anything but that!" I playfully tickle her ribs until she crumbles into a heap of giggles at my feet.

"Give! I give!" she screams.

"Shush," I whisper, because the last thing I want to do is face my mother this early in the morning. Lunchtime be damned.

"What's his name? How'd you meet him? I thought you didn't date military dudes?"

I decide to address her last question first. "I don't. I mean, I'm not dating him. I only just gave him my number last night."

Her squeal of delight is enough to tease a reluctant smile out of me. "His name is Dare."

I go on to explain how Dare and Drake came into the restaurant that first night, and how I ran into him at the auto shop a few weeks later.

"And now I want to know all about that hunk of deliciousness that was sitting across from him. Drake, was it?"

I aim a knowing smile in her direction. "Ah. That's what you really wanted, right? You don't really care about my love life."

"Because I know you well enough to know you don't have one. Hey, we've been apart for a few years, Berk, but I know you're not going to jump into anything with a guy who practically wears the words BAD IDEA across the front of his shirt. Am I right?"

I nod. "You're probably right. But…I did give him my number, didn't I? And I normally wouldn't do that. If I wanted a military man, I'd just marry Grisham, like our parents want me to. I'd never just pass Grish over for a guy just like him."

She reaches over and pries my eyes open wider, using her fingertips to hold open my lids. "Are these working right? Did you not *see* Dare? There's nothing about him that's like Grisham, not a damn thing. Dare…even his name is dark and dangerous. And I didn't spot a piece of expensive jewelry on him anywhere. And he doesn't seem like a BMW type of guy, either. Oh, and one more thing. There was no silver spoon hanging out of his mouth. He's not navy royalty, that's for sure."

Everything Mea so eloquently stated is what was already rattling around inside my own head. Dare is clearly nothing like Grisham, or any other guy I've ever dated.

And maybe it's that hint of danger I can see in him from a mile away, or his intense, brooding demeanor that attracts me to him. Or maybe it's the fact that he doesn't look at me like I'm a princess sitting on her throne that he wants to put in a box and protect.

He looks at me like I'm a goddess perched high on an idol that he wants to *worship*.

And something buried very deeply inside of me, down where the most secret thoughts and feelings of my subconscious hide, wants to let him.

As soon as I allow that thought to enter my brain, my phone begins to vibrate harshly against the wood of my nightstand.

I pick it up with a growing sense of exuberance inside of me, and read it.

INCOMING CALL FROM UNKNOWN

It's got to be Dare. Who else could it be? He's calling me? Doesn't he know the just-text-a-girl-you-barely-know rule? No one calls anymore! My eyes must be scarily wide, because Mea looks at me with panic.

"What?"

"It's him…Dare's *calling* me."

"Well, answer it, girl! Jesus, you scared me!" She clutches at her chest like an old lady having a heart attack.

"Hello." My voice is wobbly as I push the phone against my ear.

"Hey, Berkeley." His voice is the opposite of wobbly. His voice is strong, sure, deep. All of a sudden, that voice is everything. The only thing keeping me upright on my bed.

"Dare…I'm surprised you're calling me."

"Why?"

Well, that's direct.

"Because? I don't know…"

"Weren't you giving me an explicit green light last night to go ahead and call? I mean, you dared me. I don't take that lightly."

Now his tone is jovial, light and flirty. It sends the annoying crop of winged insects inside my belly into a frenzy.

"No? Well, then if I get results this quickly I'll dare you more often."

Bold, Berkeley. Very bold.

"That could be dangerous for you," he warns.

"I think I need a little danger in my life."

"I'm going to be honest here, Berkeley." My name, now my favorite word when he uses it, rolls over me like a tidal wave. "I want to see you again. Are you working tonight?"

I nod mutely, and then remember he can't see me. I swear, I wasn't such an idiot before I met this guy. Mea dissolves into another fit of giggles on the bed, and I kick her.

"Oh, no. Silence? That's a no…right? You're going to kill my ego here, Berkeley."

A delicious shiver is crawling its way up my spine at the same time a small trickle of sweat slips down between my boobs. "No! I mean, yes. I am working tonight."

"After?"

I shake my head and find my confidence. I actually do have a large stock of it somewhere. "Yes, after. Would you like to come to See Food around ten and wait for me to finish up?"

"No."

My heart sinks somewhere near my feet.

"I would love to." I can hear his crooked little smile lifting his voice. "I'll see you at ten."

He clicks off the line, and my heart is now somewhere so high I'm afraid I won't be able to reach it to put it back inside my chest.

"Well." As I toss my phone down on the pillow beside me, my smile spreads wide. "Shit just got real. I have a date with Dare tonight."

5

Dare

Drake's after-work routine is very simple: He takes a twenty-minute shower, grabs a frozen dinner to microwave, sits on the couch in a pair of sweats, and drinks a bottle of Bud.

As he enters the final stage of this custom, I'm buttoning my shirt. Drake pauses, beer in hand, on his way to the couch. His mouth falls open as he takes in my appearance.

"Why are you wearing a shirt that buttons?"

I glance down at the soft blue-collared shirt with white checks, the snap buttons down the front of it lending it a retro vibe, and then back at him. I could tell him, but I'm not ready to announce to the world that I'm trying to date a girl I'm not even in the same realm of living with, much less the same league.

"My mom sent it to me."

Drake's eyes narrow. He looks like a big, beefy, muscle head, but he's no fool, and I know it. "Which foster mom have you kept in touch with to the extent that she'd send you a shirt for no good reason?"

Damn. I had blurted out the first thing that came to me, forgetting that Drake knows my history.

"Okay. That was a lie, Drake."

"No fucking kidding?" The sarcasm drips from each word like nectar.

"I'm going to see Berkeley. It's not a big deal, just meeting up with her after she gets off work."

Drake's face settles into its normal state of being, grinning at me with an extra gleam in his eyes. "Yeah? Good luck with that, man."

"Gee, Drake. I'm so glad I have your vote of confidence here. It means so fucking much to me, dude. Come here…let's hug it out."

Drake plops onto the couch, and I follow him into the living room.

"I have all the confidence in the world, man. If you're interested in this chick, does that mean you want to stay in Lone Sands?"

I sigh, running my hands over my face as I contemplate the question I've been avoiding. "I don't know. This could still just be a stop on the train for me. You know I don't stay in one place for too long. Force of habit."

The army lifestyle suited me so well because it allowed me to move and stretch my wings. Staying in one place has never been my strong suit. You need a reason to stay. I've never had one.

"Yeah, I know your habits, Dare. And I know something else. Old habits die hard, but yours need to change. This isn't a life for anyone. Just moving from place to place all the time? That sucks. It was one thing when we had the army, but now…now things are different. And you need to make a change."

The *A* word isn't necessarily something I want to discuss. Not right now. Maybe not ever. "I get antsy."

"That just means you haven't found a reason to stay. Maybe Lone Sands will be different for you." His voice turns more serious with each word he says. "Think about it…I kind of like having your ass around."

"Just my ass? Or do you want the rest of me to stay?"

I duck as he chucks the TV remote at my head. Discharge or not, my reflexes still rival a freaking mountain lion's, and he knows it.

"What about you? You've got the garage, but is that all Lone Sands has to offer you? You've been living here for a while. You call this place home. Where's the girl to come home to?"

Drake and I will always be army brothers. Going through the daily hell that is Ranger training unifies us for life. He left the forces before I did, but our bond remained even when we were separated.

"See you later, dude. Have fun on your date."

I smirk. So I hit a nerve with Drake when I brought up the fact that he's single. I stockpile away that little piece of ammunition for later.

"It's not a date," I throw back over my shoulder as I walk out the front door.

I can't be anything but honest with myself as I drive to See Food. I want this to be a date. I know it's not, but *damn* do I wish it was. And maybe it can be. Maybe I can grow into a man that's good enough to take a girl like Berkeley out on a date.

The restaurant envelops me in a welcome blast of cool air as I walk inside, and my eyes immediately start to rove. I'm searching for blond hair that always looks a little windswept and tousled, a body that I always guess would fit just right tucked beneath mine, a face that could stop traffic, and legs that don't quit. When I see her, standing at a table near the back of the place, my whole body vibrates with a sigh of relief and a hum of straight-up arousal. God-damn.

I wait, leaning against the hostess stand, unsure if I should sit on the bench up here or just go back out to my truck. She finishes re-filling the table's drinks and heads back toward the front, pulling her phone out of the pocket of her little black apron. The army green shorts she wears are barely covered by the length of the apron, and I can't stop my eyes from raking over her generous curves as she approaches.

When she looks up, her eyes captivate mine, and I swear, they light up. Like I'm a sight for sore eyes, or exactly the person she wanted to see standing here. The thought sends hope sizzling through my chest, landing like an arrow in the center of my heart.

"Hey, you," she says as she approaches.

All I can do is smile down at her. Something tells me there won't be a time that she's walking toward me that I'll be able to do any-thing else.

"Hey," I answer. "I like your shorts. The color can't be a coinci-dence."

"It's not." A stunning pink tinge creeps into her cheeks.

"A nod for me, huh?" I widen my stance, shoving my hands in my pockets.

"Just wanted you to know I was thinking about you."

Those long lashes actually fluttered at me with that statement, and a sudden epiphany strikes. What if this girl is really an evil vixen siren who places a spell on all the men she meets? I've never been into that fantasy or sci-fi shit, but suddenly staring at this girl and all the impossible beauty that never seems to end, I'm a newfound be-liever.

I lean in closer, and use my index finger to beckon her to do the same. When my lips are only inches from her ear, I whisper, "Are you an evil vixen siren?"

Her eyes widen slightly, and then narrow with suspicion. She turns her head until her lips actually brush the shell of my ear, and an internal shiver wrecks the rest of my senses. Damn, she's sexy. At this proximity I can smell the roses, mixed with something earthy, and it's salacious. "If I was, do you really think I'd give my secret away?"

I pull back slightly, so I can meet her toffee-brown gaze dead-on. "Are there many of those? Secrets, I mean? That you're not giving away?"

She shakes her head, causing all those wild blond locks to tickle my face. "Most people in the world don't stick around long enough to learn other people's secrets. We'll see how far you get."

"That sounds suspiciously like a dare, Berkeley." As I smile down at her my heart begins to do all kinds of crazy gymnastics in my chest.

"Why don't you sit down at that booth over there?" She gestures toward the table she means, near the front door. "I'll only be a little bit. Do you want something to eat?"

I shake my head. "I'm good, thanks. I'll just hang out and wait."

She shoots me a smile as she walks away, heading off to complete her closing duties. I can't keep my eyes off of her as she sweeps under tables, rolls silverware, and does something interesting with multiple ketchup bottles.

The front door opens again and a couple walks in. The man has a headful of dark hair streaked with silver, and his height speaks to me…a man of power. The woman has blond hair coifed perfectly in a short style. I tilt my head, staring at the woman. Something clicks in my brain, and I realize she looks a lot like…

"Momma? Daddy? What are you two doing here?" Berkeley comes rushing forward, and the look on her face can only be described as panicked.

Why would she be panicked to see her parents?

I place my hands on the table to stand, because of course I'm going to shake the father's hand of the girl I'm about to take out. I may not have had parents to raise me up with values, but I learned them on my own.

Berkeley's head whips toward me as she approaches, and the slight shake of her curls has me sinking back down into the booth. I watch as she greets her parents and proceeds to have an argument with them.

From what I can hear, it's clear that they don't want Berkeley to work here. They want her to quit, and come home with them. She shakes her head, fierce as a tigress, and her feistiness makes me smile.

I had wondered myself why someone like her would be working as a waitress. Hell, I would never knock someone's job options or choices, and I don't look down on any profession. Everyone has to make ends meet. But for Berkeley to be waiting tables when she drives an Escalade, I had to wonder. Now, seeing how put-together and affluent her parents look, I'm wondering even harder.

What makes this girl do the things she does?

And that question sets off a spark of intense interest in my brain. My *brain* is interested in Berkeley now, not just my body.

The tigress sends her parents packing, and by the time she makes it back to my booth, I'm chuckling. I rub a hand over the stubble on my chin and meet her eyes.

"That was interesting," I remark, giving nothing away.

"Trust me, Dare. You want no part of my parents right now. I don't introduce them to guys I date."

"No? Never?"

"Never. They're more trouble than they're worth." She blows out a frustrated breath, which sends that cute stray strand of hair hanging over her eye flying skyward.

"I'm going to want to know more about that at some point. But what do you want to do tonight?"

"Honestly?" She puts out a hand and pulls me to my feet.

I reach out and brush the stray strand behind her ear. Just the small amount of contact sends heat coursing through my body, landing with an aching twitch in my groin. "I always want honesty from you, Berkeley."

I've been preparing myself for this all day. I'm ready to take her to see a movie, or to some swanky-ass wine bar on the oceanfront.

"Okay." A mischievous gleam enters her eyes. "I worked a double today, and my feet kind of hurt. All I really want to do tonight is kick off my shoes and drink a beer. And look at the stars."

I reach up and pull on my earlobe a few times, wanting to make sure my ears are functioning properly. She wants to…what the fuck? Finally, I speak. "For real?"

She nods firmly. "Absolutely."

I grab her hand and begin pulling her quickly out the door.

"What are you doing?" Her question is blurred by giggles and squeals. All of which I like.

"I'm getting you out of here fast, before you change your mind and tell me that what you actually want to do is go wine tasting or see a chick flick."

I stop in my tracks as I survey the tiny gravel lot. Cars are spilling out onto the street beyond. "Where's your car?"

When I look at her, she's smiling a coy smile that lets me know my guess earlier about her being an evil vixen siren was correct. "I had my friend Mea drop me off. I'm with you tonight, soldier."

It's way too soon for a first kiss. It's way too soon for a first kiss. This is my mantra as I stare at her, my eyes wandering from her eyes, to her amazingly sexy hair, to her lips, to her cute button nose, back to her lips...

When she pulls the bottom one into her mouth, my gaze is stuck to that spot. I'm telling myself that if I kiss her right now, I'll scare her away and ruin everything I suddenly want to build. I manage to tear my eyes away from the succulent lip and take her hand again.

"My truck is this way."

I'm not a small guy, around six feet, three inches. Berkeley is about a foot shorter than I am. Rather than watch her struggle to simply make it up the step rail, I grip her around the waist and lift her up into her seat. Her eyes meet mine as she settles into the leather, and we remain locked as I pull her seat belt and cross it over her torso, sliding it into the buckle on the other side of her. When I pull back, I swear I see a trail of sparks that follow. Heat explodes in my gut, and I can't remember the last time a woman made me feel like I needed to douse myself with cold water from a mere graze of skin. I close her door and take a deep breath as I walk around to my side of the truck.

When I'm seated with the engine running, I ask her where I should go. "To the 7-Eleven for our beer, and then...where do you live? Is it on the beach, by any chance?"

I smile and pull out of the lot. "It's pretty damn close."

"Perfect. Let's go to your place."

I drive. As I pull into the 7-Eleven parking lot, I glance at her. She's lounging in her seat, perfectly at home in my truck. I swallow thickly, trying to dispel the ball of instant attraction still stuck somewhere between my chest and my dick.

This girl might be the slow, epically painful death of me. But damn, what a way to go.

6

Berkeley

This beach cottage that Dare splits with Drake may be the cutest thing I've ever seen. I've always lived in large houses. Not mansions, because although my family is well-off, we're still a military family. But houses way bigger than our family of three would ever need.

This little beach cottage is a delicious change of pace, and my idea of perfect bliss in my perfect little town.

My voice is breathy when I say as much to Dare. "It's amazing. It's beautiful. It's *perfect*."

He turns; he's just gotten me down from the seat of his truck. I will never tell him this, but no one has ever done anything as sexy as physically lift me into the seat of his car before. And then actually buckle me up. When his hands wrapped strongly around my waist, my exposed skin broke out in goose bumps and a hot flush began rising somewhere deep in my belly.

"Yeah? I'm gonna go out on a limb here and guess that this house is nowhere near the size of yours."

I nod. "That's why it's so perfect."

He cocks his head to the side, his expression quizzical. "I'm trying my damnedest to figure you out."

"How's that going for you?"

"Let's just say I'd fail my first exam."

I pat him on the shoulder and walk past him. "Keep trying, Dare."

We decide to bypass the interior of the house, although one day I hope I can have a tour, and walk around to the back.

It's plain and pleasant. There's a massive deck with a huge gas grill and some comfy-looking seating. Beyond that, the yard is mostly sand with clusters of sea grass sticking up sporadically. A wooden path leads down to a walking/running trail and just beyond that? The ocean.

I sigh. My entire body relaxes at the sight of it.

"You like it?" Dare's voice is closer than expected, and I start at the sound of it. When I look up, he's right next to me, looking down at my expression. My face heats.

"It's…"

"Perfect?" He finishes with a grin.

I accentuate my accent. "Why, look at you, it's our first date and you're already finishing my sentences."

He rolls his eyes and groans. "I'm not going to embarrass myself by telling you how crazy that damn accent makes me. Okay?"

My face breaks into a smile. He's…irresistible. All that long, dark hair and those clear green eyes staring right through me. How can a guy be cute and hot at the same time? Shouldn't that be freaking illegal?

"There's some chairs down there, on the sand. Shall we?"

When he holds out his arm like an old-fashioned gentleman,

I can't do anything but grin and take it. The gesture is so out of place with his long hair and visible tattoos that I chuckle softly as we walk.

When we're settled on the sand in two lime-green Adirondack chairs, our beers in hand, we're blanketed by the most relaxing sounds on the planet. The ocean begs the shore for admittance, and the sand sends the waves rolling away every time. And beyond that…silence.

Glorious, peaceful silence.

Dare gives me a good ten minutes of it before he breaks it.

"I can't believe I live here."

I glance at him, startled. His head is resting on the back of his chair, his eyes open and staring at the velvety sky above us.

My reaction to his words is confusing the hell out of me. On the one hand, I thought he was temporary. Visiting his friend, maybe on leave. As tough a time as I'm having fighting the instant attraction I feel for him, I was relieved to think it wasn't going to take me over. I mean, shoot…I can deal with anything for a little while, right?

On the other hand, the thought of him leaving makes me…sad. Already, I like spending time with him. I like seeing his face in my places…the restaurant, my auto shop. I'm picturing what other places he can occupy.

I shake my head of all of these thoughts, because he just said he *lives* here.

"You live here?"

He turns his gaze on me, raising one eyebrow. "You didn't know that? I literally live *here*. In Drake's house. I'm a recent addition to Lone Sands."

I'm quiet, returning my gaze to the ocean. It's safe to look at the ocean. There are absolutely no surprises there. It always does just what it's supposed to do. Waves roll in, waves roll out.

I have a feeling Dare isn't ever going to do what I expect. And what a scary, scary feeling! Scary slash exhilarating.

"Hey, Berkeley? What are you thinking?"

I pinch a piece of hair between my fingers and twist. "I'm declining to answer that question on account of us barely knowing each other."

He chuckles and runs one hand absently along the side of his opposite rib cage. "I deny your decline on the basis that I want to *get* to know you." Then he grasps another strand of my hair in his fingertips and rubs his fingers together, gaze locked on me.

I close my eyes briefly, tamping down on the surge of heat pooling in the center of my body. I also fight the urge to writhe uncomfortably in my Adirondack chair. He makes me feel…hell, I don't know. He just makes me *feel*.

My *God*.

I notice a silver chain dipping down beneath the collar of his shirt, and I grab hold of the distraction like a lifeline. I reach out, taking the chain gently in my fingertips, and look up at him.

"May I?

He nods slowly, his gaze boring into mine. Out here in the darkness, where the only light comes from the floodlight on the homes behind us and the moon, his eyes are almost iridescent. The effect is mesmerizing, and I falter as I fall into his eyes.

Then I pull his silver dog tags from beneath his shirt. The metal is warm from his skin, hot really. I turn the metal over in my fingers, and I know that I'm touching something that's an extension of his body. I know it, and he knows it, and his eyes are so intent on my hands that I can literally feel them burning my skin.

"'Dare Conners,'" I read. "Wait a second, Dare is your *real name*?"

He chuckles. "I'm full of surprises for you tonight, aren't I? You thought it was a nickname?"

"Well, *yeah*! I didn't think anyone would actually be named after the action of boldness!"

His laughter turns to a full-fledged roar that rivals the sound of wind rushing in your ears during a run. The sound surrounds me.

"What the hell were your parents thinking?"

His laughter doesn't cut off abruptly, but it trails away, and I'm left wondering what I just said.

"I wouldn't know," he answers quietly.

He offers nothing more. I stare at him for another second, then replace his tags under his shirt. My fingers linger on the skin at the top of his chest. "I'm sorry."

He nods. "Don't be."

We let the silence wash over us once again.

I glance at him out of the corner of my eye after a few minutes. I want to know. I want to know the answers to all of the questions lurking behind those beautiful eyes of his. And so I know it's time for me to go.

"Dare…"

He looks over at me, his hands clasped behind his head. "Berkeley."

Dammit. Does he somehow know I have trouble continuing to speak when he says my name? Does he *know*?

"Thanks for the beer," I say, sitting up.

He doesn't. "You're welcome. Are you leaving me so soon?"

No. "Yep."

His mouth turns down, and I keep my hands firmly in my lap so that I don't brush a finger across his full bottom lip.

A low rumble of thunder rolls around us, and I glance up at the sky. A storm is obviously on its way. When I look back at Dare, his gaze hasn't moved from mine.

"Dare…"

He begins shaking his head before I've even begun my letting-him-down-easy speech. Does he read my mind, too?

"This has been a really great night…"

His hand on my chin stills me. It stills my thoughts and it stalls my words. I'm helpless with his hand on me.

"Don't do that," he says softly. "Don't give me your 'let-him-down-easy' speech. Let's pretend we've moved past that, okay? You don't want to do this again, then tell me the real reason. I don't do bullshit."

He releases my skin, but there's a burning in the spot now that wasn't there before.

It takes me a moment to find my voice, and Dare waits patiently while another rumble of thunder rolls over our heads.

"I'm…I'm super attracted to you, Dare. But I'm not available to date right now. I'll probably never be available to date. It's…complicated."

"You have a boyfriend." He says it like a fact, not a question.

"I do not have a boyfriend." It would have been the easy way out. I could have just let him believe that, but I find myself unable to lie to this sharp, sexy, honest man.

He stares at me, his expression unreadable. He rubs his rib again, and I allow my eyes to travel to that spot. He notices, and stops rubbing. When he speaks again, his voice hasn't changed. It's still soft, and still like a rough edge of a stone left out in the wind.

"So...you just aren't that into me."

I wish he'd stop searching for reasons. "Some things just aren't going to work out."

"I didn't ask you to marry me, Berkeley. I didn't even ask you out on a second date yet."

I raise my eyebrows, and he quickly regroups. "I was going to. Shit, of course I was going to. But, if you don't want to hang out again, I guess I have to accept that."

I *so* don't want him to accept it. But I nod my head, just as the sky above us opens, and we leap out of our chairs and sprint for the house.

By the time we reach it, we're soaked. We run around to the driveway, where Dare's truck is parked, and he helps me in and buckles me up while the rain pelts him.

When he finally makes it to the driver's seat, he's laughing. He runs his hands through his sopping wet hair, and I realize mine must look like a wet dog. Groaning, I pull out my hair tie and shake my mess of curls out around my shoulders.

"Shit! I didn't realize it was supposed to rain tonight." He scrubs his face with his hands, and then turns to face me. "I'm—"

He freezes when he looks at me, and my suspicions are confirmed. I'm definitely the hottest mess he's ever seen. My hair is flopping everywhere, and I'm sure the small amount of makeup I had on my face now looks like I'm starring in *The Walking Dead*.

But that doesn't matter. I just told him I couldn't see him again. Who the hell cares what I look like?

The way he's staring at me is causing my new pets, my butterflies, to take furious flight and my heartbeat to speed up at an alarming pace.

Then he reaches out and brushes that stupid strand of hair out of my eyes. The one my mother can't stand.

"I love this," he says. "I might as well tell you, seeing as how I won't get the chance again."

His finger follows an invisible trail along my cheek, pausing at the hollow beneath my eye. "And these. I fall into these every single time they're focused on me. It scares the shit out of me. And nothing scares me, Berkeley."

My breath is gone. I've lost it somewhere between his finger tracing a path on my face and the beautiful words he's speaking. About *me*.

His finger changes trajectory, trailing down until he reaches my lips. Which are probably trembling. "Do you know how long I've been looking at these? All fucking night. All night tonight, and every other time I've been in your vicinity."

His eyes drop to my lips then, and he uses his thumb to part them. Hot lava flows from my core into my every extremity until I feel like I must be catching fire. He's setting me aflame. His touch, his words, those eyes on me. I can't contain the desire that wells up inside me.

"Dare." I breathe.

His eyes flicker back up from my lips. "Berkeley."

"I guess if you're going to kiss me, you'd better do it now. You might not get another chance."

His hand curls around the nape of my neck, and I shudder. Hadn't I pictured what it would feel like if he touched me like this?

And now I know…it's heavenly and sinful all at the same time. It's hot and…

His lips crash against mine and *Oh my God*. Hot lava turns into massive, five-alarm flames, and I moan against his mouth. Shit! I didn't mean to do that.

His tongue finds my bottom lip and traces a line across it, before finding the seam and nudging my mouth open. My lips part for him so easily I'm terrified my legs will do the same if he asks me. His other hand is tangled in my hair, and even though his hands aren't on my body I can feel it tingling and buzzing in response to his lips alone.

When our tongues tangle together for the first time, he makes an appreciative noise in the back of his throat, which sends me spiraling into a sexy haze of want and need. Then he slows down, exploring my mouth for another second before pulling back altogether.

His face is inches from mine, his eyes staring so intently I could melt beneath that gaze.

I sigh, counting to ten exactly like my mother does when she's frustrated. Then I raise one hand and waggle my fingers at him.

"What are you doing?" he says with a smile.

"Putting another spell on you with my evil vixen siren song."

His chuckle is low, husky. I'm in such big trouble.

"I knew it!"

Then he drives me home, and I squeeze my thighs tightly together in order to release some of the tension this soldier has just created.

Trouble. Capital freaking *T*.

7

Dare

The incoming call is from Chase, and I curse when I read his name.

I've been dodging his calls for a week. It's been...difficult to figure out how I can help him out of his latest pile of shit when I can't stop imagining being holed up in my truck, pressed up against a very wet Berkeley.

Groaning, I roll my head back and stare at the ceiling.

The call goes to voice mail, and I glance down at my phone as it buzzes with an incoming text.

Stop avoiding me, bro. I need you.

"What are all those faces about?" asks Drake.

"My brother is at it again." I lean back in my chair, glancing up at Drake where he stands, grilling steaks on the deck.

Drake jerks around to look at me. "Chase?"

I nod.

"Fuck," he mutters. "What'd he do this time?"

I pause, because I don't know exactly what Chase did this time. I haven't called him back yet.

"I only know he needs money. Trouble with some dudes back in Florida."

Drake curses again. "You need to stop bailing his ass out, Dare."

"He's my brother. What am I supposed to do? He says it's bad."

"Of course it's bad. Nobody comes to collect unless you owe them big. Chase is into the worst kind of bullshit, Dare. You gotta cut him loose. He's not gonna learn. He's not gonna change." Drake has completely abandoned the grill in favor of a stern look in my direction, and wispy, fragrant smoke is billowing into the evening sky.

"I'll figure it out, Drake. I'll figure something out."

"You got hella cash saved, and it's for you. Your life. Don't blow it on him."

I nod. "I won't."

He turns back to the grill. "You seen Berkeley since you two went out?"

There it is. A stab of longing in my gut so sharp, I glance down expecting to see blood. I've managed to go all week without speaking her name, but Drake was about to ruin that.

"Nah." Even though my answer is neutral, the pang in my chest is anything but.

"She wasn't all she was cracked up to be once you got her alone?" He flips the steaks.

I suck in a breath. I'm pretty damn sure she's *more* than I imagine her to be. Judging from one kiss, she's fucking lethal. A kind of lethal I've never dealt with. Berkeley isn't in my wheelhouse.

I haven't been able to decide what I'm going to do about her.

There's no way in hell I'm just going to let her write me off after what happened in my truck when we got drenched. I don't know what she meant by "not available," but that kiss said it all. I need more of Berkeley. And I'm not going to let her brush me off that easily. Not when I don't even know the real reason.

The E.V.S. Recovery mission begins tomorrow. There's no way in hell I'm letting that evil vixen siren just walk away from me.

When I start awake, golden sunlight is streaming in through my window and my sheets are twisted and sticking to me. I half-crawl, half-slide over to the window to peek through the blinds. The ocean greets me a mere football field away, lapping gently against the shore, and I gape in disbelief. Then my mind begins to clear, and I realize I'm in Lone Sands.

My time in Africa haunts me. But only in my dreams. I've conquered the beast during the daytime, but I can't seem to control my nightmares. I squeeze my eyes shut, willing the memories to fade, and I suck air in through my nose, then push it out through my mouth.

I plant my feet on the floor and let my head fall into my hands. When I feel calm enough to rise, I pad barefoot, only wearing the boxer briefs I sleep in, across the hall to the bathroom where I take a piss and wash my face. My eyes are bloodshot when I glance at my reflection, and I realize that it's going to take more than a rinse to wash away the stink of my demons.

I pull on a pair of workout shorts and head to the garage, where Drake has a gym set up. I tape my hands and pull on a pair of boxing gloves.

Then I proceed to pummel the shit out of a heavy bag, punching it as hard as I can until my breath comes in heavy gasps and sweat pours off my body.

An hour on the bag, thirty minutes lifting free weights, and I'm good to go.

I've never been a trusting person. Growing up in foster care after losing both your parents in a car accident at the age of seven will do that to a kid. But after what happened to me behind enemy lines in a continent where I had no friends, aside from the men I lost and the ones I couldn't make it back to, that almost broke me. It leveled my body and murdered my spirit. I clawed my way out, but only a shell of the Dare I used to be returned from that hellhole.

And the tiny amount of trust I'd built with the army?

Gone.

So I don't know why I've decided to pursue Berkeley, a girl I've met a handful of times and been on one date with. Something about her just soothes my soul. And a soul like mine needs a salve.

Somehow, I know I can't trust her not to reach into my chest, pull out my heart, and crush it in her fists.

But I can't walk away.

An hour later, I push open the door to See Food. Freshly showered but not shaved, I smile at the lady who I've gathered owns the place, and she comes rushing forward.

"Table for one, sweet thing?"

I give her a grin, nodding. "Thanks."

"I take it you'd like to sit in Berkeley's section?"

Nodding again, I wink at her. "Am I that transparent?"

She tucks a strand of her short, black hair behind her ear and nods. "As a window."

She seats me and leaves, and I wait while my heart thumps forcefully against my ribs.

I see her before she sees me, coming around the corner from the kitchen, her arms laden with plates for one of her tables. My eyes stay locked on her perfect form as she carefully maneuvers around the restaurant until she's just five tables away. She still hasn't seen me, so I have time to thank God for creating cutoff jean shorts that show me every delicious, curvy inch of Berkeley's legs, and to marvel at the fact that I know what her full, strawberry-colored lips taste like.

She smells like roses, but she *tastes* like tangy, sweet marmalade.

When she finishes delivering her food, she turns to my table, to me, and freezes. Then she straightens, pulls the stunned look from her expression, and walks casually over to my table.

I smile up at her. "Hey, Berkeley. How's the shrimp today?"

Her eyes narrow. "Fancy seeing you here, Dare."

I thought this would be difficult, but now I can see that it's just gonna be fun. "I'm eating. Isn't this still a restaurant?"

She shifts, calling attention to her legs again, and my eyes betray me as they leave her face to trail over her body. *Fuck*, her See Food shirt today is a ribbed tank with a picture of a crab on the front. The tight fabric accentuates her generous rack, sitting high on her chest as if on display. I swallow.

"Yeah, but why *this* restaurant?"

"Because you're here," I say simply.

Her lips part, but no words escape, and I turn my attention to my closed menu. "You already know what I want, right?"

I'm aware this statement has two possible meanings, and I wonder which of them she'll answer.

She glances at the door to the kitchen, like she's considering dumping my table onto someone else. But since the only other waitress I see running around is her boss, I doubt it'll happen. Her gaze shifts back to mine, and I hold it, hoping she can read my intentions in my eyes.

I'm here for you, Berkeley. Only you.

She sighs. "Okay. I'll bring you your usual."

As she turns, I reach out and grab her arm. She stiffens, turning to face me. "No Killian's. It's kinda early. Just bring me a sweet tea."

She nods and walks away. I smile.

When she returns with my drink, her boss is on her heels. "Break time, Berk."

She whirls, a glare on her face. "But I just—"

The lady, who has a bouquet of flowers in her future from a grateful ex-Ranger, shakes her head. "Sit. Have lunch with your friend. I got it covered, and Daniella will be here any minute."

Berkeley glances between her boss, and me and blows the stray piece of hair I've grown to love so much out of her face. "Fine. Have Boozer make me a crab cake. Thanks, *Lenny.*"

Yeah, thanks, Lenny.

She sits down across from me, her mouth set in a stubborn line.

"Lucky turn of events," I offer.

She holds her angry stare for about another five seconds before it crumbles, and she bursts into laughter. It's infectious, and I'm laughing, too.

"How'd you pull that off?"

I shrug, eyeing the dark shadows beneath her eyes with a frown. She hasn't been sleeping?

"Maybe I've picked up a little of your siren magic."

She leans forward, placing her elbows on the table, and giving me a clear shot at her cleavage, which I take advantage of. When I meet her eyes again, she's staring at me with a mixture of frustration and curiosity.

"I thought I made it clear last week. I thought you got the message, since I haven't seen you since."

"You haven't seen me since because I've been strategizing. I didn't get any message, other than when we kiss, the whole fucking world stops moving. So we shouldn't *stop* kissing. We should kiss *more*."

Her eyes drop to my lips, and I go instantly hard in my jeans.

She does that to me with a *look*.

Sexy siren indeed.

"So, what? You're just going to keep coming in here until I kiss you again?"

"If that's what you want."

She shakes her head, and I change the subject.

"You haven't been sleeping well. Is something stressing you out?"

The bluntness takes Berkeley aback, her eyebrows twitch in surprise. "How did you know—"

I just wait, toying with the straw on my tea while I read her face.

Finally, she sighs. "My parents want me to move out to San Diego. My dad's a pretty powerful guy, and he's making all kinds of arrangements without my consent."

My chest clenches as my heartbeat kicks up. "Why would he do that?"

She hesitates, averting her eyes. "I told you I'm not available, didn't I? My life is…complicated."

"If you don't want to go, you just don't go. That's pretty simple."

"Yeah." She sighs. "That would be pretty simple, except you don't know my father."

That's true, I don't know her father. Right now, I'd really like to meet him, though. Because it's really, really crazy, but I *don't want her to go.*

It must show on my face, because hers softens. "I'll think of something."

My lip twitches, and my chest expands.

Suddenly, she reaches for my arm across the table. "I've been dying to read this."

I glance down, and her fingertips are burning into my tattooed arm. The heat spreads, traveling through the limb and beyond. "Go ahead."

Her lips move minimally as she reads the cursive script, and I add it to the list of "Berkeley's Adorable Character Traits" that I'm building in my head.

"'My Country, My Sacrifice, I Protect What's Mine.'" Her eyes are serious when they meet mine again. "That's beautiful."

I shrug again. "It's true."

We sit, locked in each other's gazes for about a minute before Lenny brings us heaping plates of food.

"You can't survive on just a crab cake, sweetie," she chides Berkeley gently.

She's loaded Berkeley's plate with not only two crab cakes, but also hush puppies, succulent-looking asparagus spears, and a baked potato.

Berkeley rolls her eyes but smiles warmly at her boss as she retreats.

"She's nice," I remark. "Treats you like family."

Berkeley nods. "She's been a second mom to me ever since I started working here. When I was seventeen, I needed a home away from home. She and Boozer gave me that, and I've loved them ever since."

I nod, and we eat in comfortable silence. I know how hard it is to achieve comfortable silence with someone, because I've only ever experienced it a couple of times. Drake and I can go hours without talking, while sitting in the same room. Neither of us is bothered by it in the least. And Chase, when we're on good terms. We don't need words to have a conversation.

Berkeley makes these little noises of satisfaction when she eats that are slowly driving me insane. She seems to live so fully, appreciating everything she gets like it's the last time she'll ever get it. I'm having a hard time keeping my eyes off of her.

When she finishes, she pushes her plate a few inches away from her and sits back in the booth. I sigh with relief, because I don't know how much more of her sexy, unabashed eating I was gonna be able to take.

"You have the day off from the garage?"

I nod. "Yep. I have every Sunday and Monday off. Why, are you free?"

She gives me a warning look. "Dare—"

I wave her off. "I know, I know. Unavailable."

I lay enough money on the table to pay for my meal, and then I stand up.

A shadow crosses her face, and I almost park my happy ass right back in the booth. "You're leaving?"

I nod. "I think I've worn out my welcome for the day. I'll see you tomorrow, Berkeley."

Her brow furrows. "Tomorrow?"

"Are you working?"

She nods.

"Then I'll be here on my lunch break."

I check my phone on my way out to my truck. One text message, from Chase.

You can't leave me hanging like this. These dudes aren't fucking around.

8

Berkeley

"He's either crazy, or he's insane."

Mea's statement is so matter-of-fact, I almost miss its absurdity.

"Mea. You do realize both of those words mean the same thing?"

She waves me off. "Well, what other explanation is there? He's had a meal with you at your place of employment every single day you've worked for *two weeks.* What other explanation is there?"

It's true. Dare has turned up during every shift I've worked, whether I'm working lunch or dinner. If I'm waitressing, he's there. At first, I didn't know what to make of it. He'd come in, and we'd talk. Lenny would push me to sit down and eat with him, and I didn't fight it.

Then, I grew to expect his visits. I looked forward to them. When the door of See Food opened, I would look up expectantly, because I kind of couldn't wait to see Dare's gorgeous face as he entered.

Now I'm just confused. I don't know what he's doing. Hell, I'm not sleeping with the guy. We only kissed once. And maybe that kiss meant more to me than any other kiss in the history of kisses, but he couldn't feel the same way. He's a dude, for one.

And he's an *army dude*, for another!

That's one topic we haven't discussed. I haven't brought up the army, and neither has he. I'm smart enough to know that he's not still in, or he wouldn't be here. So the army is his past.

Does that change anything for me? I swore off dating military men. But technically, Dare isn't a military man anymore.

I say as much to Mea, and her face gets all scrunchy, like she smells something bad. "He's still a big fat red flag, Berk. You don't even *know* him. And he's so…mysterious. And dark. And sexy. All of those things make for a very, very bad combination. You could never introduce him to your parents. And if Grisham lays eyes on him…World War Three might break loose."

All valid points. Mea's absolutely correct on all counts.

But still…

Tonight I'm off work, and I haven't seen Dare today. I glance wistfully at my phone. Our lunch and dinner dates haven't morphed into texting or calling, and I'm missing him.

Shit. I've fallen into seriously dangerous territory here.

My bedroom door flies open, and the Admiral is standing there, filling up my doorway in all his domineering glory.

"Berkeley."

"Yes, Daddy," I counter, glancing at Mea.

"We need to talk." He glances at Mea, too. "Alone."

She turns to me and rolls her eyes, facing away from the Admiral of course, and rises to her feet. "Call me later, Berk."

When she's gone, the Admiral comes to stand beside my bed, and

I give him my full attention, a stone sinking to the bottom of my stomach.

"Grisham's downstairs."

"He is?" That's not terrible news. I haven't seen Grish in a few weeks. Hanging out with him tonight will be fun, take my mind off of the army-man-who-shall-not-be-named.

"He is," the Admiral confirms. "He's leaving in a few weeks for California, you know."

I nod. "I know."

"I think he expects you to go with him."

I sigh in exasperation. "Really? On what planet—"

The dark look in the Admiral's eyes has me recanting and changing what I was about to say. "I mean, I don't think so, sir. Grisham and I are just friends. I've told you that before."

"Friendship is for children, Berkeley." The Admiral's usual booming voice is subdued tonight. "You don't have time for it anymore. It's time to start your life. And your life is in San Diego, with Grisham. It's what's best for you."

I can feel the flush forming in my neck, rising quickly to my face as I grow more heated. "And don't I have a say in what's best for me?"

He closes his eyes, as if he's having an argument with a petulant child. I want to growl, I want to throw something. But then I would be acting like the petulant child he thinks I am, so I simply glare. "I'm an adult. I can make my own decisions."

"Go down and see Grisham." The Admiral turns and walks out my bedroom door. "We'll talk tomorrow."

The growing sense of dread in my stomach should have abated with his exit, but it didn't. It keeps growing as I change out of my ratty old gym shorts and throw on a jean skirt and a tank top and join Grisham downstairs in the foyer.

He smiles, but it's not a normal Grisham smile. Grish's smiles are always warm, tender, and full of understanding. They light up his whole face. This smile is nervous and wobbly and doesn't quite reach his eyes.

He holds out his hand. "Walk?"

I nod, taking it and letting him lead the way outside and down to the sand.

We walk, silently absorbing the darkness around us, the twinkling stars above us, and the ocean's dull rumble beside us.

"What's up, Grish?" I finally ask.

He stops, shoving his hands in the pockets of his ridiculously expensive jeans. He doesn't meet my gaze, instead focusing his eyes out at the invisible horizon.

"Berkeley." His voice is quiet, so quiet I almost can't hear it over the crashing of the waves.

Oh, no. Oh, God. This can't be good. Grisham has never been as lively and as surly as me, but he never sounds this serious, either.

"What, Grish?" I whisper.

"God, Berk. I know, more than anything that you aren't ready for this. But our parents…they think it's time, Berkeley. The pressure from our dads is almost killing me. I can't go off to San Diego in a few weeks without at least honoring their wishes. I don't want to lose you—"

His voice breaks on the last word, and instant tears spring to my eyes. I haven't thought about what our fathers' pressure must be like for him. He must feel it so much more strongly than I do, because he's a man, and they have stringent expectations for his life. Probably more so than they do mine. I just thought that since he's basically followed every directive they've ever given him that he was doing what made him happy.

"I thought I would have more time. More time to help you see that, in the end, this really is what's best for both of us. Because I love you, Berkeley. I always have. I always will. You're my best friend, and I want to spend the rest of my life with you. On our terms, not on theirs."

He finally looks at me, and my heart is squeezed to a pulp in my chest. His eyes are anguished, because he knows. He *knows* I'll never be able to give him the answer he wants.

He pulls out the ring anyway, right out of his pocket. And gently takes my hand, closing my fingers around the warm metal circle. "Just think about it, Berkeley. Okay? You're it for me, and I could be it for you, too. You just haven't thought about me like that yet. Start thinking about it now, Berk."

Tears are in danger of pouring out of my eyes, but I take a deep, shuddering breath.

No. No, I can't marry you, Grisham. You know I can't.

That's the answer I should have given him.

But looking into Grisham's eyes, the boy I've known since I wore diapers, I can't do that to him. I can't break him that way, not when he's already cracking under so much pressure from our dads. So instead, I say, "I'll think about it Grish."

The music pounds in my ears, and the tequila flows like liquid fire in my veins. It only took one call to Mea, during which she could barely understand me, for her to have a car waiting outside of my house to take me to where she was.

It turns out, she was at a bar.

"Another." I indicate my empty shot glass and gesture to the bartender.

He shakes his head, frowning at me. "Switch to a mixed drink. No more shots."

I place my hands on my hips, and sway with the minimal movement. Sighing, I nod. "Give me whatever."

I grab my drink from him and stick my tongue out. Childish, yes. Satisfying, yes.

When I turn around to face the sea of people in the bar, Mea is there, tugging on my arm. "Come on, Berk! Dancing is therapy!"

So I dance. I drink, and I dance. I do both of those things until the look in Grisham's eyes as he proposes to me no longer burns a hole in my brain. And the only face I can see is Dare's.

I pull my phone out to check it, but of course there's no message from him.

"What happened to my life?" I wonder aloud.

Mea frowns and shakes her head. "Not tonight. No mopey Berkley tonight. We'll tackle this problem tomorrow, I promise."

I nod, and sway on my feet again. "I gotta go home. I'm trashed."

She nods, concern flickering across her gaze. "I'll get Mikah."

I shake my head. "No. I'll just call a cab. I don't want to make anyone else leave."

"Berk, it's one in the morning. It's not like our night just started."

I shake my head again. "Cab. Come see me at a decent hour tomorrow, 'kay?"

She huffs out a sigh and crosses her arms. She really is such a cute little pixie. "'Kay."

I give the cabdriver directions and lay my head against the window as I ride. The cool glass soothes my hot, sweaty skin, and I close my eyes. I'm going to have to fix this situation with Grisham tomorrow. He has to know that I can't marry him. Our fathers bullied him into asking me, anyway. Right now, I kind of hate both of them.

When we arrive, I glance out the window and my eyebrows knit together. Damn, I'm either more drunk than I thought or I'm just freaking pathetic. I reach in my pocket and pull out the contents of my pockets. Phone, ID. No cash.

Shit! I must have used it all at the bar.

"Um…" I stall, looking at the cabdriver as he glares impatiently at me in his rearview mirror. "I'll be right back."

"Hey!" he shouts as I lurch out of the car. "You pay! You pay before you go!"

His thick Middle Eastern accent is difficult to understand, but I get the gist. He's not letting me out of his sight until he has his money.

So I run, I run for Dare's front door and start pounding on it.

Yeah, Dare's door. Apparently, my mind is so focused on this man, I gave the cabdriver his address instead of my own.

And now I'm here. At one-thirty in the morning.

On the fifth pound, the cabdriver has reached me, grabbing my wrist in a vise hold.

"You pay." His voice is demanding as he hisses at me.

"Let go!" I scream, probably louder than is necessary.

The door flies open, and Dare stands there, looking sleepy, dark, and dangerous. His eyes widen when he sees me, and his gaze locks on my wrist where the cabdriver is gripping me.

He reaches out, grabs the guy's wrist, and wrenches mine free. The cabdriver protests, but Dare's cold voice cuts him off.

"Touch her again, and you lose that hand. I'll pay you. Wait here."

I shiver at the authority and the quiet ferocity in his voice, and he wraps an arm around my waist and pulls me inside with him.

I stand beside the front door and inhale a deep, shuddering breath while he jogs down the hallway. When he returns with his wallet, he shoves a wad of cash at the cabbie and shuts the door.

Then he turns to face me.

And I have a chance to fully take him in. Dare is shirtless and shoeless. Dark gray pajama pants cover his lean, muscular legs.

And *oh, wow*.

He's a full-blown, darkly delicious *man*. My abdominal muscles clench as I stare. His pecs must be as hard as boulders. His tattoos are standing out in the dim light on cut, sculpted biceps, and I can't stop my eyes from finding the sharp, sexy lines of his obliques.

My eyes land on the long, shiny line of scarred skin running from his hip bone, along his ribs, and stopping just below his left pectoral.

Through the alcohol-induced haze in my brain, I realize that this scar is what he's been rubbing when his hand absently moves to graze his side.

I *will* kick myself if I remember this in the morning, but my mouth opens, and I say, "You're beautiful."

His mouth turns up in that crooked smile that makes me shiver, and he opens his arms.

I run into them, resting my face against his chest. I inhale, and his scent envelops me. Fresh soap, musk, and darkness.

"What are you doing here, honey?" His voice is a murmur right at my ear, and I want to cry from the relief of just being with him right now.

Honey. I melt like the endearment he just used.

"Do you want the long version or the short version?" I sniff.

He pulls back and looks at me. "You're loaded?"

Shit. I must be slurring. I sigh, nodding.

He frowns. "Usual occurrence?"

This time, I shake my head.

"Okay. Then you've had a bad night, and I don't need to know the details right now. I'm going to pick you up, okay?"

I nod again, biting my bottom lip, and I'm lifted into the air. I cuddle into his chest as he carries me to what I assume is his bedroom. He lays me gently down on the bed, and disappears.

I look around me. There's a lamp lit on his dresser, and the room is neat and clean. When I turn on my side and inhale, his scent envelops me and again, I have the urge to cry.

He returns, carrying a glass of water. "Drink."

I do, finishing nearly the entire glass. He hands me two aspirin, and I take them.

Then I settle back on his pillows. "I'm sorry, Dare."

His eyes darken until the clear sea-foam is more of a teal, and he's sitting beside me in one fluid movement. "I don't want you to ever be sorry for choosing to come to me when you need me. Ever. Okay?"

With wide eyes, I nod.

"Sleep," he orders. "We can talk in the morning, if you're up to it."

He retreats, and all I want to do is reach out and grab him. "Where are you going?"

"The living room couch."

"Don't do that," I beg. I've been reduced to begging. I should be ashamed of myself, but I'm too drunk to care. Thank God.

He raises an eyebrow. "Berkeley?"

My voice is soft and pleading. "Stay."

He scrutinizes me. "You sure?"

I nod, because all I want is to feel him beside me.

Tonight has been a doozy of a blow to my heart, and my liver. I'm a little bit broken and busted, but when Dare slides into bed beside me, circling his strong arms around my middle, and molding his large, hard body to mine, the tears that have been threatening to come rushing out in his presence finally decide to fall.

I sob silently into his pillowcase, and he squeezes me tighter.

"I'm here, Berkeley," he says, and my name is once again a beautiful song that only he knows how to play.

Then he presses a soft kiss to the back of my neck, and I fall asleep surrounded by Dare.

9

Dare

*L*isten, fellas!" *Olsen shouts to be heard over the noise of the Black Hawk's rotors. "We get in, take over the airfield, and send the troops the all clear. Any resistance, you know what to do. Those weapons* will not *make it out of the C.A.R. Understood?"*

"Hooah!" Our answering cry is shouted in unison.

My adrenaline is coursing through my veins, not because of the impending jump. I've jumped out of more airplanes and choppers than I can count. It's because of the mission. Completing a mission consumes me, it infiltrates my thoughts and my dreams until I can carry out my actions in my sleep.

One minute until drop zone. Forty-five seconds until drop zone. Thirty seconds until drop zone.

And then I'm falling. I plummet toward the earth, just the way I've done countless times before. My team is around me and we all stealthily hit the ground. We've done our research, we've scouted this location. We know exactly what to do. We journey for a few minutes through covered jungle toward our destination. But then suddenly, there's a shout in the trees around us and men are upon us like ants. They're every-where. How did they know?

It's an ambush. And my guys are dying around me.

I awake drenched in my own sweat, trembling. I heave for every breath I take, and no matter how much air I gulp it doesn't seem to be enough. I feel like the fire from the burning helicopter is swallowing me whole as the pieces of the wreckage fall down all around me.

Then I feel a searing blaze of heat, a different kind of heat, hit my shoulder. Another flash strokes my neck, and another. Another just beneath my ear, and I finally open my eyes.

Sunlight attacks me from the window, and in the golden light it's clear that I'm dead. Because a motherfucking angel sits on top of me.

"Dare." Her voice is gentle as she leans down and places a kiss on the hard plane of my chest. I shudder, and it has nothing to do with the dream.

"Wake up, Dare," she says. "You're at home. You're safe."

I grab ahold of her and pull her down to me. Her head settles against my chest, and my breathing steadies as her wild blond curls envelop me and the smell of roses and stale smoke pervades my senses. I finally internalize her words, realizing that I'm in my room at Drake's and that the angel in my bed is actually Berkeley Holtz.

In my bed. *Holy fuck.* The previous night comes flooding back.

"Are you okay?" My voice is morning-rough, and I stroke her mess of curls with one hand while I tilt her face up to look at me with the other.

Her expression cracks into an ironic smile. "I am, now. I was terrified that *you* weren't okay."

Shit. "I'm sorry, Berkeley. I'm fine…I wish you hadn't seen that."

I push her hair out of her eyes, rubbing my thumb along her cheekbone. "Headache?"

She shakes her head. "Nope. Aspirin did the trick."

I raise a brow. "Yeah? You were pretty tanked last night. Want to tell me what happened?"

Her eyes cloud over. "I shouldn't have shown up on your doorstep, I know—"

"Uh-uh," I interrupt her. "Don't apologize for that. I didn't mind."

That is a vast understatement. If she needs me, I will be here. I know that, it almost doesn't matter what she asks me to do. I want to be the one she calls when she is scared, or lonely, or upset. A warm pleasure enters my chest just thinking about it.

"Well, I don't even know how I ended up here. I guess I just automatically gave the cabdriver your address." She looks embarrassed, and the expression causes her to bite the corner of her bottom lip.

"You cried," I say softly. "Before you went to sleep. Why?"

I have to know. I remember the sound of her sobs, and the way her body shook. With each one I grew angrier, and more possessive. I want to hurt whoever made her cry like that.

Her voice is so small my ears strain to hear her. "My dad...he's impossible. Something happened last night that broke my heart. Now I'm going to have to fix it, and I don't know how. It's all just a giant mess."

Her answer is vague, and I don't want to push her. Confusion nearly numbs my tongue, and my blood freezes up in my veins. "Broke your heart?"

She looks up at me. "Not like that. It's a long story."

I nod slowly. I'm all too familiar with long stories. "I like long stories. But I understand if you're not ready to tell me yours."

She looks grateful, and nods. Then her expression turns almost shy. "I've really liked all our meals together over the last couple of weeks. I…I wouldn't mind if that continued."

"Yeah? I don't know…lunch with an amazingly sexy girl every single day is getting old. I might need a break."

She slaps my chest, and I laugh. "Fuck! Ouch. Fine. Every day I get to eat with you is like the new best day of any given week. You wanting me there just makes it even better."

She smirks. "That's more like it. For a second there, I thought my magic was wearing off."

She gets quiet, and I just lie here, listening to her steady breathing. When she looks up again, her face is serious. "So how long have you been suffering from PTSD?"

Reeling, I stare down at her. My mouth is open in shock, and I hold her steady amber gaze. "How did you know?"

She doesn't blink. "I'm familiar with the symptoms."

Now I'm really taken aback. Has she dated a guy in the military? Is that why the no-military dating rule? As I stare into her eyes, I can feel her gaze deep in the depths of me, like she's reading me from the inside out. It's uncomfortable, but I find myself wanting to let her see everything I have.

Almost everything.

"I'm recently discharged. I was injured about five months ago while deployed. Since then."

She nods. "I figured you weren't active duty. Do you want to talk about it?"

I give her a wry smile of my own. "It's a long story."

And just like that, we've begun building a relationship with a foundation of secrets. I should know it'll come back to bite me in the ass, but with Berkeley lying on my chest first thing in the morning, I can't bring myself to care.

Suddenly she sits up straight in my bed as if she's been shot with an arrow.

"Oh. My. Word." Each word is a stunned breath from her lips.

I sit up with her, attempting to pry my eyes from the cleavage spilling out of her halter-top and failing. Berkeley's rack should have its own website. It's glorious.

"What?" My tone is amused.

"What is that heavenly smell?" she whispers, her eyes wide.

I sniff, and grin. "Bacon. Eggs? Drake's basically a breakfast chef. You want some?"

"Oh, Dare." She breezes out of the bed, standing beside me in seconds. "You'll learn. I *always* want breakfast."

She heads for the door, and I spring out of bed, grabbing her hand and yanking her back around to face me. The force sends her flying straight into my chest, and my arms go around her as I cradle her close. The electricity between us sizzles, and she lets out a small whimper of surprise.

I close my eyes, getting myself under wraps. *Jesus*, her noises.

"Slow down, Berkeley. You're not walking out of my room like that."

She glances down at herself. Her short denim skirt is askew, hot pink toenails adorning her bare feet. In that skirt, her shapely legs stretch on forever, and although her halter-top covers her stomach, it still shows off her cleavage.

I love my roommate, but he gets to see none of that. I want to keep Berkeley's sexy all wrapped up for my own private viewing.

"This wasn't exactly a planned visit, Dare," she protests. She folds her arms over her chest and shifts her weight to one foot, which is damn cute. "I don't have a change of clothes."

"Then we're lucky I live here, aren't we?" I stride to my dresser, poking through clothes. I finally toss her a black army T-shirt and a pair of gray sweats that fit me snugly.

She wrinkles her nose at the sweats. "I'm going to roast."

I eye her meaningfully. "Roasting is better than smoking, at least in this house." But I replace the sweats with shorts.

Biting her lip to hide her smile, she unfurls her arms. I bend down and press my lips to her forehead.

"Did I mention this morning ranks up there in my top five?"

"Top five best mornings?"

I nod, smiling.

She leans forward, rising up on her toes. She reaches both arms around my neck and pulls. When my face is only inches from hers, she whispers. "One day I want to hear that list."

Then she pats me *on the ass.*

I growl as I back out the door. This girl…she's gonna kill me.

When she walks out of my bedroom, wearing my clothes, I've had time to warn Drake that she's here. But I haven't had time to prepare myself for what it feels like to see her rocking *my shit.* The caveman in me wants to beat my chest and grab her up. I want to walk over to her, grab her face in my hands, and kiss the mess out of her. I want to stake my claim, pronounce to the world that this gorgeous, sexy, funny girl is *mine.*

Instead, in the interest of not coming off as a complete psycho, I play it cool. I smile at her.

"See, Drake? I told you she was here, and not a figment of my imagination."

Drake shakes his head as he dishes a mound of bacon onto a serving plate. "Well, fuck. I just knew you were making that shit up."

Berkeley grins. Her whole face lights up when she smiles like that, and the sun's rays streaming in through the window have nothing on her.

"Good morning, Drake," she says.

"Good morning, sunshine."

My smile grows, because I know Drake is thinking the same thing I am.

We eat breakfast, and then Berkeley goes to retrieve her phone from the dresser in my room. I watch. I know I'll never be able to keep myself from watching her walk out of a room.

Drake mutters a curse, and I glance at him. "What?"

He snorts. "You. Shit, dude. It's all over your face. Did you—"

I hold up my hand. "Don't, Drake. You're my friend, and I love you. But if you finish that sentence, I'm gonna have to come across this table and fuck up your beautiful face. I don't wanna do that, Drake."

He splutters, sending orange juice flying over his plate.

When Berkeley returns, she's holding her phone and her expression is exasperated.

"I gotta go," she says.

I stand. "Let's go, then."

Once we're settled in the truck, I keep throwing glances in her direction. She's staring out the window, with a tiny little smile on her lips.

"Berkeley. If you keep sitting over there with that sexy smile on your face, I'm going to turn this truck around and bring you back to my house."

She looks over at me, and I see the crimson flush creep up from her neck to her cheeks. I add it to my mental list.

"We're almost there," she says. "You can just drop me off right over here."

She points to the curb ahead, just outside of a neighborhood with gigantic homes built directly on the oceanfront.

I look at her like she's lost her ever-loving mind. Which she has, if she thinks I'm leaving her by the side of the road. I continue driving right on past the extravagant neighborhood sign.

"Which house?" I ask.

She sighs, and then points me in the direction of her house. I pull into the long, circular driveway and look over at her.

"I'll call you later."

She nods, and the corner of her lip disappears into her mouth. "Thanks, Dare. For last night."

I nod. The front door of the house opens, and the impeccable woman from the night I took Berkeley home appears. She stands in the doorway, arms folded.

"Huh. Momma doesn't look too thrilled."

"What else is new." Berkeley sighs. She reaches over and squeezes my hand. "See ya."

I watch her as she walks up the driveway and up the stone steps to the house. She breezes past her mother, who spends another second staring at me before slamming the door shut.

Then I drive away.

The strangeness with Berkeley and her mother barely affects me as I drive home with a grin plastered on my face. While driving I decide that I'll finally call my brother today.

Chase might be a pain in my ass, but he's my brother, and he deserves for me to at least hear him out.

As a teenager, I got into my fair share of scrapes. Unwanted

90 Diana Gardin

kid in the system in Florida, I had to find my own way. Make my own friends. Without any guidance. Sometimes I made the wrong choices. Sometimes I found myself in deep shit with guys bigger and tougher than I was. Chase always had my back. Some scuffles were more serious than others, and if Chase and I hadn't backed each other up, we may not have made it to where we are today.

Where I am today is a pretty good place, all shit considering. Where Chase is? Not so much. He can't seem to stay on the right side of the law. When we turned eighteen and I enlisted, I tried to talk him into doing the same. I told him that we could travel the world together, do something important with our lives. He declined, stating that the world was too big for him. Rather than get lost in the great unknown he'd rather stay in Florida and take his chances with the devil he knows.

No sooner do I have that thought than I pull into my driveway to the sight of a strange car parked behind the Challenger.

When I open the front door, Drake is sitting on the couch with his arms crossed and a deadly serious expression on his face. Across from him, next to the ornate stone fireplace, stands my brother.

I no longer need to return his phone calls.

Chase, and possibly the problems he's currently dealing with, have come to Lone Sands.

10

Berkeley

I'm allowed to move five paces into the foyer before my mother explodes.

"Berkeley *Jane Holtz*!"

I turn, facing her wrath head-on without even cringing. I'm so proud of myself that I smile before I forget my mother is about to rip me a new one.

"Momma—"

"Don't you *dare* 'Momma' me! You've been out all night, probably with that Mea and her crew of misfits, and you arrive home this morning in the passenger seat of a *pickup truck*—"

I bite my bottom lip to keep from bursting into hysterical laughter. This is beyond ridiculous. I'm twenty-two, not twelve.

"At least it wasn't a motorcycle," I offer. Then my mind drifts away to a world where sexy-as-hell Dare owns a Harley.

My mother's mouth drops open. The shock and disgust are written like a story all across her face. "You're *joking* about this? It isn't funny, Berkeley! What if your father had been home to see you arriving with…who *was* that?"

Here we go. "Nobody. Just a friend of mine."

She shakes her head in disbelief, her elegant blond bob barely shifting with the movement. "Get upstairs. I can't even look at you right now."

I nod. "I have to shower and change, anyway. I'm working the lunch shift."

Her mouth opens to argue, but I don't wait to hear it.

I'm just done.

When I get out of the shower, I have a waiting text from Dare.

You working lunch or dinner today?

I smile, typing out my response.

Both. I'm on for a double. My feet are gonna be so sore 2nite.

I get dressed in a pair of ripped jeans that I absolutely love, and a tight purple See Food T-shirt. In the spirit of pissing off my mother, I throw on a pair of black Chuck Taylors, because I know how much she hates them.

My phone buzzes, and I frown a little as I read Dare's message.

I'll make it in by dinnertime later. I'll miss my lunch date, tho.

The dude won't make lunch with me, after I spend one night at his house, and I'm feeling *disappointed*? I give myself a mental shake, and then I actually slap both of my cheeks with my palms.

Get it together, Berk-baby. He's not yours.

He's not mine, but in my head, I picture him the way he was last night. The way he looked when he opened his front door to me. My toes curl in my sneakers and my muscles all tense up at the memory. He was darkly sexy. I didn't even know that combination appealed to me. Maybe it doesn't. Maybe it's just Dare that appeals to me.

And the way he cradled me in his arms as I fell asleep, and the way I kissed him out of his nightmare this morning. The low murmur of his voice as he spoke to me while I lay against his chest. The territorial look in his eyes as he observed me walking into the kitchen wearing his clothes.

I wish he could be mine.

Then I think of the look on Grisham's face when he asked me to marry him, when he knew full well I didn't want to. And my happy thoughts crumble into a pile of rubble all around me.

I pulled out my phone to send another text.

We need to talk, Grish. I'm working all day today. 2moro?

I head downstairs, thankful that my mother is nowhere to be found, and climb into my Escalade. When my phone buzzes, I look down at it.

Headed to Cali for a couple of days with my dad. Talk when I get back.

I nod, sighing as I pull out of my neighborhood. A couple of days to breathe and think. That can only be a good thing.

When I arrive at See Food, Lenny is sitting at a back booth, cradling her head in her hands. The restaurant isn't open yet, so we're alone. I know Boozer is in the back, prepping his cooking materials for the day.

"Oh no, Lenny," I croon sympathetically. "A migraine?"

She nods miserably, shielding her eyes from the dim restaurant lights overhead.

"I'm going to get right on the prep work, then. Why don't you just go lay down in the office? Daniella will be here soon, and I know we can handle the lunch crowd without you. Maybe by dinnertime your head will feel better."

She looks up with a look of pure gratitude. "You're the best, sweetie. Thank you."

Her skin is pale and she looks a little green underneath the chalky pallor, so I shoo her away and head into the back of the kitchen to help Boozer finish prepping.

After a solid forty-five minutes of cutting meat and seafood, chopping vegetables, and making sure the walk-in freezer is stocked for service, I leave a thankful Boozer in the kitchen and go flip the sign on the door to OPEN. I send Daniella a grateful smile for completing the dining room prep herself, and tie on my apron.

The first customer in the door is Mea, and I laugh as I seat her. She's practically bouncing on her toes as she walks beside me, and I make her wait an entire minute before I finally ask the question she's dying to answer.

"What are you so happy about?"

She squeals, and I roll my eyes. "I rented an apartment today!"

My mouth falls open. "I had no idea you were moving out!"

Then I narrow my eyes in suspicion. "Wait…do you have a job that I don't know about? You know, other than the one where you sell jeans and shirts for a living?"

Throughout college, Mea never stopped working at the job she began in high school. She worked retail at the mall, in one of the most popular clothing stores. She worked at a different local store when she was away at school, but now that she was back she worked in Brunswick County again.

"Actually…" She dragged out the word like it had about eight syllables instead of just four.

I raised my eyebrows, waiting for her to spit it out.

"I just got promoted to manager! It turns out that stuck-up bitch that used to manage the place was stealing money from the register every night! Lucky for me, huh?"

I grin. "Yeah, lucky for you. Congratulations! When can I see the new place?"

"Um, as soon as possible? I'm looking for a roommate. There's a girl I knew from school who lives here, too, and I'm trying to convince her to move out of her parents' mansion and come pay rent with me."

"Okay," I agree. I know now isn't the time to ask Mea why she isn't pursuing something with her recently acquired theater degree, which suits her so perfectly.

I leave her to go get her drink order and tend to the growing number of tables quickly filling up in my section.

By dinner shift, my feet are aching so severely I'm limping instead of walking, and my back feels like I've been carrying boulders down a mountainside rather than waiting tables at a popular seafood restaurant. My hair is falling limply around my face, and I'm sure whatever trace of makeup I had on before I left the house this morning is long gone. Despite all of that, my butterflies begin to dance around in my stomach as I anticipate Dare's impending visit.

As if on cue, his dark, beautiful form enters the front door about halfway through my shift. When I see him, I forget all about my usual play-it-cool act and run straight into his strong, willing arms.

He makes a pleased sound deep in his chest, which rumbles against my neck where his face is buried, and I sigh with satisfaction.

"That's a hell of a greeting," he murmurs against my skin.

"Well, a girl misses her soldier when he's been away all day." My voice is a little breathless as I pull back to stare up into his perfectly handsome face. A dark shadow of stubble graces the line of his jaw, where it connects with his neck, and I reach up to run my fingers across it.

"No shave today?"

He smiles, staring down at me. "I've had a lot on my mind today."

The corners of my mouth begin to rise, and then another guy, one that I've never seen before, steps out from behind Dare.

"Hi there," he says, sticking out a hand. A brilliant smile touches his lips. "I'm Chase. Dare's brother. You must be Berkeley."

I can't stop my eyebrows from shooting upward, and my mouth from dropping open. I had no idea Dare had a brother. Then again…I don't know Dare very well, do I? A wash of unease settles over me as I shake Chase's hand. I catch Dare's eye and he gives a minuscule shrug.

"Well, let me get y'all to a table," I finally say, turning to lead them toward the back of the restaurant. As I let Chase step around me, Dare grabs my arm, gently swinging me around to face him.

"I didn't know he was coming. I'll explain later." His gaze is apologetic, and I know he's read my expression and wants to ease my conscience.

I shouldn't feel uneasy at all. There are plenty of things about my life I haven't shared with Dare. Including a proposal for marriage and parents who have my entire future mapped out for me.

Chase is tall, though not as tall as Dare. Their hair is similar in its dark color, although Chase's may be closer to the color of toffee, rather than milk chocolate. His eyes are drastically different from Dare's clear light green ones. Chase's are dark as a night sky, the darkest, deepest shade of brown I've ever seen. I can't read anything in them, and it strikes me that he could be hiding anything in those deep, dark abysses. His hair curls around his ears, where Dare's reaches all the way to his collar.

After I seat them and take their drink orders, I inform Dare that I won't be able to eat with them tonight.

"Yes, you will," says Lenny as she breezes by me on her way out of the kitchen. "I'm feeling better. You deserve to sit and eat, and then to go on home, sweetie. I'll do your side work tonight. Thank you so much, Berkeley, for helping me today."

I smile at her. "You're sure you're okay?"

She crosses her heart with her index finger. "Swear."

Dare stands so that I can slide into the booth next to him. As I slip by him, my chest bumps against his and his eyes burn holes into mine. I try to contain my shiver and fail.

"So, Berkeley," Chase begins once I'm seated across from him. "How come I'm only just finding out about you?"

"Chase." Dare's voice is quiet, but his warning is crystal clear. Chase completely ignores it, staring at me.

I glance back and forth between them before I answer. "I'm not sure, Chase. Does Dare usually talk to you in great detail about all of his friends?"

Chase whistles. "Damn, bro. Friend zone? I thought I taught you better than that. I thought traveling the world with fatigues on would have taught you better than that."

I narrow my eyes at Chase. Dare and I may not be together, but I won't stand for anyone to talk about him like he has no game.

Because that's just a dirty damn lie.

"I didn't say he was in the friend zone...friends don't usually spend the night in the same bed, do they, Dare?" I glance at him and smile sweetly.

He chokes on his Killian's, which Daniella has just delivered, and thumps his chest with a fist. "Nope. Mine never do. Do yours, Chase?"

Chase just shakes his head, turning his attention to the menu.

Dare leans over, his warm breath tickling my ear. "Nice one, vixen."

I'm dying for Dare to explain the dynamic I'm reading between him and his brother. They don't really favor each other in the way I'd expect brothers to. But also, there seems to be a tension between them that I can't understand.

We put in our orders when Daniella comes back, and dinner goes off without any more drama. When we're finished, Dare lets me out of the booth and I stand, stretching.

"I know you're probably tired," says Dare as Chase begins walking toward the front door. "But I'd like to keep you company tonight. That okay?"

I hesitate. I try not to be held captive in those striking eyes, but I get lost in them every time. "Dare...last night was...kind of amazing. But as far as my complications go, nothing has really changed. In fact, my life has recently become even more complicated. I don't want to drag you along for the ride."

His eyes narrow dangerously. "But what if I like rides? Especially really, really fast ones?"

I laugh.

"Just hanging out, Berkeley. Remember? No marriage proposals."

My stomach turns an impressive somersault.

"I have an idea for tonight…humor me," he continues. "You have your car here?"

I nod.

"Okay, follow me back to my place so I can drop Chase off. Yeah?"

I can't say no. Damn, why can't I say no to this guy? I let my gaze sweep over his large form, and I know exactly why I can't.

"Okay." I nod, biting the smile off my lips.

Once outside, Chase is waiting next to Dare's truck. I give him a wave as I walk to my Escalade. Chase whistles for the second time tonight.

"Shit, Dare," he drawls. "She's out of your league! You know that, right?"

"Yeah," Dare replies, staring at me as I climb up into the car. "You're not telling me anything I'm not painfully aware of."

God, I hope Chase's visit in Lone Sands is a short one.

11

Dare

Keeping my hands off of Berkeley, especially after she spent the night in my arms, is growing increasingly more difficult. Tonight she's wearing ripped jeans and Chucks, and I had no idea sneakers and denim could be so fucking sexy on a woman. But with Berkeley's curves poured inside of the jeans and the tight purple T-shirt that reads YOU WANT SEE FOOD? GET IT YOURSELF, my hands are clenched into sweaty fists under the table just so I won't grab ahold of her luscious flesh.

"What the hell, Dare? You got a girl and didn't tell me?"

I grit my teeth as I continue trying to ignore Chase's interrogation. I am beyond irritated with my foster brother. He'd shown up in town before I had the chance to return his endless phone calls.

"Chase, how do you know your problems didn't follow you here? I don't need that kind of headache in my life right now, man. I just got settled."

Chase scoffs. "You think I'm an amateur? I've been doing this shit a long time, bro. Nobody followed me. They'll be pissed I skipped town, but I'll roll back in with their dough and all will be well."

I glance over at him. "And that's where I come in, right?"

"Dude, I know you've saved up some crazy bank from your soldier days. You never spent a dime, always staying in the barracks and shit. You hoarded money like a motherfucker, didn't you?"

Everything he said was absolutely true. You get paid well to put your life on the line, especially after you rise in the ranks. I had no family to care for, and no expenses outside of my cell phone. Everything I made when I was overseas was tax free, and I saved money religiously. I'm glad now that I did it, because I've been thinking about what kind of life I want to start for myself now that the future is looking brighter.

Until Chase came to town. As much as I love my foster brother, his timing has always been shit.

"How much?" I sigh. I want to get it over with. Chase isn't in town for a friendly visit, and I can't pretend that I don't want him out of Lone Sands as quickly as possible. I've got more important matters to attend to. Like convincing the future Mrs. Conners that she is the future Mrs. Conners.

Fuck, where did that thought come from? I don't know Berkeley well enough to think she could one day be my everything. But damn if the thought comes as naturally as a breeze over the ocean.

This girl is messing with my head. And I don't even hate it.

As I'm fumbling with my own thoughts, Chase spits out the amount of money he owes for his gambling debt.

The truck swerves dangerously into oncoming traffic, and I yank the wheel back hard to the right, narrowly missing a collision with a minivan.

"Jesus *fucking* Christ, Chase!"

He merely nods. "I know. I fucked up. But you got it, right?"

I nod slowly. "Yeah. I've got some of it. But I can't give you that kind of money, Chase. It would clean me out."

He grips my arm. "I wouldn't ask, Dare."

His voice has gone soft and quiet, and his grip on my arm is desperate. "I wouldn't ask unless I desperately needed it."

I growl, running a hand through my long hair. "What kind of guy is this, Chase? He going to kill you if you don't pay?"

Chase nodded. "That's pretty much the gist of it."

"*Goddammit*! Why do you do this to yourself? What if you didn't have me to bail your ass out all the time? I've had it with this shit, Chase. I'm trying to start a life here. I can't keep getting into your messes with you. You need to stand on your own feet."

"You're gonna give me this lecture *now*, Dare? I know, okay? I know I mess up all the time. It's pretty much all I know how to do. But if you help me with this, I swear I will turn shit around. I fucking swear it."

I just shake my head as I pull into Drake's driveway. The Challenger is parked in front, so I know he'll be ready to weigh in on this issue. He's less than thrilled that Chase showed up unannounced.

I've told Drake enough about Chase over the years that Drake pretty much can't stand my foster brother. I can't blame him; Chase is a total and complete mess. But we've been through a lot together. More than two young boys should have to suffer through.

Berkeley pulls in behind me in her sweet SUV, and I glance in the rearview. "I'll see what I can do, Chase. No promises."

He nods. "Well, I'll stick around until you figure it out."

Chase heads for the front door as I turn to face Berkeley. When her mile-long legs exit her car my heart begins thumping a steady, anxious rhythm in my chest.

I can't help it. As I greet her beside her car I grab her up into my arms and squeeze. She's so soft and round to my hard and sharp, the contrast is an addiction I don't want to kick.

I'm gonna let this girl become my habit.

"Hey," I say into the crook of her shoulder.

"Hey." Her voice is breathless as she answers, and the fact that I affect her the way she affects me gives my body a purely male reaction.

"You're a terrible driver," she whispers into my chest.

I chuckle. "That wasn't my fault."

"Yeah? Did Chase reach over and grab the steering wheel, forcing you to swerve like a drunk grandma?"

Shaking my head, I pull back to look down at her. "Nah. A crazy-hot blonde with wild hair caught my attention in my rearview."

I laugh as she immediately reaches up to stroke her mess of curls, and she glares at me. "Wild hair?"

"Did you miss the part where I called you hot?"

She smirks, and the dimples in her cheeks wink at me. I keep my hands firmly around her waist, but I can't help it that they tighten their grip. Those damn dimples are my Kryptonite.

"What are we doing?" she asks.

That reminds me of why I asked her to come out tonight. "Come with me," I say, leading her around to the back of the house. I hope to God my text to Drake when I left the restaurant sent him running to complete the arrangement I set up on the deck earlier this evening.

As we round the corner of the house, I smile, because my mission has been completed. The shocked gasp that escapes the girl beside me as she takes a look at what's on the deck is enough to make me pull her faster across the yard and up the steps.

I've littered the place with candles of various sizes. I found some lying around in Drake's cabinets, and purchased the others between arguments with Chase today. As soon as Berkeley told me this morning that she was working a double, I knew that I wouldn't be able to see her at lunch because of Chase's impromptu visit. I wanted to make it up to her, and I hated the thought of her aching muscles and tired feet after standing up and waitressing all damn day.

I've piled a lounge chair high with soft cushions, and sitting on the wood in front of it is a metal tub with a soothing footbath.

"Ohmygod." Berkeley sighs. I want to take that sigh and put it away for later, so I can get it out and listen to it again and again.

My fucking habit.

"Sit," I instruct her, pushing her gently into the chair and kneeling in front of her. Her eyes widen as I untie her Chucks and pull them off of her cute little feet. Each of her toenails is painted a different color. Blue, pink, purple, and slate gray alternate between her toes, and I smile at the sight of them. A hot blush creeps up her neck to her cheeks, and my grin grows wider.

I caress each foot gently across the top and place them in the water one at a time. The water's temperature is perfect, not too hot and not cold, either. I'll have to offer up my soul to Drake later, but I can't be bothered with it now. I'm too busy watching the sexiest look of ecstasy wash over Berkeley's face.

"I can't believe you did this." She moans.

"Why?" I sit back on my heels and just stare up at her like a goof. Her eyes fly open, where they had been drifting closed only seconds before. "Because it's so thoughtful and sweet. I've never had anyone do anything like this for me before."

Lone Sands-1. Dare-1.

"Berkeley…are you telling me that I'm your first, again?"

She nods, a teasing smile playing on her lips. "Yup. I guess my evil vixen siren magic is working just as I planned."

She closes her eyes again, and I get up to occupy the chair beside her. "Relax, vixen. Tonight is all about me taking care of you."

Her answering sigh makes me feel like I'm winning at something…for the first time since I was blown out of a helicopter crossing over hell.

We sit in silence for a while, staring up at the stars. The sky is so velvety black out here at night, away from everything city-like. The ocean is our backdrop of sound, and I think that maybe staying like this, in the dark, staring up at the stars will become our thing.

"God, it's beautiful. I wish I could paint this. I've never actually been able to capture the night sky the way it truly looks."

My eyes slide over to her, and then they narrow. "What do you mean, 'paint it'?"

She turns her head so that she's looking at me, but she doesn't bother to pick it up off the chair. She's so completely blissed out. Something deep inside my chest takes flight, knowing I've made her feel that way. Then I allow another thought to enter my mind. What if I had the chance to make her feel that way with my hands? With my mouth? With my body?

The thought sends a sizzle of heat straight through my body, and I immediately return to the subject she's just broached.

"Paint. You know, like with brushes and colorful liquids? On a canvas?" Her eyelids are heavy as she teases me, and I swallow hard.

"You're an artist?"

She scoffs. "Well, I mean I *paint*. And I really love to do it. Sometimes there're feelings and emotions raging around inside of me that I don't know what to do with. When I was in middle school and I picked up a paintbrush in one of my art classes, I felt a complete release come with each stroke I made. I've been doing it ever since."

I stare at her. I'm sure my eyes are filled with wonder. "Can I see?"

"My art? You want to see a piece I've done?" The almost shy tone to her voice is back, and she sucks hard on the corner of her lush lip. Jesus. I want to suck on that lip.

"I want to see *every* piece you've ever done."

She flushes that sexy crimson, and I reach over to brush the hair out of her eye.

"You know you're very, very cute when you're embarrassed."

Her dimples dot her cheeks. "Yeah, well…"

For the first time, she's at a loss for words, which I find uproariously funny. When I settle down, I ask her again.

"So, can I see?" I don't know why, but I have a sudden urge to see what this funny, beautiful girl has created with her hands and her mind. The desire is literally pulsing inside of me.

"I don't know. I don't keep any of it at my parents' house. I can't stand it when they don't get it the way I want them to. I have some pieces on a gallery wall at my university. My art professor promised he wouldn't remove them anytime soon." She offers me a shy, tentative smile. "Would you want to—"

"Yes," I answer before she finishes. "Just…yes. Can we go the next day you're off work?"

Her dimples appear in her cheeks. "Yeah. It's about an hour's drive to UNC Wilmington from here. You up for a little road trip with me, soldier?"

I reach over and grab her hand where it's resting on the arm of her chair. "I'm probably up for just about anything with you, Berkeley."

I reach down and feel the water her feet are still soaking in. It's cooled off considerably, so I grab a towel from the little table beside me and pull her feet out one at a time. I take my time toweling them dry, and then leave one of her legs in my lap. Even though I love her ripped, tight jeans, I wish that today had been a day she was wearing a pair of her short shorts.

As I begin to rub her feet, using my thumbs to apply pressure to first her heel, and then the ball of her foot, she moans. I drop my head back, undone.

"Hey...Berkeley?"

"Mmm?" Her eyes are closed again.

"Those noises you're making...they're likely to make me forget about respecting your 'complications.' They're likely to make me turn that lounger into a bed and lay you out on top of it. And then I might inexplicably end up laid out on top of *you*. I don't want to be a dick, but if you can....refrain from making those little moans. That would be fucking great."

Her body tenses, and she's quiet, but I can see her peeking at me through one eye. "You don't know how much I wish I didn't have those complications right now, Dare."

Jesus. My name on her tongue does things to me that have never been done before. I can't get enough of this girl. Her face, her voice, her humor. Her laugh, her dimples, and now that I've found out she's an artist...I just want *more*.

She suddenly sits up, the muscles of the leg in my lap tightening as she levels her gaze at me. "What's up with Chase?"

I sigh, moving my kneading hands up to her ankle. "He's my brother. He had my back a lot growing up. We always come through for each other, no matter what." I try to keep my expression neutral.

She nods thoughtfully. "You two, for being so close, seemed awfully tense at dinner."

I close my eyes briefly. I don't want to go into detail about Chase and his issues, but I don't want to hide anything from Berkeley either.

"Let's just say that he's got problems that I wish he didn't have. After high school, I picked a path that had to keep me on the straight and narrow. He chose a different path. He's still on it, and it irritates the shit out of me."

Her brow furrows. "He's in trouble with the law?"

"Sometimes. At the moment, he's in trouble with someone worse than the law."

She sucks in a deep breath. "And you have to get involved?"

"It's complicated, Berkeley. I get involved when I can in order to keep him out of trouble. But I don't know if I'm going to be able to do that this time."

She nods, but her expression is full of apprehension.

"Do you have siblings?" I ask her.

She shakes her head, her curls bouncing back and forth with the movement. "Only child. Hence the brattiness. I do have a close family friend who's sort of like a brother to me." A shadow crosses her face, and I trace her jawline with a finger.

"What would you do for him if he were in trouble?"

Understanding dawns on her features like a painfully beautiful sunrise. "Probably anything."

"You see my dilemma."

She nods, biting the corner of her bottom lip.

"Be careful," she whispers.

I lean closer until my face is only inches from hers. At this range, my self-control is almost nonexistent. The scent of roses washes over me, and every muscle in my body wakes up.

"You worried about me?"

She nods.

"You know I was a Ranger, don't you? I think I can handle myself with my brother's issues."

Her eyes grow wide, and I almost fall into their whiskey-colored depths. Her skin pales slightly, losing some of the normal rosy blush. "A Ranger? Shit, Dare! I just thought you were infantry."

I chuckle. "See? We're getting to know each other better already. Complications be damned."

She stands up. "Complications indeed. I better go. The footbath and rub was amazing. You get a reward the next time I see you."

My brows rise as I stand up beside her. "And what day is that again? Your next day off, we're road tripping."

She smirks. "Thursday, then. Can you get off work?"

I answer her smile with one of my own. "I live with the boss, remember?"

Today is Tuesday. In two more days, I will have Berkeley to myself for an entire day.

And now I have a new mission: to obliterate her complications.

12

Berkeley

I'm not sure why I agreed to this, other than the fact that Dare Conners, the ex–Army *Ranger*, for God's sake, is utterly irresistible. I don't parade my paintings around for guys I date. Shit, I'm not even supposed to be dating Dare! He just snuck his way into the inner workings of my mind somehow, and now I can't shake him.

Damn him and his funny quips and his ridiculously hot body and his perfect face and his subtle internal darkness.

We pull into Wilmington in my Escalade, because Dare didn't insist on driving. I even purposely tested him, asking him if he minded me driving. He said no. I had to ask again to reassure myself I wasn't hearing things. I've never dated a guy who didn't insist on driving everywhere we went together. I've never seen my mother and father ride in the same car together where the Admiral wasn't at the helm.

I glance over at Dare as we drive into a gas station. "Hungry?"

He shakes his head. "No, but I could go for some caffeine. Let me get you something?"

I shake my head no, and he shows me a couple of bills. I stare at them.

"What's this for?"

He arches an eyebrow. "Gas? Does it usually take about eighty-five to fill this mother up?"

He thinks he needs to pay for my gas? I begin shaking my head, but his strong fingers enclose around my arm and force me to meet his gaze.

"Berkeley, let me get the gas. I'm the one who begged you to take this trip, right? I got this."

It's like he hypnotizes me or something whenever he has me pinned in that unusually green gaze of his. I nod, all out of arguments.

It dawns on me that I'm *never* out of arguments, except where my father is concerned. I scowl at my handsome navigator. "Fine. But I'm going to suggest a road trip next, and you're going to let *me* pay for the gas."

I take note of the fact that the Carolina humidity is causing the hair around his neck to curl slightly, almost as if it's beckoning me to touch it. To brush it off of his thick, solid neck. Saliva fills my mouth, and I swallow thickly.

His lip curls crookedly, and my heart flutters in its cage. "I think it's hilarious that you don't see how that's still a win-win for me, honey."

Chuckling, he exits the car and heads into the store.

Around the same time that Dare disappears inside, I hop out to pump the gas. I know he would do it for me when he comes back out, but I'm anxious to get to the university, so I'm already pulling the pump out of its holder when a carful of college guys drives up beside me.

I see them all look, and I roll my eyes as I punch my information into the automated cashier machine. I'm taken totally by surprise when the boldest one in the bunch comes strutting right up to me. I instantly picture a puffed-up peacock in my head, and I snort quietly.

"Hey, sexy," he says.

I almost gag. Oh, my God. *Seriously?* How did I ever date college guys, even when I was in college?

I ignore him completely, pulling my sunglasses down over my eyes and reading the meter.

"Don't be like that, sweetheart. I was just wondering if you knew where the party was tonight."

Out of the corner of my eye, I see him drag his eyes slowly down the entire length of my body, and I shake with a disgusted convulsion.

Finally, I can't take it anymore. His friends in the car beside us are whistling and being generally obnoxious, and I've had enough of the whole game.

"Not interested. Here with someone. 'Kay?"

He glances around, and his grin only grows wider. He fingers his spiky blond hair and steps closer to me. "Funny. I don't see anyone, sweetness. So it looks like you're here with me."

He reaches out then, wraps an arm around my hips. His fingers brush the bare skin of my thighs, and I gasp at how forward he's being. Then he yanks me toward him until my body is pressed flush against his. I can see how watery blue his irises are and how dilated his pupils are. *Drugs. Perfect.*

I start looking toward the building for Dare, and suddenly he's there. He towers, literally *towers*, over my intimidator and yanks his arms free of my waist. Shoving me behind him, he glares down at College Boy. The guy backs up, holding his hands up in front of him as he eyes Dare's solidly muscular build, angry glinting eyes, and the silver chain holding his dog tags around his neck.

"Sorry, dude. Didn't know she belonged to you." The college guy continues muttering his apologies as he slinks back to his now-silent buddies.

I glance up at Dare with a shaky smile. "Thanks, hero."

His eyes are still glinting furiously as he stares down at me. "Never. Never will I let someone touch you like that when you're with me. And if it happens when you're not with me, I need to know about it. Okay?"

Oh, I get the message loud and clear. And I'm conflicted. Should I be offended, because this is the twenty-first century and modern woman and all of that? Or should I be totally hot and bothered that the pure male energy of this man just scared off a carful of punks like that?

My current reaction? Definitely the latter. My stomach clenches tighter as he leans in and gets up in my personal space.

"You okay?"

I nod. I'm definitely more than okay, except for the rubbery feeling in my legs and the jitters fluttering around in my stomach. But Dare doesn't need to know all of *that*.

I've been protected my whole life. It's not a new feeling for me. But the strong, almost oppressive desire I feel to *be* protected by Dare? To be a woman that he wants to hold on to and cherish? That desire is overwhelming. I shake my head to clear it and climb back into the car.

When we arrive on campus, I park outside the Arts building and we head inside. A strange, giddy feeling is starting to creep over me as we get closer to the gallery. I *love* this place. I spent four years of my life in this building, creating and designing, and it was the best four years of my life to date. Sharing it with Dare isn't something I expected to get behind, but now that I'm doing it, it just feels *right*.

God, wait until Mea hears that. She'll cackle her tiny little head off, and then she'll make fun of me for weeks afterward. Yeah, probably gonna leave that out of the next bestie chat.

Just before we walk inside, my phone chimes with a text notification. I pull it out and check it.

Back in town. Want to talk 2nite?

Reality hits me when I read Grisham's message. I sigh, putting the phone back in my pocket.

Dare's eyes narrow slightly when he looks at me. "Problem?"

I shake my head. "Not really. Just a…complication."

His eyes darken even further, but he says nothing else.

I lead Dare down a main hallway until we come to a sign that says ART GALLERYwith an arrow pointing down a path to our right. Suddenly, I'm full of nervous energy. What if he thinks my paintings suck? What if he starts thinking I'm some weird, artsy chick after this? What if…

"Hey," he says, right up by my ear. His lips commit the barest of grazes against the sensitive skin, and a shiver rocks through me. "I can't wait to see them."

I need those words. I need them to allow the calm to enter my system again. I nod, and then we're walking into the university Art Gallery.

It's a plain, rectangular room with stark white walls. The high ceiling boasts several skylights, which bring an array of natural light into the space. Hung on the walls around us are paintings in all shapes, sizes, and colors. Littering the floor in the center are pedestals holding impressive sculptures.

I sigh when the familiar sense of peace cloaks me. I haven't been here since graduation, and God, I've missed the place.

I lead him to the wall where three of my pieces hang. I nibble my thumb as he wanders along the wall, just staring.

He stares first at my painting of a purple lily, floating in a sea of blue with a glinting of the sun reflecting off of the water. Then he moves on to a bright sunburst, filled with hues of brilliant oranges and blazing reds. The last painting is a portrait. It's of a young girl with wild blond curls, running in a clear green pasture, her arms extended out behind her, as she appears to have not a care in the world.

That girl is me, only the *me* I always wished I could be.

I'm holding my breath without realizing I'm doing it. I might as well be stripping down naked in the middle of this room for this man. That act would be no less revealing, no less *exposing*, than showing him my artwork.

When he finally turns to face me, his eyes are a swirling cloud of dark and unreadable emotion. He stands perfectly still, just sizing me up with his penetrating gaze. I shift my feet, dying to know what he's thinking but too terrified to ask.

Then he eliminates the distance between us, wraps me in his arms, and presses his lips to mine.

The kiss is unexpected, and it's not the gentle sweetness of our kiss just out of the rain. His lips move hard against mine, his tongue prying my lips open in order to taste, no, to *take*, what's inside. My hands clutch at his biceps as he grips me tightly to his chest, and I rise onto my tiptoes so I can meet his relentless lips with my own. This kiss is Dare's rawness unleashed, and where our first kiss left me breathless, this one is going to leave me *soulless*.

My knees buckle beneath me, and his strong arms remain steady around my waist.

Then, just as quickly as he took me, he releases me, and I stumble backward. He catches me by both wrists before I can lose my footing, his eyes burning straight into mine.

His chest rises and falls swiftly as his fingers curl around mine. "I've never seen anything so beautiful."

His words are a weight off my shoulders, and an arrow in my heart. We stare at each other for another long moment until I have to pull my gaze away for fear of being swallowed completely whole by the consuming energy that is Dare Conners.

"Thank you," I whisper.

He pulls me to his broad chest, and I cave into him. His musky, soapy scent washes over me, and I inhale shakily. He just smells like Dare, dark and sweet at the same time. I inhale deeply, and I feel him do the same against my hair.

"Thank you for showing me," he says softly. "Now I'm gonna have to work on getting you to make one for me."

Oh, the man is so clueless. He could probably ask me to paint a picture of him while I stand naked in the freezing rain and I'd agree. The less he knows about how much I'm starting to like him, to crave his company more and more, the better. Wouldn't want him using such knowledge to his advantage, would I? Then I'd really be screwed.

It's a little later than lunchtime, and our stomachs are growling, so I take him to eat at a diner I used to love when I lived in town.

"What's good here?" he asks with a teasing lift of his lip.

I bite back a smile, remembering the first question he ever asked me. "Everything's good here."

His grin grows wider as he puts his menu down on the table. He clasps his hands together on top of it and leans back in his seat. "Well, then, let's get one of everything."

And we almost do just that. We get a number of dishes to share, and all the fried yumminess is as delicious as I remember. Stuffed, we sit back and stare at each other. I'm suddenly feeling forlorn at the thought of having to end this day with him.

He must be reading my expression, because he says, "We don't have to go home yet."

I know I have to get back to talk to Grisham. There's no way I'm going to accept his proposal, and the sooner I tell him the better. The thought occurs to me that I should probably tell Dare about Grisham, but I just don't want to put a damper on this amazing day. I've seen so many sides of Dare today. I've seen his scary-protective side, and I've seen him happy. I've seen him full and satisfied, and I've seen him emotional. I just want to keep seeing all of the facets that make up this fascinating man. So I don't bring up Grisham.

"We still have the ride home," I say instead.

Frowning, he nods. He doesn't say anything else, and my heart melts a little. He lets me remain in the driver's seat of whatever this is between us, and I can't describe the way that makes me feel. Growing up with a father with as much power and sway as mine has, it's been a rare occurrence for me to feel like I'm in charge of anything. I haven't even told Dare that my father is in the navy, so I don't know how he knows what I need. He just does, and it's simultaneously freaking me out and has me wanting to throw myself in his lap.

Oh, the contradictions that are my feelings for Dare Conners.

13

Dare

I just spent the best day ever with the girl I never saw coming. And I was a U.S. Army *Ranger*, for Christ's sakes. There isn't *anything* I can't see coming. Everything about her throws me off my game. Her wild curls, her epic-movie-length legs, her casual, sexy style. Her rosy scent, her dark, smoldering eyes, and her spunky attitude. I've never met a girl like her. It's like all those qualities combined were created to fit inside my world.

As I get ready to go out with Chase and Drake tonight, a new thought makes me cringe. With Chase around, my world really isn't safe enough for Berkeley. The idea of putting her in danger because of my brother enrages me. A sense of innate, primal territoriality engulfs me just as sure as if I'm covered in flames.

A knock sounds on my door, and I look up into the open doorway. Drake stands there, his face all broken up into one of his goofy-ass grins.

"Ready? I need a shot, like yesterday. Can we go, or are you still *primping*?"

I've never primped a day in my fucking life, and Drake knows it. My hair is still damp from the shower, and it'll dry while curling up all around my neck like it always does. I'm wearing a low-maintenance T-shirt and jeans, and I shove my feet into a pair of black combat boots as Drake stands there watching.

"Look, man, I know you're jealous. But if you want me to give you some tips on how to look your very best, all you have to do is ask."

"Fuck you." Drake throws the insult over his shoulder as he walks back down the hallway.

"No thanks, Drake, maybe after a few beers!" I call back with a chuckle.

The three of us pile into the Challenger and weave our way through Lone Sands. It is a touristy destination, so there are several places we could choose from to go drinking tonight. I texted Berkeley to let her know our plans, but I haven't heard back from her yet. I know I've just spent most of the day with her, but the absence of her by my side feels wrong. Like I'm missing a limb. Considering I've been close to missing a limb more than once, I consider myself an expert on the subject.

We pull into an overflowing parking lot, and I'm reminded that this is the first time I've been out with my friends, to have fun in a place as ordinary as a bar, in longer than I care to admit. A smile that starts inside my heart touches my face, because this place could be home for me. When was the last time I had a true home? Before my parents died? Before I lost everything I ever cared about when their car went over the side of that bridge? Before I nearly ceased to exist in a country I'd never even visited before I nearly died there?

We have to stand in line for a few minutes at the door, but the line moves quickly and we're inside in no time. We choose a high-top table near the bar and sprawl out. I look around, and the place rocks a relaxed atmosphere, a beachy vibe that can't be faked. I sigh, utterly relaxed, and think that the only thing missing is Berkeley.

A waitress in a short khaki skirt, flip-flops, and a bikini top stops by our table. Chase's eyes nearly pop out of his head, and Drake offers her an appreciative grin.

"What can I get you boys to drink tonight?"

Since my comrades are too busy ogling the generous cleavage spilling out of her top to answer, I decide the first round is on me.

"We'll take a pitcher of whatever you have on tap, something dark. And keep 'em coming."

She shoots me a flirty smile, and then spins around to get our pitcher.

"So smooth, asshats." They deserve an endless amount of smack talk for that, but I leave it alone.

Drake shrugs. "She's smokin' hot."

Chase agrees, shaking his head to clear it. "So, I meet your girl and she looks like a sweet slice of heaven, and then I come here and the freaking waitress just walked out of *Penthouse*. I might never go back to Florida. The hot girls here are so close you can reach out and touch 'em."

I glance at Chase. Something's not right. He's talking a big game right now, but it's obvious there's no real heat behind it. My radar goes crazy, signaling that I need to find out what's up.

Drake shoots him a sharp look, too. I know Drake isn't happy about Chase being here, because he knows he's hitting me up for cash. But he's been tolerating his presence because he's my best friend. I don't know how long his patience can hold out, though.

"You'll find your own slice of heaven when you get your shit together back home." My voice is low, with a note of warning.

Chase has never been one to heed warnings. "Yeah, but I don't have my brother back there. Maybe I should start fresh, ya know? Lone Sands seems like my kind of place."

Drake opens his mouth, unable to contain himself any longer. "You're about the last thing Dare needs in his life right now, dude."

Chase regards him coolly. "Yeah? What makes you the expert?"

Our waitress interrupts Drake's response by slamming our pitcher down in front of us. She *thunks* frosted mugs down in front of each of us and says she'll be back when our pitcher needs a refill.

Drake and Chase go right back to ignoring each other and looking around the bar, and I groan inwardly. These two are gonna be great company tonight. I drain half of my beer in a couple of gulps, then stand.

"I'm gonna take a piss," I announce. "You two. Either become BFFs in the time that I'm gone, or at least learn to tolerate each other. Because if you don't, I'm cutting our night short when I get back."

I pull my phone out of my pocket to check for missed messages or calls. I sigh when I see there's nothing.

Guess it's going to be a Berkeley-Free night.

Two pitchers of beer later we're all feeling a little looser, although Drake stopped drinking after two mugs. He's grumbled twice about not being the driver next time.

Chase is still sitting at the table with us, which surprises the hell out of me. Normally by now he would have begun making his rounds. He always finds a table full of girls and pulls himself a comfy seat right in the middle of them. Chase has always been the social butterfly. He has this magnetic personality, a charm about him that just draws in members of the opposite sex like waves to the sand. I've never been able to hang with him when it comes to meeting girls. It was another story when I met Berkeley; I couldn't *not* talk to her. But usually, I'm more standoffish. I've always let women come to me.

But Chase is a hunter, and he likes the game. If he didn't have such a knack for getting himself into trouble by hanging out with the wrong people I'm pretty sure he could be anywhere he wanted in life. He could have a successful career; he's smart enough. He could have a woman in his life that loves him; he's lovable enough. But instead, he makes one bad choice after another, leaving me to clean up his messes.

Tonight is so different, I know something's off. He's just sitting here, draining beer after beer and acting like he sees nothing and no one around him.

When he gets up to go to the bathroom and disappears around a corner, I contemplate going after him.

But then Drake and I are suddenly joined at our table by a slim, rough-around-the-edges-looking girl whose jet-black hair is cut into a short, uneven cut that's streaked with purple hair chalk. She gives us both a hard look, and then darts a furtive glance around the bar.

"Can we help you?" Drake's amused tone draws a glare from our new little guest. She's like a dark, Goth-looking pixie. Who's scared shitless of something. Or someone.

"No. And I can't help you, either. But I thought you should know…your friend over there?" She jerks her head toward where

Chase disappeared. "Doesn't have much time left before they get him. They know where he is, and they want their money. Got it?"

My eyes narrow and I reach out and grab the pixie's wrist. "You're talking about my brother, Chase?"

Her eyes lock on my hand where it's grabbing hers, and she frowns up at me. She's obviously refusing to speak again until I let her go, so I do, but lean in farther to peer into her face.

"*Who* knows where he is?"

She takes another furtive look around. "Look, I shouldn't even be sitting here. My boyfriend...I just know what I know, okay? And you look like nice guys, and I hate all this shit anyway. I just thought I'd warn you. Do what you want with it."

Before I can grab her again, she's up and moving away from the table like a stormy little cloud. I cut my eyes to meet Drake's.

Drake's face is unusually hard, and he shakes his head slowly. "He's fucking out, man. I want him out, tonight."

I emit a frustrated groan and run one hand through my hair. "I understand that, Drake. But shit...he's my *brother*. I'm supposed to just let him go back to handle this shit himself?"

"No way in hell I'm letting you go down with him, Dare. You know me better than that. Chase made this mess himself. He's gotta deal with it. Did you hear what she said? She said *they want their money.* That sound like he's told you the whole story?"

Fucking Chase and his shady mess. I look around the bar, running a hand through my hair agitatedly, and then back at Drake.

"No, I guess he hasn't."

I glance toward the door, where the pixie disappeared, thinking about what my next move is going to be. As I'm staring absently at the exit, the face I've been missing the entire night walks in the door.

The tightening in my chest that was caused by the redhead is loosened when I see Berkeley's curls and brown eyes coming into the bar. Maybe she got my texts and just decided to meet me here instead of answering them. I stand up, ready to go over and get her, when the guy entering behind her places a hand on the small of her back. He guides her farther into the bar, and then they swing off to the right. They continue walking until they find a small table for two in the corner, and they sit. She never even glances my way.

I sink back down in my seat, heavy lead suddenly filling my limbs.

So, Berkeley decided to come out tonight. But she's not here to meet me. She's here with another guy.

Drake sees my face, and opens his mouth to ask what I saw, but I hold up a hand. I pick up my half-empty mug and drain it before I speak.

"Berkeley's here," I finally manage to spit out.

Drake's eyebrows lift. His dark, closely shaved head swivels around to search for her. "Yeah? You gonna go get her?"

I want to go get her. I want to yank her away from the *motherfucker* who had the gall to touch her and ask her what the hell she's doing. But I don't have the right to do any of that. We never said we were dating. Shit, she even told me her life was complicated. But having the fact that she's with someone else, maybe that complication she was talking about, thrown in my face when I'm not expecting it is tearing me apart right now.

I take a deep breath, blowing it out slowly as I focus on Drake's face. "She's not here alone."

Now his grin disappears and he locks his gaze on my face. "A dude?"

I nod.

He sits back in his chair, tapping his middle finger against the side of his cheek. "Go talk to her."

"I told you, she's not alone."

"Who gives a shit? You spent the whole fucking day with her. Not to mention all the other times it's just been you and her. She owes you an explanation, and if the dude wants to cause a ruckus, I'll be right behind you. Go talk to her."

I nod, standing. Somehow, my heavy feet carry me across the bar and to the secluded table where she's chosen to sit with...him. Somehow, I get my face together so it's not all broken-looking, and smooth it over with what I hope is a passive expression.

"Hey, Berkeley."

She looks up, surprise filling her features. Her amber eyes go wide, and the corner of her bottom lip is immediately caught between her teeth.

The guy she's with is military. There's no way to disguise it, I can just tell. He's a different brand of military than Drake and I are, though. He's got the telltale short haircut, and the straight posture that goes with someone yelling at you a hundred times to stand up straight. But that's where the similarities end. He's wearing clothes that probably cost more than my entire wardrobe. A crisp pair of expensive jeans and boots that look like he's only worn them once. A T-shirt with shiny shit spelling out the letters of the brand. He's probably a little younger than me, and by the look of his unblemished, unlined face, he's seen a hell of a lot less horror than me.

He's just starting out. Probably hasn't seen any action yet. Maybe he went to college first. Yeah, that's definitely it. He's a prep school guy, then straight to OCS to be shot out of the gate as an officer. I earned my ranking by way of a much tougher route.

"Dare," she says, her voice strained. "This is my *friend* Grisham."

She emphasizes the word *friend*, and I don't miss it. I relax a little until the guy stands up and offers his hand. His face is tight, he doesn't like the fact that I've broken up their little party, or the way she introduced him.

"Grisham Abbot," he says gruffly. "Berkeley's *friend*, for now. But if I have anything to say about it, she'll be my *fiancée* soon. You are?"

Son of a *bitch*. I see red, and I know that if I don't walk away from their table right now, I'm gonna hurt him. And that would hurt Berkeley. She told me they were friends, and he thinks they're more. It's a situation I can't get into the middle of, not when my vision is starting to blur with the rage piling up inside of me. Maybe she'll explain it to me one day, maybe not.

All I know is I have to get out of here. Now.

So, without even looking at her again, I turn around and walk away.

Away from the table, away from the girl.

Just away.

14

Berkeley

After I drop Dare off at his house, I head home to change before I text Grisham back. I pull into my driveway and groan a little because I can see that my oldest friend has chosen the impatient route, rather than waiting for me to text him back.

Grisham's pristine, shiny black Audi A5 is sitting in the driveway. But he's nowhere to be seen, which means he's inside with my parents.

I trudge up the walkway and into the house, closing the door quietly behind me. Voices drift toward me from the kitchen, so I make my way to the back of the house.

When I walk into our ornate kitchen, Grisham is seated in an upholstered, high-backed barstool at the island, while my mother stands across from him looking delighted. The Admiral has put in a rare appearance as well. He stands at the other end of the counter from my mother. They all look up as I enter the room.

"Berkeley." My mother's frowning, which puts her Botoxed forehead in some serious danger. "Where have you been all day? You've been keeping poor Grisham waiting."

Grisham shoots me an apologetic half-smile. "I wasn't trying to rush you, Berk. I'm just anxious to talk to you, and I figured I'd come on over and scoop you up."

The Admiral's two cents boom across the granite countertop. "Why didn't you tell us about Grisham's proposal?"

Now I grit my teeth and stare at Grisham pointedly. He told my parents? He *knows* better! He knows better than anyone that keeping my parents in the loop is strictly against my policy. Now I would have to deal with their reaction to my refusal that much sooner. Dammit, Grish!

He reads the look in my eyes and averts his. Oh, he's going to get it. And he's fully aware of his impending doom.

"Momma, Daddy. Grisham and I need to talk. So I'm going to go shower and change, and I'll be right down, Grish. We're going *out*."

He nods, and I escape up the stairs. I have no qualms about leaving Grisham alone with my parents, now that he's spilled the beans. They all get along swimmingly, they're like a second set of parents to him. Just like his are to me. Everyone is going to be so disappointed in me, and our mothers are going to milk their heartbreak until the cows come home. Well, it can't be helped. I'm not going to marry a guy I'm not in love with. There's more to life than that.

Maybe at one point in my life, I would have considered it, just to make everyone around me happy. It would make my parents happy, Grisham's parents happy. It would make Grisham happy, because there's always been more to our relationship for him than friendship, even though I've never lead him on. But would it make me happy? Long ago, I could have probably convinced myself it would in the long run. But not now. Something in me has changed since I graduated from college. I have a goal of designing for my own firm that's actually in my grasp, if I reach for it. And Dare…holy hell. How could I go into a platonic marriage with my best friend now that I know what true heat, true passion feels like? When Dare looks at me, he sets my skin on fire. Then he touches me, and my entire body bursts into flames. When his lips touch mine, what's left of me just melts into a puddle of want at his feet. No one has ever had that effect on me. If I didn't have to go and let Grisham down easy tonight, I'd be whining in Mea's ear about what it all means.

I can't act as if my dreams haven't begun to shape my future. I can't act as though being with a man like Dare hasn't changed my vision of what I want out of life.

Once I've showered, I leave my hair damp and hanging around my shoulders in curly tendrils and throw on a pair of white shorts and strappy sandals. My mother will pass out if when I leave the house with Grisham I look anything less than like the princess she thinks I should be. My brown blouse pulls the amber out of my eyes and plunges in a low V in the front.

When I come back downstairs, my parents have disappeared and Grisham is still waiting for me at the island in the kitchen. His blue eyes run over every inch of me, making my skin feel tight because, well, he's *Grisham*. One time I shoved a mud pie in his face for refusing my elegant play-cooking when we were eight.

"You look amazing," he says. The genuineness leaks out of his words, and I smile at him.

We walk out of the house together.

In his car, I squirm as he drives through the town. I always feel a little vulnerable when I ride with Grisham. I'm used to riding around town in something akin to a tank, and now that I've ridden with Dare, I get the same feeling of protection when I'm up in his truck. Whether from the size of the vehicle or from the presence of the man, the jury's still out.

"You eaten?" asks Grisham, glancing at me out of the corner of his eye.

I shake my head.

"Well, then I'm taking you to dinner."

I nod this time. We don't say anything else as he directs the Audi to a nice restaurant that overlooks the ocean. Grisham's only been to See Food a few times, and I know it's not his usual scene. Grisham, like me, has grown up with the finer things in life. But where I'd rather things be simple, he craves all things expensive and fine. But it's just a part of his personality that I understand, despite the fact that it's not my ideal. I do *get* Grisham, even if I don't claim him as mine.

We're seated at our white cloth-covered table and scanning our menus before he asks.

"So, you're going to turn me down, aren't you?"

I close my menu and open my mouth just as our waiter comes to stand beside our table.

He rattles off the specials in a smooth, knowledgeable voice, and I listen without really hearing him. When the man asks me what I'd like to order, I look up at him blankly.

"She'll have the mahi-mahi," says Grisham matter-of-factly. "Side of parsley potato mash and grilled asparagus. I'll have the porterhouse with steak fries. Thank you."

He orders for me so seamlessly that I smile in response. "You know me so well."

His eyes are such a bright, clear turquoise that most girls would be in danger of falling overboard into them. But I'm still too stuck on another pair of eyes of a vastly different color to be enthralled with Grish's.

He leans toward me, his expression earnest. "I do know you so well, Berk. And I want you to remember that while you're breaking my heart. No one has known you as long as I have, or knows the ins and outs of the feisty girl you are like I do. I know what you look like when you're ecstatic about something, and I know what you look like when you're devastated. I can read you like a book, and that's because you're the best chapter of the best book I've ever read. I know you think I'm not the guy for you, but you're wrong, Berkeley. You're so damn wrong."

His eyes fall to his clasped hands after that, and mine fill with tears. God, I really do love him.

"But I'm not in love with you, Grish. Don't you want that? You deserve it. You deserve to meet a girl that falls into a heap at your feet, that can't wait for your hands to meet her skin. You deserve a girl who's yours and only yours."

He raises his eyes and narrows them. "Who are you into, Berkeley? I noticed you didn't answer your mom when she asked you where you were today."

I sigh. "I was out with a guy. A guy that I like very, very much."

Grisham sits back in his seat. His cheeks are flushing a brilliant scarlet, a sign that he's upset. "So you're not picking me because you want someone else? That's fucked-up, Berkeley."

I reach across the table and grasp his large, warm hand in mine. "No, it's not. Don't be angry with me, Grisham. We've been friends for too long to let it end like this. You're my best friend, you always have been. And you always will be. But that's all we can ever be."

He doesn't say anything else until our food arrives, he just holds my hand silently, tracing small circles on my skin.

When we finish our dinner, he finally meets my gaze. "I think since you shattered my world today, you should at least go out with me while I drink my sorrows away."

I can hear the teasing tone in his voice, and I know that we're going to be okay. There's never been anything that Grisham and I haven't been able to get through to the other side of, and now I know this will just be another one of our scrapes that we manage to survive together.

"Okay."

We drive down the road to one of the busiest bars on the strip. I move to open my car door, when Grisham reaches over the console and grabs my arm.

I look at him questioningly, and his face is lit green by the interior lights on the dashboard. "I didn't say I was giving up, Berk. You know I'm not a quitter."

Well, shit. That I'm not expecting. Grisham is an extremely competitive guy, and apparently I've just lit the ultimate fire under his ass. The determined gleam in his eyes lets me know that I'm playing with a man who is used to winning at life, and I sigh in frustration.

"You have to respect my wishes, Grish."

He nods. "I do. But you also have to respect my right to do everything I can to change those wishes."

"Gah! You are so stubborn sometimes. And this is the worst time for stubborn Grisham to make an appearance!"

He grins, his perfect rows of teeth on display. "I love you, Berk. I gotta do everything I can until the fat lady sings."

Silently, I thank the navy powers-that-be that he's going to be moving to San Diego in a matter of days. Then I give him a sardonic grin.

"I'm going to need a drink, then."

I walk into the very crowded bar, and Grisham leads me with a hand on my back to a secluded table. He gestures me into a seat, and I roll my eyes dramatically at him before I sink into it. He signals the waitress and orders himself a bottle of something imported, and an enormous margarita for me.

I narrow my eyes at him. "You think getting some tequila in my veins is going to change my answer? You're such a rookie, Grish."

He throws his head back and laughs. "Even if it doesn't change your answer, it's just fun to watch you get loose. It always has been. And I'm usually too buttoned up to get loose with you. If I have to leave the Audi in that lot out there and call us a cab later, I will."

My eyes grow wide with mock shock. "Grish, what are you saying? Leave your precious baby here to fend for itself? I'm shocked at you!"

"The things I'll do for you, girl."

I'm suddenly jerked to attention when a deep, rough voice that I've come to know so well greets me. "Hey, Berkeley."

The familiar rush of heat to my core that comes from hearing my name roll out of Dare's mouth accompanies a light feeling of excitement from the surprise of seeing him here. But when I look up into his eyes, they're full of hurt that I can only assume comes from seeing me here with Grisham. My desire to reassure him is instant and overwhelming.

"Dare, this is my *friend* Grisham."

I can see the relief wash over his face and the beginning of a smile when Grisham decides to take matters into his own stupid, stupid hands. He stands up and offers his hand to Dare.

"Grisham Abbot," he says puffing out his chest like a penguin. "Berkeley's *friend*, for now. But if I have anything to say about it, she'll be my *fiancée* soon. You are?"

I will kill him. I will murder Grisham Abbot tonight by running him over repeatedly with his beloved Audi, and they will never, *ever* find the body.

The look on Dare's face is enough to terrify me, and it should absolutely be making Grisham wet his expensive pants. But Grisham just stands there, not allowing his gaze to leave Dare's face. I'm trying to stand, to get my damn chair to scoot away from the table, but my limbs are so heavy with dread that I'm having trouble making them work.

And then Dare is moving away from the table, walking quickly as the sea of bodies parts before him.

I finally stand, and slap Grisham hard on the arm. "Grisham *Avery Abbot*! You did that shit on purpose!"

He shrugs, plopping back down into his seat as the waitress wearing a bikini top two sizes too small brings our drinks around. "What? Who was that guy?"

"He's the guy I've been seeing! But you knew that, didn't you?"

He shrugs again, and I want to slap him repeatedly in his smug face. "How would I know that? He's not your type, Berk. You don't do dark and dangerous. What is he, an MMA fighter?"

"He's an ex-Army Ranger, Grisham, and now you've pissed him off. Your funeral!"

He reaches for my arm as I turn away from him, but I pull it out of his reach. Then I hurry after Dare.

When I catch up to him, his wounded expression is enough to send my pulse racing to the moon and my heart to clench so tight within my chest it hurts.

"Let me explain," I plead.

We're standing just outside the bar, still too close to the waiting line of people for my taste. I move over into the shadow of the brick wall on the opposite side of the door, and I sigh in relief when he follows. He leans against the wall, staring at a spot just over my head. His face is hardened, and I would think he wasn't affected if it weren't for the heavy rise and fall of his chest.

"Dare," I say tentatively. "Grisham is not my fiancé. He's not even my boyfriend."

His light-green eyes flare as they finally lock on my own. "Then you and he have a communication problem. Because he sure as hell thinks there's more to it than you do."

I nod, a little frantically. "Grisham and I have been best friends for…like, ever. Our parents go way back, and we've just been thrown together our entire lives. My parents are very…controlling. They've always thought they could decide every detail of my life, and I've had my work cut out for me carving things out for myself. Well, the latest thing they've decided is that I'm going to marry Grisham and become a navy officer's wife just like my mom. And so a few days ago, Grisham proposed."

My voice trails away as his eyes widen and his mouth goes slack.

"Your dad…he's navy?" he asks quietly.

I nod.

"That's why you have an issue dating guys in the military?"

I nod again.

"Why didn't you tell me?"

I sigh, tugging at a stray curl. "I don't know…it never really seemed like a time to bring it up. My dad…you've seen him. He's not just navy, Dare, he's an admiral. He's used to controlling everything and everyone. I'm just something else he gets to control."

Dare blows out a heavy breath, and then he reaches for me. I go very willingly into his arms, and his crushing embrace nearly drags a sob from my chest. He buries his face into my neck, inhaling deeply.

"Nobody can control you, baby." He breathes into my ear. "You're too strong."

I feel anything but strong as my knees wobble under me and a shiver runs along my back. I feel like with one more breath in my ear, one more sweet word, one touch of his lips, he could break me into a million, tiny little pieces.

"I'm sorry," I whisper. "Grisham proposed to me because he thinks he wants to marry me. But I told him no."

I feel his chuckle. It's mirthless, but it causes his body to vibrate. "That guy? Isn't taking no for an answer, Berkeley."

I nod. "Yeah. Grisham's pretty used to getting whatever he wants. But he knows he's met his match when it comes to me."

"Does he know…"

"That I've been seeing you? He does now."

Dare's quiet for a minute, just holding me still in his arms. Then his muscles tense, and I pull back so I can see his face.

"You think he'll go to your dad?"

There's no fear or apprehension in his question. There's just a cool sense of his own brand of determination. I shrug.

"I'm not sure what Grisham will do in this situation. I've never been in it with him before. The Admiral is definitely going to lose his mind when he finds out I turned Grisham down and I'm not going to San Diego with him. But I don't know how much Grisham will want him to get involved."

Dare's gaze is made of steel and ice when it meets mine. "Are there any other 'complications' I need to know about, Berkeley? Because I think at this point, we should pretty much put it all out on the table."

I can feel a flush creeping up my cheeks. "No more complications on my end. How about you?"

A shadow crosses his eyes, and the pregnant pause tells me that there are definitely things he hasn't told me. "Dare?"

He shakes his head and takes a step back. "I think we've dealt with enough tonight. Let's take a breather from it all, all right?"

My mouth falls open as I stare at him. "Are you serious right now?"

His stare is unwavering as he nods.

I cross my arms over my chest and take a deep, calming breath. I can't believe he's taking a step back after I just came clean about all of my drama. Now that he knows my father's position and that another man wants me, has he lost interest? It's a lot to handle, true. But I just thought we had something more important than all of that.

Could I have been so completely wrong about Dare Conners?

15

Dare

I slam the heel of my hand into the dashboard, but the accompanying pain isn't nearly satisfying enough.

"Hey!" shouts Drake. "Do you know whose car you're in right now?"

I ignore him completely and slam an open hand into the dashboard one more time for good measure.

"Fuck," I growl. "Fuck!"

"Yeah, man, we get it," drawls Chase from the backseat. He reaches up and pats my shoulder. "How's this girl got you so twisted up? I mean, she's hot as shit and all—"

I turn around and grab the hand he used to touch my shoulder, squeezing it until I feel his bones crushing together.

"Dammit!" he screams.

I release him. "You're my brother, and I love you. But if you talk about her like that again I'll break a bone."

Chase mutters to himself in the back, "Mental note: Don't mention the *B* word, or Dare goes bat-shit crazy."

Drake cuts his eyes toward me. "Slap your hand on my car again, dude, and *I'mma* break some bones."

That's fair enough, so I nod. Then my scowl returns.

I let her walk out of there with another guy. Sure, it's a guy she says she's not interested in. But he's definitely interested in *her*. And the look he tossed over his shoulder at me as he left the bar with my girl was a smug grin that I *need* to physically remove from his face. I need it like I need fucking air.

As soon as we get home I sink onto my bed and text her.

Are you okay?

I wait, every muscle in my body flexed tight, for her to message me back.

I left her so I could give myself some space to think of how, and when, I was going to fill her in on my situation with Chase. Even though I've been keeping it from her for her own good, it's no longer fair for me to keep my secrets when she's shared all of hers. I want to tell her everything. I just also want to keep her safe. Thinking about bringing her into Chase's unstable world makes me want to break things. A lot of glass things.

Once again I'm struck by how utterly crazy being around a girl like Berkeley is making me. I try and pinpoint again, just like the night I met her, what exactly it is about her that strikes such a deep chord within me. It's not specifically her looks, although when she enters a room the most sensitive muscle in my body stiffens in response to her. It's not merely her sense of humor, even though when I'm with her it feels like someone has turned on the sun and my cheeks end up sore from all the stupid-ass grins she pulls from me. The strength and self-possession she exudes are addictive, and her easy affability leaves me wanting more and more time with her. It's a combination of all of those things, her very particular brand of *Berkeley-ness* that is putting me in danger of falling for her.

My phone vibrates, and I snatch it up.

I'm fine.

Shit. Okay. I decide it's time to lighten the mood a bit. We've had a heavy, emotional night. I could tell earlier that she'd been through a lot, and I didn't help matters by melting down when I saw her with *Grisham*.

I find her name in my phone contacts list and press SEND.

She answers on the first ring, which brings a slight smile to my lips.

"You still don't know that guys don't call girls anymore." Her voice is all cute and grumbly. I gulp down the intense desire that washes over me like the downpour that ignited our first kiss.

"You must know by now that I don't follow social cues," I say into the phone. "Two-word answers over text aren't going to work for me tonight."

She sighs, and a pause stretches between us on the phone. My fingers itch; they bend and flex as I picture her soft skin beneath them.

"It's been a rough night, Dare."

"Are you alone?" The question tumbles out of me; I hadn't even planned to ask it. But I need to know she's not still with Grisham. Once I know that, I'll be able to think clearly again.

"You don't even need to ask me that, Dare." Her sigh is weary. "Answer something."

"Anything."

"You didn't let me in on whatever you were holding back tonight.

I get it. It took me this long to share everything with you. But now that I have…are there many more secrets you're not giving away?"

I hear my own question for her being thrown back at me, and I run a hand through my hair while I grin like a fucking idiot.

"Most people don't stick around long enough to learn other peoples' secrets," I say. God, I want to touch her so bad right now.

I mouth her next words right along with her as she speaks them. "That sounds suspiciously like a dare, Dare."

I shoot up off the bed like someone has lit a rocket under my ass. I stride for my bedroom door, throwing it open.

"Be outside in ten minutes, Berkeley. When I pull up, I want you in my truck."

Her voice is breathless as she answers, and she doesn't even think to argue with me. I like that. No, I fucking love that.

As she speaks, I can tell she's moving around. "Where are we going?"

"I'm bringing you back here. I need you next to me tonight, Berkeley." I realize my voice is rough as my truck's engine roars to life, and I try to soften it. "I know I need to open up to you, but I don't know when I'm going to be able to do that. I will do it though, Berkeley. You are so worth opening up to. I just…tonight I just want to feel you beside me."

"Ten minutes?" Her voice is barely a whisper.

"No. Eight."

I clasp her hand firmly in mine and lead her out of the entryway and down the hall.

"Aw, hell." Chase's voice, coming from the living room, doesn't faze me as I tow Berkeley behind me into my room. We haven't really spoken since I picked her up, but this thing between us doesn't always need words to fill the space. It's big enough to fill it all on its own.

I pull her inside my room, shutting the door behind us, and I just take her in, standing in my most personal space for the second time. It hasn't been too long since she was last here, but all I've done in the meantime is picture her here again. It's maddening, this attraction that eats me up from the inside. And *damn*, does it turn me into a little bitch.

She stands there, that stray chunk of hair falling into her eye again, and I reach out for her wrist and pull her toward me. When she's flush against my chest, and looking up at me with those big, sienna eyes, I bend and kiss her. I kiss her like I need her, like she's all I need.

When I pull back, her lips are puffy and her eyes are blazing at me.

She's wearing form-fitting black pants that cut off just below her knees, and a tight tank top that hugs her generous curves to a point that's literally painful for me. She kicks off her flip-flops by the door, and turns away from me to climb up on my bed. Wordlessly, I turn off the light and crawl in after her.

"Why'd you pick me up, Dare?" she whispers in the darkness.

We're facing each other, inches apart, and I reach an arm out to wrap around her waist. Her body is so soft and supple against my hand, and I reach the other up to stroke her face.

"Because if you weren't here, I would have driven myself crazy all night trying to picture where you were."

She nods slowly; I can only see her outline in the inky blackness of my room. My eyes aren't yet adjusted to the dark.

"I hurt you tonight, even though I didn't mean to." It isn't a question, her voice is sad.

"I should have trusted you before I allowed myself to hurt."

She shook her head. "Maybe I haven't earned that kind of trust yet. Evil siren vixen magic can only go so far."

My smile is invisible to her, so I pull her hand to my mouth and kiss the flat of her palm. "You'd be surprised at how far that magic can take you, Berkeley."

She sighs.

"You know this isn't a booty call, right?" I'm suddenly worried that she'll think I asked her here just to get laid. I want her more than I want my next meal, but she's no booty call.

"Shit! It isn't?" She huffs, starting to sit up in bed.

I pull her back down, and her lips crash into mine. Her mouth, total sweetness, opens to me, and I dive inside. My tongue takes its time stroking hers, exploring where I've been too determined and frantic to take the time before tonight. I know that I have her all night, and that no matter what happens tomorrow, she's mine while she's here with me.

She's all round curves and I slide my hand along the outer edge of her from shoulder to thigh and back again. A soft moan slips from her mouth and into mine, and my body responds by tightening, hardening, stiffening.

She rolls onto her back and I stalk her, covering her body with mine while I hold myself above her. Our lips part and she stares up at me, her eyes glinting in the darkness. I bend to kiss her again, harder this time, my tongue lashing against hers as she pushes her chest against mine. I groan as I feel her nipples driving through her thin tank, and she grinds her hips into my erection.

Jesus. I want to find my way around her body like I'm making a map, but she's making it impossible to slow down the frenzy working in my body.

I leave her mouth to trail my lips along her jaw, pausing to inhale her rosy scent. I want her surrounding me, her smell, her feel, her taste, all of it. And I want to make her feel incredible, better than she's ever felt. When she leaves me in the morning, I want her to be completely and utterly satisfied.

And completely and utterly mine.

My hand skates across her stomach and down her thigh, bunching in her pants before making its way up again. I reach the hem of her tank, and look down at it. When I look back up at her, her eyes are blazing, and I pull the tank up and over her head. She lies there, her breasts exposed to me in a black lacy bra, and my breath hitches at the sight of how ample she is, how fucking *beautiful* she is. She's made like a goddess, and an errant thought that maybe she *is* a siren enters my head.

Chuckling slightly, I dip my head down to kiss the swell of her breast, and she gasps.

"You think this is *funny*, soldier?"

I keep my lips on her chest as I shake my head from side to side, creating friction with my mouth on her fiery skin.

"I find nothing about this funny," I murmur. "I was just thinking that if you actually use magic against me, I hope you never stop."

She smiles playfully, that corner of her lip finding its way into her mouth, and I pull it into my own mouth instead. Her answering moan is the fuel I need, and my hand travels south until it's resting on her hip bone and playing with the drawstring on the top of her pants.

"Dare," she gasps, and I still.

"Too much?" I try not to pant, but I meet her gaze. If she's asking me to stop, I need to see her eyes when she says it.

Her dimples appear as she presses her lips together, but I don't tear my gaze from her eyes.

"If you want me to stop, Berkeley, just say it. We have…time."

She reaches up and her fingers tangle in my hair. It's an amazing feeling, her fingers grazing my scalp as she plunders. "There are secrets between us. So I can't…I can't give myself to you. Not yet."

I want to curse, but I don't. I nod, because that reason is so valid and reasonable that I can't argue it. I wouldn't want to.

"Okay," I whisper. "One day soon, there won't be anything between us. I promise."

I don't make promises often. But I swear, I'll keep this one so close to my heart that breaking it will also break me.

I crawl up beside her and take her lips again, kissing her long and hard, until we're both so exhausted we fall asleep.

16

Berkeley

Y ou did *what?*"

The Admiral's voice was deadly calm as he asked me to repeat what I'd just said.

"I turned down Grisham's proposal. I'm not marrying him, Daddy. Grisham and I are friends, that's all."

I can feel the rigid set of my jaw as I finish, staring steadily at my parents as they glare at me from across the kitchen table.

My dad puts down his fork and wipes his mouth with his napkin. He steeples his fingers above his plate of eggs, meeting my stare with an angry one of his own.

Momma speaks up. "Berkeley. What are you saying? Of course you're going to marry Grisham! He picked out a beautiful ring. His mother and I have already been discussing the event!"

My mother's tone is a little hysterical. I know I'm crushing all her well-planned hopes and dreams. But seriously? Did they never even notice that Grisham and I aren't boyfriend and girlfriend? Have they never noticed that we don't kiss or hold hands? Are they really this freaking blind? Jesus.

The Admiral only stares, chewing his last bite of food so slowly and thoroughly it must be liquefied as it finally slides down his throat. When he speaks, his voice is low and even. Oh, boy. The Admiral is scariest when he's calm, cool, and collected. I brace myself.

"Sweetheart," he begins. Oh, God. Every time he calls me sweetheart, I live to regret whatever ill-advised decision I've recently made. "Sweetheart, do you really think your mother and I have planned out a promising, *secure* future for you only to let you throw it away? You're not thinking clearly right now. You and Grisham will work this out. He'll be here during the annual children's hospital fund-raiser, the garden party your mother has spent hours organizing. It's only a few weeks away."

Shit. Shit, shit, *shit*. I completely forgot about the garden party fund-raiser. It's a navy function, officer-level only, and each family pays a donation in order to come and have dinner in our backyard. It's exhausting for my mother to painstakingly plan each year, and I'm always required to attend.

Momma sighs. "I already bought you a dress. I knew you'd forget."

I nod. "Fine. But what I said about Grisham stands. We're not going to end up together. I wish you two would just accept it."

A thought formulates in my brain then, twisting and turning itself into an exciting idea. My heartbeat flies away from me as I consider it.

I haven't seen Dare for over a week, since I spent the night with him. We didn't have sex, but lying in his arms while he tasted me and touched me was causing lingering dreams of want. I miss him, but I can't continue this dance with him when he doesn't trust me enough to let me in on more of his life. So I've backed off considerably, and he's let me.

But now, I'm thinking there's a garden party I'd like to invite him to.

Having Dare with me as my date will shock and appall my parents, but what better way to introduce him to them than with a party full of onlookers? They'll have to behave.

I leave them stewing. Hell, what can they do? I've finally asserted my independence, and I'm nearly airborne with the satisfaction of it. *Damn*, why didn't I tell my parents what was up long ago? I'm a freaking adult, for God's sake. This isn't the nineteenth century. I'm not participating in an arranged marriage.

I hightail it to Drake's garage to see Dare. I'm off work today, but I know he isn't. When I arrive, I park in the lot instead of pulling up to the quadruple set of garage doors. The same young guy who pulled my car in for me when I had my oil changed and discovered my favorite new addiction in Dare is standing at the counter. His face breaks into a flirty grin when he sees me, and I restrain myself from rolling my eyes. The guy has never seen Dare and I together, so he can't know that Dare might physically remove that grin from his face if he catches him.

"Hey," I say politely. "I'm looking for Dare."

His smile falters a bit, but then he plasters it right back in place. Spunky one, this guy. "Dare? Like, you want him to answer a question about that sweet ride you've got out there?"

I narrow my eyes, walking up to the counter and placing my palms flat on the top of it. His eyes grow big and round, and it's just a smidge fun how intimidating he finds me. Okay, it's super fun.

"Nope. More like...I want him under my hood."

Now I just feel sorry for the guy as he splutters, choking and pounding his fist on his chest. I look through the glass door behind him and spot Drake. I walk around the counter, ignoring Mr. Flirty, and catch Drake's eye. I point to the door, and he grins, waving me in.

"Thank you," I say sweetly to the choking artist.

I put my index finger to my lips as I enter the bay, hoping Drake will understand that I don't want him to alert Dare to my presence. He raises his eyebrows but complies with my request, pointing toward a blue VW Jetta where a pair of muscular legs covered in navy coveralls are sticking out from beneath.

I tiptoe over, easygoing in my Chucks, and stand directly next to Dare's legs. I use my toe to nudge one booted foot, and wait. I know he's partial to my legs, so I hope the bare-leg view in my cutoffs is something he'll enjoy.

There's a pause, and then I hear his intake of breath.

"*Goddamn*," he mutters as he slides out from under the vehicle. He stares up at me, his lips quirked up in his sexy half-grin, his long, nearly black hair splayed out around his head. God, he's beautiful.

"Hey there." Now it's my turn to take in a quick breath as his rough voice meets my ears. My thighs immediately clench together as I register the hot pulse of electricity that travels between us when we lock eyes.

I kneel next to him just as he sits up on his little scooter, wiping his hands on a rag that's lying beside him. I reach out and rub my thumb lightly over one of his cheeks, erasing a dark smudge.

He turns his head, eyes still locked with mine, and takes my finger into his mouth. When I feel his teeth bite down gently, I reach out a steadying hand to clutch his thick bicep.

He releases my finger, taking my hand in his. "Did you come here to start trouble, honey? Because I haven't seen you in a week."

I hope my voice doesn't fail me. I shake my head slowly, so lost in this sexy moment with him that it takes me a minute to shake clear of it.

"You know I can always start a little trouble, soldier. But I'm here to talk."

He stands, pulling me up with him with my hand still clasped tightly in his. He leads me past Drake, who coughs "Get a room" as we pass. I glare at him, and he grins.

Dare leads me through the building and back out to my car. He leans me against the driver's-side door and boxes me in with his arms braced on the shiny black paint on either side of me.

"You've got my attention," he says casually. "But I don't know how long you have until I have to taste you. Start talking."

"You're not mad I've made myself scarce this week?" I whisper. "I'm sorry. I miss you, Dare."

"Times up," he mutters, before taking my lips. He kisses me hard, pinning me to the side of my car with his hips. I lose my freaking wits, moaning as I feel his hardness pulsing against my belly. Damn. Damn. Damn. What did I come here for? I have no idea, I'm lost in his soft lips and his punishing tongue and, oh *God*, his teeth as he uses them to nip at my bottom lip.

Finally, I gasp, my thoughts swirling hazily around my brain as I brace my hands against his chest and push.

He rears back only a few inches, his green eyes blazing dangerously as he focuses on mine.

"Berkeley." His voice is husky as he utters my name, and I swear I could fall apart right here on the scalding hot pavement.

"I-came-to-ask-you-to-be-my-date-to-my-mother's-garden-party." The words tumble out in a rush, because if I don't hurry and get them out I'm going to spend the rest of the day plastered against him, our lips and bodies fused together. Somehow, a week's break has ramped up the attraction between us, made me the fuse to his lit match, ready to ignite as soon as we touch.

His eyes widen, and then he chuckles. "Somehow, I doubt that your parents will be thrilled about that. What's going on?"

"I'm sick of them." I sigh. "I'm a damn adult, I can make my own decisions. And one decision that I really want to make, Dare, is you. Will you come?"

He contemplates, absently raising a hand to brush the hair out of my eyes, and then leaning forward to brush his lips against mine. He does this as if it's second nature, as if it's not even a conscious effort on his part.

"If you don't go, my parents are going to spend the entire night pushing me onto Grisham," I warn him. Somehow, I have a feeling that will light a fire under his ass.

His eyes narrow as he presses himself firmly against me once more, taking my face into his hands. "Not happening. I'll be there."

Those are his words before we are lost in another round of the hottest kissing I've ever experienced. Only with Dare. Only with my soldier.

"Do you have a tux?" I ask against his lips.

He groans. "Of course not. I guess I better have one by…"

"Three Fridays from now," I offer.

He sighs heavily. "Three Fridays from now. I'll be there, Berkeley. Promise."

I smile, reaching behind me to open my car door. As I climb up,

I feel his helpful hands on my waist, squeezing me firmly as he lifts me into my seat.

I look out at him and smile.

"That's weeks away, Berkeley. Are you going to make me wait until then to see you again?"

I shake my head. "Can't. A week was long enough. Come have dinner at the restaurant tomorrow. We can hang out after."

He nods, closing my door. Just before it shuts, he says, "I'll see you then, beautiful."

Breathless. Dare's words, his hands, his lips, his *presence*. It all leaves me feeling breathless. It makes me wonder how long a girl can go without taking in air.

17

Dare

"This is different, Dare." Chase's voice carries over the roar of the waves as they crash into the sand where our legs are stretched out in front of us.

I have the day following my encounter with Berkeley off at the garage. Chase and I decided to spend it surfing. Our surfboards sit beside us in the damp sand. Chase never travels anywhere without his, and I'd purchased a new one as soon as I'd arrived in Lone Sands.

"Oh, yeah?" I pull my legs in until I can rest my forearms on my knees, my bare feet digging into the sand. "Oh, good! I must be completely wrong about the fact that you made a bad bet and lost money that you never had to begin with. Again. Thanks for setting me straight, bro."

Chase throws his head back and groans. "I did *not* miss your dry-ass sense of humor. At all."

I stare at him, waiting.

"I mean it. I didn't just make a bad bet, Dare. I hadn't been gambling for a while. I got my shit straight. And then I met this girl."

Now it's my turn to groan. I want to take both sides of my hair and just pull.

"A girl." I shake my head, sending droplets of water flying in all directions from my saturated hair. I'm thinking the worst.

"Yeah, a girl. I met her when I was playing a sanctioned poker game. I was trying to go legit. You know, playing the circuit whenever I could. Poker's the only thing I'm good at, Dare. I'd just finished my game, and…there she was. This beautiful redhead. She smiled at me, and I was done. Then I bought her a drink, and talked to her. She was bright and open and full of this light that I've never seen before.

"The way I've seen you look at Berkeley? I know I must have had that dopey-ass grin on my face the night I met Shay. We talked all night, until the place was closing. And then…then her boyfriend showed up."

My groan was lost in the waves, but Chase didn't miss the way my eyes screwed up and my fist went to my mouth. The word *idiot* came to mind, but I restrained myself.

"He grabbed her, Dare. Hard. Jerked her up by the arm, and I was out of my seat. I got in his face, told him to let her go and stop talking to her the way he was. Then she looked at me…she looked at me, and the look in her eyes told me that she was leaving with him, and that if I didn't stop what I was doing it was going to be so much worse for her. And then they left.

"I asked around about her after that. All I had was her name, but it didn't take too long before I got her story. Her boyfriend is a major dealer and loan shark back in Florida. He uses her like he owns her, and roughs her up all the time. He has her doing dirty work for him most dudes wouldn't do, Dare. She's also not the only chick he stakes claim on. So I made it a point to get in on one of his games."

I'm shaking my head, staring at Chase like he'd just descended from the sky on the end of a rainbow. I've never heard him talk this way. He's usually only out for himself, and trying to see how far he can stretch whatever little bit of luck he's run into. The way he's talking about this girl is totally new and unrecognizable to me. I think my mouth is hanging open, but I'm too worried about what his next words might be to push it back into place.

"I bought a place at the table and showed up early. I had my eye out, but I didn't see her until about halfway through the game. She came in the door, and I thought her eyes were going to pop out of her head when she saw me. I folded immediately, and met her in a back hall where we could talk.

"I asked her about her boyfriend. His name is Chavez, and he treats her like shit. He holds an old bet of her brother's over her head, threatening every time she wants to walk out on him to make good on collecting. She's stuck, and she's miserable. She deserves better.

"So then…you're not gonna like this part, Dare."

I sigh. I don't like anything about this story, so I can only imagine that the next part is going to spin my head around in circles.

"I started seeing her. Behind Chavez's back. We would just, you know, chill. Eat lunch or dinner. Watch movies. We just spent time together. And every time I saw her…I fell harder for her. So I came up with a plan."

I bury my head on my arms then. Never, *never* has Chase come up with a plan that ended well. His plans were often the reason why I ever got into trouble growing up. He comes up with these ideas that he thinks are foolproof, and then they end up coming around to bite him in the ass.

"I know that this guy, Chavez, loves money more than he loves Shay. So I made a bet. I told him that I'd win in the poker tournament that was running through town at the time. And when I won, I'd turn the money over to him. In exchange for Shay."

I suck in a breath. As I level my gaze at Chase, disbelief runs rampant through my head. "You bet *her*? Shit, Chase, I thought you said you cared about this girl."

He nods firmly. "I do. That's why I had to get her freedom. She's like a prisoner with Chavez. I had to do something."

"Well, obviously, things didn't go like you planned. You didn't win?"

Chase shook his head, anger coloring his face. "Fucking Chavez rigged the game." He spoke animatedly, using his hands to demonstrate his agitation.

"He rigged the game?"

"Yeah. He rigged it. So I lost everything, including Shay. And now, I know he's hurting her. I owe him the money, but of course I don't have it all. That's why I came to you. It's not just another dumb-ass scheme I was trying to work. Shay's life depends on this. If I can get enough money together, I want to try again. To free her."

I blew out a breath I didn't know I was holding and shook my head slowly. "Damn."

He finally tore his dark eyes away from mine and stared out at the ocean. "Yeah. Damn."

We let a few minutes of silence slide by, just watching the waves, the horizon beyond, the clouds shifting lazily in the too blue sky. I close my eyes and try to imagine what I'd do if Berkeley were the one in trouble. If she were being controlled by someone, unable to escape her situation. The thought sends anger burning through my blood, causing my skin to become fiery and slick with a sheen of sweat. I would never let anyone hurt her. By nature, for whatever reason, all I want is to protect her. For her to be safe and happy. It's funny to think about. I've never needed to protect anyone but myself, and Chase when he needed it. My brothers in my Ranger Battalion didn't need protecting. We all just watched one another's backs. Somehow, Berkeley broke into my bubble of independence and singularity. If what Chase feels for Shay is even a fraction of that, I understand his sentiments fully.

"Stay here while we figure it out," I hear myself saying. Drake might murder me, but this Chase, this protective, focused Chase, isn't the Chase I grew to know. He's different, and his reason for needing my help is legitimate. I won't turn my back on him.

He nods, visibly relieved.

"We gotta be able to outsmart a thug like Chavez, right?" I give him a half smile. "We need to get out of here. I need to get cleaned up so I can meet Berkeley later."

We pick up our boards and set off for the little bungalow just behind the beach.

I enter See Food and earn a giant smile from my new friend Lenny. She's evidently a big encourager of Berkeley and me, and I'll take all the cheerleaders I can get. Judging by the look on Berkeley's mother's face the day I dropped her off and from what I hear of her father "the Admiral," I'm not sneaking in under the radar where they're concerned.

"How ya doin', Dare?" she asks kindly.

"Not too bad, Lenny," I say, returning her smile. "Is our girl almost ready to clock out?"

Berkeley comes around the corner from the kitchen then, busily untying the apron strings around her waist. When her eyes collide with mine, her face breaks into a gorgeous smile that sends my heart flipping around in somersaults.

Fucking *dimples*.

"All done, Lenny!" she calls brightly as she makes her way toward me. I restrain myself, stopping just inside the entry to the restaurant and opening my arms. If I had let myself, I would have run to her and scooped her up. I still have some semblance of my self-respect, even though more time with Berkeley is likely to send it crumbling to pieces.

"What are we doing tonight?" She breathes as she folds perfectly into my arms.

Sliding her arms around my waist and looking up at me with those big brown eyes, she's causing my thoughts to muddle, making me forget exactly what I have planned for tonight. I shake my head slightly.

I slide my arm down until it's around her shoulders as I guide her to the door, holding it open while I push her through gently.

"Did you remember to pack a change of clothes?" I ask her as I open the passenger door on my truck.

She hops up with my assistance, then grins down at me from her perch on the seat. She nods excitedly. "Yeah. What are you up to, Dare?"

I reach up and brush a thumb across the little wrinkle in her forehead. "We're going camping."

I shut her door and let that sink in as I walk around to my side of the truck and climb in. After I've started the ignition and back out of the parking spot, I turn to her as I pull out onto the road.

"Camping?" Her mouth forms the word as if it's foreign to her.

"You've never been?"

"Of course I have," she says, smiling. "I just…didn't expect it. Just you and me?"

I nod. "You can call Mea if you want."

She shakes her head, her smile lighting up the truck in a way the lights on the dash never do. "Just us is good."

She shoots me a bemused glance as I pull into the driveway at Drake's.

"We're camping in your bedroom?" she asks, her eyes glittering.

"No, smart-ass. We're camping on the beach."

Her eyes widen, and I smirk as she nods. She's surprised, and the sparkle in her eyes lets me know it's a pleasant one.

We bypass the inside of the house and weave around the side yard and into the back. We follow the walkway down to the sand, and Berkeley's gasp is all I need to feel alive and fierce, like I'm the man she needs in her life. The feeling leaves me almost drunk with joy.

"You gotta stop surprising me like this, Dare," she murmurs as her eyes reflect the flickering light from the torches. "I'm going to end up spoiled."

I roll my eyes. "Have to keep treating you to the life you're accustomed to, Berkeley."

The private beach behind Drake's is set up with a small tent. I had the camping gear already. Sleeping outside is second nature to me, although I've never done it on a beach. I know that Berkeley feels smothered by her parents, and I wanted to give her a sense of sleeping outside, with not only the great big sky above her, but also the big, wide ocean stretching out beside her.

I reach out for her and wrap her in my arms. She leans back against my chest, staring at the tent and the pile of wood I'd set up just in front of it.

"This is amazing," she whispers. "Thank you."

I nod, nuzzling my lips into her neck. She smells so sweet, I'm tempted to nibble on her warm skin as an appetizer. But I'll wait. The night is young.

"You sit on the blanket," I say, nudging her back toward the plaid spread I've set beside the little fire pit. "No beer tonight. You can open that bottle of wine and pour us some glasses, and I've got some cheese and French bread in that basket over there."

She gets busy on the task while I light the fire. The night is warm, but a cool breeze has kicked up down here by the ocean, and I want every excuse to be able to keep her wrapped up in my arms.

"So," she says, when we're settled and staring at the fire. "Did your parents take you camping a lot when you were a kid, or is this solely a product of the U.S. Army's training?"

The question is completely innocent and natural, but my body tenses at the mention of my parents. I've never shared my story with a female, I can't even think of a time that someone has asked about my family. I take a deep breath and let it out slowly.

"Dare?" Berkeley tilts her head back to look up at me from where she's situated against my chest. "What's wrong?"

I shake my head, glancing down at her. "Uh, nothing. No, my parents didn't take me camping. They probably would have, if they'd gotten the chance. My parents died in a car accident when I was seven."

Her bottom lip disappears instantly into her mouth, and the crease in her forehead deepens. "Oh, Dare. I'm so sorry."

I bend down and kiss the top of her head. "I should have told you the night you met Chase. It's just not an easy subject to talk about."

"Who raised you and Chase?" she asks tentatively. "Grandparents?"

I bark out a laugh, harsher than I intended. I can't remember how many times in my screwed-up childhood I'd wished for grandparents to swoop in out of nowhere and take me away from this foster family or that one. I've heard there are some great foster homes out there, but I was never lucky enough to be placed in one. I saw way too much violence and heartbreak at way too early an age, and it forced me to build walls around myself for my own protection. It made me strong, but it also crippled me emotionally.

"No. Actually...Berkeley, Chase isn't my blood brother. He's my foster brother. We met in the same for-shit home when we were eleven, and he's been like blood ever since." I glance at her out of the corner of my eye, gauging her reaction. If there's pity in her eyes, I'd rather not face it head-on.

"You don't have to talk about it, Dare. Not if you don't want to."

God, I don't want to. I grab her offer like a life raft and change the subject.

"Your parents are the ones who took you camping?"

She shakes her head, a rueful smile playing on her lips. "Hardly. Can you picture the Admiral, camping with his family? No, we vacationed, but it was usually in the middle of some base tour he was taking. He didn't have time to disconnect and hang out in the woods."

I nod thoughtfully, trying to picture Berkeley as a little girl. She probably adored her father, and craved his attention. My heart aches thinking of all the times she probably didn't get it.

"So who, then?"

"I went a couple of times with friends' families. I haven't been much."

"Ever camped on the beach?"

She shakes her head. "Nope. This is my first time doing this."

I lean down and whisper in her ear. I feel gratified when she shivers in response. "Me, too."

"So, um…," she begins. "I've been meaning to ask you, you know, if you're seeing anyone else right now? Because if you are, I don't have any reason to, you know…" She pauses, and then rushes on the way she does when she's nervous. I know what she's asking, and I could put her out of her misery. But she's just so fucking cute. "It's fine if you are, I just wanted to know upfront. Because I'm not, you know—"

I grin, because I can listen to this girl babble for the rest of the night. Her modest sexiness knows no bounds. But I can't let her keep going; I have to tell her how I feel. No matter how cute her babbling is.

"Berkeley," I interrupt.

Her face colors, and I know she's embarrassed. The thought sends a giddy burst of energy through me.

She looks up. "Yes?"

I tilt her head back with my index finger under her chin and catch the nape of her neck with my other palm. When her startled eyes are staring up into mine, I answer her question.

"How could I be seeing anyone else when you are all I think about, every single day since I've met you? I'm way too into you,

Berkeley, to want anyone else. And you saw how I reacted when I thought you were seeing someone else. So…no. This? It's fucking exclusive. Okay?"

"Okay." She has time to breathe before my lips find hers.

The kiss is deep and intense. I always mean to go in soft and gentle when I kiss Berkeley, but somehow, the message gets lost in translation. The connection we share is something that sizzles with electricity and heat, and I can't contain the fervor my body feels to be melded with hers. Her lips move against my mouth just as ardently as mine, and we're matched perfectly. She tastes like redemption and bliss, and I can't get enough.

When she pulls back, gazing up at me, I feel something inside of me shift. We just declared exclusivity, which means Berkeley is *mine*. No matter what her overbearing father says, no matter what her *friend* Grisham wants, she belongs to me. The idea sends me soaring off somewhere among the stars, and my chest constricts with the seriousness of our declaration.

Have I ever belonged to someone? Not since my parents died. And never in this capacity. It leaves me feeling…changed. This girl is altering me from the inside out. And I *like it*.

Suddenly, with a gasp, Berkeley is under me, on her back against the blanket. I search her face for a second, asking silent permission, before I lower my head and trail my lips along the line of her jaw.

"This," I murmur roughly as my lips find the sweetest spot in the curve of her neck and suck. "This is what I think about, when I'm in bed at night without you."

She moans, and shifts under me so that her hands are free to rove my back. She bunches up the shirt under her fingers, and I decide it'll be easier for her if I just rip the damn thing off. When it hits the sand behind me, I return to the sweetness that is this girl.

"And this," I inform her as my mouth finds the delicate angle of her collarbone. My hands are acting on their own, one finding its way under her shirt and raising it upward. I glance down, and all I can see is miles of bare skin and lace-covered mounds of heaven.

"Fuck," I mutter. "I need this off, Berkeley."

She lifts, and I remove her shirt just as quickly as I did my own. Then I lower my mouth over one perfect, hardened nipple.

"Oh, God." Her voice is silk in my ear, and her taste is like the ripest, plumpest piece of fruit I've ever had. I suck, bite, and lick until she's a writhing mess underneath me.

But I remember what she said that night in my bedroom. I move to her other breast, not wanting to play favorites, and she utters my name like she's about to disappear into sweet oblivion. I remember that she isn't ready to give herself to me, so I stay north of the snap on her shorts.

"Dare." She sighs as my mouth plants hot kisses along her rib cage.

"Mmmm."

"Touch me."

I still, hovering in place on top of her. I glance down, and her whiskey-colored eyes are boring into mine with fierce seriousness.

I don't break the magnetic hold of her gaze, but I need to clarify what she's just asked me.

"Where, Berkeley? Where do you want me to touch you? Ask me fucking anything. I'll do it."

My words draw a ragged breath from her, but she keeps my gaze steady in hers. Then I feel her hand moving between us, and I glance down.

Berkeley is unzipping the tiny pair of shorts she's wearing.

Jesus Christ.

"Touch me," she says again.

I will never, ever make her ask me twice again.

I cradle her head with one hand, trailing the other down her ribs, her stomach, and past the top of her panties. They're purple, with a lacy front that lets me see everything going on underneath.

She gasps as my finger draws down slowly, until I can feel the dampness, the *heat* radiating from the softest parts of her.

Goddamn. I want this girl.

I close my eyes, because she just feels too amazing. Dipping beneath the thin fabric, my finger slips inside her.

"Dare!" She jerks violently, and I lay my lips to hers.

"Shhhh," I whisper. "I got you, honey."

Her breath is coming in pants as I use the heel of my hand to rub against the bundle of nerves that I know will slowly drive her insane. I keep whispering in her ear, and I keep rubbing, and I keep the finger inside her thrusting until she's a quivering mess of noises in my arms.

"I…Dare…fuck," she murmurs.

Shit. That statement nearly makes me lose my shit right then and there, but I keep it together. This is about her, not me.

One more thrust with my finger and she's falling. Right into pieces in my arms, and I'm there to catch her.

I always plan to be there to catch her.

Somehow, bringing Berkeley pleasure leaves my knees feeling weak, my body poised and tensed for more. But we both have some kind of unspoken promise to…wait. Berkeley's body calls to me like she's got my number memorized by heart. She fits perfectly into my hands, molds magically into the plane of my chest. My imagination runs away with me. What will she feel like when they're no barriers between us? Just Berkeley? The thought sends my pulse racing, sets my blood on fire. My body desperately needs to know the answer to that question. My head can wait.

Later, when we're snuggled together in a sleeping bag inside my tent, she yawns and her voice is a barely there whisper.

"Dare?"

"Yes, baby." The nickname rolls off my tongue like I've been using it forever. In fact, I've never used it.

"How is it possible that you're making me feel safe and free all at the same time?"

My breath catches. She's freaking incredible. I kiss her cheek as her breathing evens and deepens. She won't hear my answer if I give it, and I know it wasn't a question she needed an answer to anyway.

I wish that falling asleep with a smile on my face was a guaranteed way to keep the nightmares away.

It isn't.

18

Berkeley

"Dare?"

It's morning again, and we all know how functional I am at this hour. *What hour?* Any hour with the letters *a.m.* directly following.

So I'm groggy and confused when I feel his body convulsing beside me.

"Dare?" I say again, louder.

Holy crap. It's his PTSD. He's having a nightmare, and he can't wake up from it.

I shove him onto his back from his side and climb on top of him. His eyes are squeezed shut tight, and he's mumbling in his sleep as his body shakes with violent tremors.

"Dare!" I scream it now. "Wake up!"

His arms reach up, and he grabs my shoulders. Hard. I gasp with the force of it, but then use my palm to slap him across the face. Also hard.

His eyes fly open, wild and panicked. The brilliantly clear green draws me in as his glance darts to his hands still gripping my shoulders. His eyes widen and he instantly releases me.

"Shit, Berkeley! I'm sorry. I'm sorry. Did I hurt you? Shit."

I shake my head firmly, not even considering that there's a tiny hint of pain where his hands gripped me so firmly. It doesn't matter. He matters, and so does the pain he's in.

"I'm fine." I shake my head dismissively. "Have you talked about them?"

He slowly sits up, gripping my hips to keep me seated on his lap. "Talked about what?"

"The dreams. Did you talk about them when you were in therapy? You must have done some therapy after your injury, right?"

He eyes me warily, and silence stretches out between us like a rope. I grasp the end of it, pulling myself back to him before he's able to retreat from my question.

"They're not going to stop, Dare. Not unless you share them."

I read the panicked look in his eyes and instantly soften my tone. "I'm here. When you're ready to talk about them. Okay? I can listen."

He keeps his eyes locked on me, and then finally runs a hand through his disheveled hair. He nods tiredly. "Yeah. Maybe one day."

I tilt my head to the side, assessing him. "One day soon?"

He hesitates and averts his gaze. When he looks up again, he looks sadly at my shoulders. I glance down to see I have red marks where his fingers gripped me. No bruising will result, and I don't want him to worry about that. I grip his chin in my hand.

"Hey," I say firmly. "You didn't hurt me, Dare. But *you* are hurting. Every night in your dreams. And that's not okay with me. Let me help you."

I can see the torrent of emotions as they flicker through his eyes one by one. I know he's never talked about the things that haunt him at night. He's gone through something so awful he can't even spill the words from his lips. But if he doesn't find a way to expel it, it will consume him. I'm certain of that. And I can't sit around and watch it happen, now that I know him.

"I don't want to drag you into my hell, Berkeley," he finally says. His voice is soft and sad. It causes a painful ache to spread through my chest that doesn't even compare to the slight sting in my shoulders. "It's…they're my demons to battle, not yours."

I reach out and run my fingers though his hair, settling my hands on the back of his neck. Leaning my forehead against his, I say, "Your demons are now my demons."

The troubled expression that flits across his eyes gives me pause, but before I can comment it's gone. Maybe I imagined it.

"Breakfast?" I say hopefully.

He nods, pulling me up and out of bed with a devastating, lop-sided smile.

I creep into the house, shutting the door behind me as quietly as I can. I'm not exactly hiding that I spent the night out once again, but my mother doesn't need to see me coming in the house looking all sleepy and disheveled, either.

"Good morning, Berkeley."

I whip around at the sound of the Admiral's voice, and my blood freezes in my veins. He's standing just inside the entryway, his arms folded casually over his chest as he leans against the paneled wall.

"Oh, good morning, Daddy," I stutter. His presence is…unexpected. So much so that I fumble for words.

"You were out early this morning," he remarks. His tone is still casual, but it's taken on an edge that alerts me: he knows exactly what's what. "Or should I say you were out late last night?"

My face falls, my eyes scanning the ground in front of me, as if I'm an errant child who's been caught stealing a cookie.

Then I straighten. I shouldn't have to feel this way. I'm an adult, and adults don't need to explain to their parents where they're sleeping. Even if one of said parents is a scary, all-powerful commander in the U.S. Navy.

"Since I was out so late, I just decided to wait and come home this morning. No big deal, Daddy." I attempt aloofness as I walk past him toward the stairs. The small smile that plays on my father's face nearly brings me to a halt, but I continue up the staircase anyway, wondering what in the world he could be smiling about this morning.

I'm still thinking about it when I open my bedroom door, because the Admiral should have been *way* more pissed about the fact that I spent the night out and he had no idea where I was. Maybe Momma told him I'm seeing someone. That seems unlikely, because—

"So you're sleeping with him now?"

The accusatory tone in Grisham's voice, actually the fact that Grisham's voice is coming from my normally empty bedroom at all, rips a shrill shriek from my mouth as I enter the rom.

"What the *hell*, Grish? Are you trying to give me a heart attack?" I clutch at my chest as I stare openmouthed at him.

His blond hair is falling handsomely across his forehead, and it shifts slightly as he shakes his head. His chiseled face is shadowed, and he frowns at me slightly. He's not even a little bit apologetic that he just scared the bejesus out of me.

"Where have you been?" he demands instead. "Your parents said I could wait for you up here when I came to take you to breakfast this morning. But they didn't have a clue where you were. That's not safe, Berkeley."

I sigh, moving toward the bed and plopping down beside him. "I was safe, Grisham. I was with Dare."

"The guy I met the other night? Shit, Berkeley!" My eyes widen slightly because Grisham's never once cursed at me. "All night? I knew you were talking to the guy, but you're spending the night with him now? I don't even understand you right now!"

I inspect his angry face carefully before I speak. Me spending the night with a guy shouldn't make Grisham flip out like this. There's something else going on. There has to be. "What's wrong, Grish?"

He turns away from me, toward the window. Then he stands and walks over to it, staring out at the ocean beyond. Agitated, he runs a hand through his hair, and then turns to face me.

"After next week when I go to San Diego, we'll be the farthest away from each other we've ever been, Berkeley. That means something to me. We've been best friends since we were babies. Can you make some time for me? I want to…be with you as much as possible before I leave. Is that too much to ask?"

My mouth falls open, and then the guilt sets in, tensing all the muscles in my body like tightly wrapped coils. I nod silently, just staring at the beautiful boy-turned-man who's always been here for me. I could never turn down his request, and I don't even want to. There's too much history with Grish and me to leave him hanging now.

"Of course, Grish," I say feebly. "I want to spend as much time as possible with you, too. I'm sorry…I haven't been thinking straight lately. I'm off work today. What do you want to do?"

A golden smile lights up his face, crinkling his eyes at the corners, and I smile back gratefully in return. Grisham has always forgiven my fallacies as if they were merely sand sifting through his fingers. No matter what happens, how far our parents go to try and control us, I know he's my rock. I want to be the same for him.

"I want to go surfing," he states.

I sigh. Just imagining the bruises I'll acquire while trying to remain standing on a long board make me cringe. I am not athletic.

I repeat, I am not athletic.

Grisham knows this but takes every opportunity he can to get me on a board. I'm suddenly glad he's moving to a place where he doesn't have to lose surfing.

"Of course you do."

He grins. "I'm going to run home and get changed, then I'll come back and pick you up. We'll go to that spot I love, behind the Morocoke Dunes. Be ready in an hour. You still have the wet suit I gave you?"

His smile is infectious, and I can't help but return it. "Still have it. See you in an hour, Grish."

As soon as he leaves my bedroom, I flop down on my bed and groan. I'm happy about spending the day with Grisham, but I wish we were doing something that wasn't going to leave me black and blue.

Then I think of Dare. Shoot. I won't be around all day. Should I tell him that I'm going surfing with Grisham? Judging from the way he reacted when he found me with Grisham at the bar the other night, he wouldn't be thrilled about the fact I'll be alone with him all day.

Oh, well. Dare is going to have to get used to it. Grisham is my best friend. And he's leaving soon. I'll have to be around him.

But I let my phone stay put on the nightstand. I'm not in any hurry to inform Dare of my day's plans.

I jump as my phone chimes. I stare at it suspiciously. Is Dare psychic?

I lean over and read the words on the screen. When I see Mea's name, I relax.

Want to meet me at Smash tonight for drinks and dancing? You can bring Dare. Or...Grisham? Girl, I can't keep up.

I glare at my phone. Mea is so not funny. My fingers whip across the letter keys as I type my response.

Oh, you are hilarious. Can you wait a minute while I stop laughing? YES, Smash sounds good. I'll ask DARE if he wants to come.

There, that should work. I'm spending the day surfing with Grisham, but I'll be dancing the night away with Dare at Smash if he wants. Everyone should be appeased.

Maybe the next week, before Grisham's departure, won't be as tough to navigate as I thought.

19

Dare

I put my phone down on the workbench beside me, smiling as I imagine spending the night on a dance floor with Berkeley in my arms. I texted her to ask what she was doing with herself today, but I haven't heard back yet. She has the day off work, and I hope she's spending it relaxing and not worrying too much about her parents and their lame expectations.

Berkeley is such a free spirit. I've learned that about her in just the short time I've known her intimately, and her parents should be slapped in the face repeatedly for not respecting that. Trying to make Berkeley into something she isn't is almost criminal, and I'm going to have a hard time keeping my thoughts to myself at that garden party in a few weeks. My mind flies away from me as I think back to the art she'd shown me at her university. She is so damn talented, and everything she touches becomes beautiful and perfect.

"Oh, God," says Drake. He slides up next to where I'm sitting on the garage floor on a little red stool. "You're thinking about Berkeley, aren't you? Shit, Dare, there's heavy-ass machinery you're working with in here. Get your head on straight."

His tone is half-teasing, half-serious. "I got this, Drake. Mind your own business. And if you're jealous of Berkeley, you can just say it. You don't have to pretend you're worried about me dropping a Chevy on my head."

I shoot him an understanding smile, and he slaps me in the back of the head. "Not jealous. She can keep you, for all I care."

"I love you, too, Drake," I say with syrup in my voice. "Hug it out?"

He shakes his head as he rolls away to where he's rotating the tires on a Fiat. "There's something seriously wrong with you."

"I'm getting therapy," I promise him. "Her name is Berkeley, and she's hot. Hey, you want to go to some club called Smash with us tonight?"

He narrows his eyes. "Just you and Berkeley?"

I shrug. "I bet Chase will want to come. And her friend Mea will be there. I'm guessing some other girls, maybe." I raise my voice a little. "Hey, Will! Bring me a monkey wrench, will you?"

Drake cocks his head to the side. "Is her friend Mea hot?"

Considering, I think of Mea's light brown skin and exotic, almond-shaped eyes. Her wild curly hair is similar to Berkeley's, but a dark chocolate brown instead of honey-blond. It's hard for me to see past Berkeley when I'm with her, but I'm not blind enough to have missed Mea's contemporary beauty.

I nod. "Yep."

Drake gives me one of his enormous grins, and I picture Mea being blinded by it. It could be good, him meeting her tonight. "Then I'm all over it."

"Okay, but you're not going to be all over *Mea*, right?" I'm suddenly nervous that Drake alienating Mea with a love-her-and-leave-her magic act might be dangerous for my own relationship with Berkeley.

"Right." If his grin could get any wider, it just did. Shit. Now I'll have to babysit not only my wild-card brother, but also my commitment-phobic best friend. The upcoming night is looking less shiny and fun and more tedious already.

"Can I come?" asks Will from where he's searching the drawers of the tall tool cabinet against the nearest wall.

"Fuck, no!" answer Drake and I in unison.

After work, Drake and I shower, change, and grab a quick bite in the kitchen with Chase before we all head out in my F-250. It means I won't be able to drink more than a beer or two, but it's better than folding my long body into the Challenger.

"You know you're being ridiculous about my car, right?" Drake flicks a glance in my direction from the front seat. "It's big enough for your tall ass."

I keep my eyes on the road as I reply. "You're just saying that because you're short."

He chokes, and I reach over and pound his massive chest with my fist. "I'm not short, Dare. Six feet tall isn't short."

I humor him with a smile. "Okay, big guy. Chase, you good back there?"

Chase has his long legs stretched out behind the passenger seat. I glance in the rearview, and he gives me a thumbs-up.

"What does Mea look like?" asks Drake, redirecting my attention.

"You'll see in a minute," I reply. "This isn't a double date, Drake. Be cool."

"This is funny. You, telling me to be cool?"

I ignore him as I pull into the packed parking lot at Smash. I inspect myself before we walk toward the line wrapping around the front of the building. I've chosen a plain black T-shirt and dark jeans and a pair of charcoal-colored boots with a light dusting of scuff marks on the toes.

Chase's attire is similar, but Drake's decked out in a long-sleeved button-down with blue-and-white pinstripes and designer, faded blue jeans. His crisp white Steve Madden casual sneakers are accented with navy blue, and the cologne he wears could probably be identified by name by most of the girls in this club. I shake my head at him, amused. Drake takes style very seriously.

"What?" he snaps when he catches me looking.

"Nothing," I say innocently. "I just wonder if you're going to punch in the face the first guy who steps on your shoes."

He scowls for just a second before it's replaced with a grin. "Hopefully a girl will step on my shoe. Then I can just tell her she owes me a dance."

I nod. "You always have all the answers, Drake."

A tiny arm grabs mine just as I'm about to walk past the front of the line, and I turn to find Mea gripping me tightly. She smiles up at me, and then tugs my arm again. I follow her, beckoning the guys to follow me.

"These guys are with me, okay, Dan?" She addresses the bouncer standing beside the door with his arms crossed. He raises his eyebrow at her, and then scans each of us in turn. Finally he shrugs.

"Okay, Mea."

She reaches up on her tiptoes and kisses his cheek, and he grins. Then, nodding at me, she gestures inside. "After you, boys."

"Thanks." We file past her into the club.

Inside, it's bigger than the nondescript building gave it credit for. We pass an enclosed coat-check, and then it opens up to a cavernous room with a bar curving along the back wall and a stage closer to the front. The stage is empty, and a DJ is taking up residence in a booth a few feet away from it. I'm assuming that since there's no band, girls will be dancing on that stage once things really get going. The lighting is dim, but not dark, and I'm able to see faces clearly as I look around. Following Mea to the bar, I spot a head of wild, blond curls. She doesn't turn as we approach, and I'm able to close the gap before she knows we're here.

"We're back!" sings Mea.

Berkeley whips around, and I'm right *there* in her personal space. Her nostrils flare slightly as she looks up at me, and her eyes burn into mine.

"Hey," she says breathlessly as the electricity crackles between us.

"Hey," I whisper, bending in to take her lips. I can't help it. She makes me weak for her, and I can admit it.

When I pull back, she smiles. "I missed that today."

"Yeah? What'd you do today?"

Her eyes fall, but before she can answer, Drake elbows me in my ribs.

I swear, then turn deliberately toward where he and Chase are standing behind me. He flicks his eyes toward Mea and then back to me.

"Mea," I announce formally. "This is my friend and roommate, Drake. And this is my brother Chase."

From her significantly lower vantage point, she eyes Drake and Chase carefully. "Hey. Nice to meet you both."

They nod. Chase shoulders his way closer to the bar to ask for a beer. I hold up a finger, indicating that I want one, too. I eye the cup in Berkeley's hand. "What's that?"

"Screwdriver," she says. "Have I told you I'm kind of obsessed with orange juice?"

I laugh, spacing out over the way her lips wrap around her straw. "No. But I'm not surprised, considering how much you love breakfast."

I look her over, finally able to tear my gaze away from her eyes and her lips. She's poured into a tight, black dress with a lace overlay. Her shoulders are bare, and there's a pair of pink heels on her feet.

Holy. Shit.

If she was aiming for "Give Dare a Coronary" when she got dressed this evening, she's damn near achieved her goal.

She catches me eyeing her and smiles almost apologetically. "Yeah, this? Mea made me wear it."

"You look...amazing," I manage to choke out. "Uh...where's the rest of that dress?"

She rolls her eyes, glancing at Mea and jerking a thumb toward me. Mea smiles cheerily. "I told her when she dressed me that I can barely breathe."

I nod slowly. "Me neither." I lean closer, letting my breath linger somewhere near her ear. "Are you coming home with me?"

Her answering smile is flirtatious. "Maybe."

I groan a little as my muscles clench. "When you know how I can turn that answer into a firm, resounding yes, let me know."

She nods. "Will do."

I scan her body again, and my eyes land on the purplish bruise darkening her thigh. "What the *hell* happened to your leg, Berkeley?"

She sighs, holding out her leg so she can eye the bruise. "I landed on a rock."

I open my mouth, but she tugs on my arm that isn't holding my Killian's. "Dance with me?"

I follow her wordlessly to the dance floor, but our conversation isn't over. She left me this morning without a scratch, and tonight she's got at least one bruise I can't account for. Nothing about that is okay with me. I set my mouth in a firm line.

As soon as she stops in front of me and begins moving to the beat reverberating around us, I spin her around with one hand and pull her back so that her ass is resting against my thighs. Then I lean down, speaking into her ear so that she can hear me clearly.

"Berkeley, where did that bruise come from?"

I don't know what I'm expecting her to say, but her actual answer nearly knocks me on my ass.

"Surfing."

I rear back, looking down at her as she continues to sway against the front of me. I can feel my body answering to her writhing movements, but my brain is stuck on rewind and I can't make myself move with her.

"You surf?" The disbelief in my voice is evident.

She leans back, meeting my surprised gaze. "Unfortunately."

She leaves it at that, and I reluctantly do, too. Or not so reluctantly, since my body finally begins to move against her like it's always been meant to do exactly that. There is so much more I want to ask her, but the questions dull to a whisper as I move with her, dance with her. The music changes, I lose count of how many times, and I'm still tethered to her by the fiery connection we've shared since I laid eyes on her that first night. The feeling that I was brought to Lone Sands for a reason, for *this* reason, nearly swallows me whole as I inhale the sweet scent of Berkeley swirling around me.

I'd put off Drake's offer to join him in North Carolina since I'd gotten out of rehab for my back, and if I'd come any earlier Berkeley would have been away at school.

I'm not used to being in the right place at the right time; it's a completely new situation for me. I'm feeling pretty damned lucky right about now.

Berkeley turns in my grasp, winding her arms around my neck as she gazes up at me. Her eyes are sparkling, two tawny diamonds glittering in the dimness of the club.

"Hey," she says, her dimples creasing the smoothness of her cheeks.

"Yeah, hey." I smooth my thumb over her defined cheekbone.

The little wrinkles in her forehead let me know she's pondering something.

"I can't wait to get you alone so I can ask you what you're thinking about," she finally says. "You look very far away right now."

I shake my head gently, staring at her. "Just feeling really lucky right now. For like, the first time ever. It's a pretty weird feeling."

She nods slowly, dropping her arms from my neck and grasping my hand. She rises to her tiptoes so she can be heard. "I want you to tell me about a time in your life when you didn't feel so lucky. It's safe to talk about it, Dare. Your luck has changed. You have me now."

A ball of emotion gets stuck in my throat. I thump my chest a few times, trying to clear it. When I can, I lean toward her, indicating her empty cup. "Another drink?"

She nods, and we head to the bar, where we walk up on a heated argument.

"Don't be stupid," Drake is saying in exasperation. "Just take the drink. Shit, I was trying to be *nice*."

"First of all," Mea shoots back, "I don't take drinks from guys I don't know. Second of all, I can buy my own damn drinks. Third of all—"

I'm looking dumbfounded between the two of them when Berkeley breaks in. "Whoa, girl. Easy. I'm sure Drake was just trying to be a gentleman. What's up with you?"

"Nothing," says Mea, glaring at Drake. "I've just had about all I can stand of guys like him, that's all."

She turns on her stiletto and flounces away, leaving us staring openmouthed after her.

"I'm so sorry, Drake," says Berkeley. "I don't know what that was about. She's not usually like that."

"Yeah, but you've been away at school, right?" I muse. "Maybe she's changed."

"No, she hasn't," says Berkeley firmly, shaking her head. "She's still Mea. But maybe I need to find out what crawled up her ass while I was away."

Drake nods. "Yeah. That sounds like a plan. You want her drink, B?"

Berkeley beams at him. "Sure. Thanks, Drake."

I shoot Drake a glare. "Yeah, thanks Drake."

He grins. "Hey, I'll always take care of your girl for you when you need me to, Dare. That's what friends are for."

My eyes narrow and my lip curls. "I'm not going to be needing that service, but thanks, buddy. Glad to know you're around." I slap him so hard on the back he splutters on the sip he just took of his beer.

"Where's Chase?" I ask, glancing around the bar area.

Drake shrugs. "I didn't sign up to babysit him."

I search the room, keeping one arm snug around Berkeley's waist as I do. I can't see Chase anywhere, and I'm immediately nervous. I've just let go of Berkeley, turning around to ask Drake to keep her company for a minute, when a deep voice snaps my attention right the fuck back.

"Let's go, Berkeley."

Her head whips around, and so does mine. We're confronted with the tall, solid form of the man she calls the Admiral. He stares down at his daughter, and then glances around the club, clearly disgusted and angry.

"I've had enough of this," he says, glaring at Berkeley. "We're going home. And then I'm locking you in your room until you can figure out how the daughter of an Admiral is expected to behave. Because this sure as hell isn't it."

His words are sharp like nettles, and I can see the sting of them as Berkeley's head snaps back in surprise and hurt. My instinct is to grab her by the waist again, and push her behind me slightly, angling my body toward her father like a shield.

"Berkeley," I say quietly, not taking my eyes from his. "Are you ready to go?"

When I glance back at her, her eyes are wide as they dart between her father and me. Finally, she focuses on him. "What are you doing, Daddy? I'm just out with my friends. I'm not doing anything wrong!"

He shakes his head impatiently and reaches out. He clasps her wrist in his hand so roughly I hear her gasp, and I zero in on the spot. I reach out, wrench her wrist free from his grasp, then shoving his hand back at him.

The Admiral stares at his hand, and then at mine. When he raises his eyes to meet mine, they're lit with a smoldering anger I know from experience is dangerous.

"I don't know you, son, but you seem like a smart man. Touch my daughter or me again and I'll end you. Understand?"

I understand, all right. I know men like the Admiral. Hell, I've *worked* for men like the Admiral. Men who parade around on a high from the power they've achieved, who know that anything and everything is possible for them. They move people in their lives around like pawns, in order to get what they want.

I narrow my eyes. My anger is radiating just beneath the surface of my skin, causing my blood to zing through my veins. The adrenaline is rushing so loudly in my ears I can't focus on anything else. "She doesn't want to go. I suggest you go ahead and back away from her."

He takes a menacing step forward, and then Berkeley flings herself out from behind me and steps in front of him. "Okay, Daddy. Let's go." She throws a warning glance back at me. "I'll call you, Dare."

I step forward, lifting her chin to look at me. "You don't have to do this. You can stay. I'll protect you."

She shakes her head, raising her chin a fraction of an inch. She glances back at her father, and then meets my eyes with a pleading gaze. "I'll be fine. Promise. Later, okay?"

Everything inside of me is screaming at me to keep her safe. Her father should be safety for her, but he isn't. I can feel it so deeply within me that it hurts. I don't want to let her go. I don't want to allow her to slip free of my grasp.

With everything in me, *I don't want to.*

She sees the battle going on in my eyes and leans up to kiss my lips. Her lips brush against my chin, and I hear the whisper of the words against my ear as I lean into her. "Trust me."

I nod mutely, releasing her. She turns away from me then and follows her father to the door. He turns around once, locking eyes with me. His eyes narrow in anger, and he throws one last frown in my direction before he turns and follows Berkeley out of the club.

I sag against the bar, placing my hands on my head and pulling at my hair in frustration. "Fuck."

"Yeah, you said it," says Drake calmly. He leans back beside me, taking a swig of his beer. "Well, that was intense. You good?"

"Drake, I'm so far from good right now. I want to go after them."

"Not smart," he advises. "That dude, her father, is no slouch. He's an admiral, huh? He meant business. You'll be lucky if you get to set eyes on Berkeley again, dude."

I turn to stare at him. "And you think that's okay with me?"

He shakes his head, slowly. "No. But we'll figure something out."

Chase appears next to me then, out of nowhere.

"Where the hell have you been?" I ask louder than I intended.

He stares at me in surprise and holds up his phone. "Outside. I was talking to Shay." He furrows his eyebrows as a shadow crosses his expression. "I'm worried about her. I hate that she's there, alone with him."

"Yeah, well you can join the Worried Boyfriends Club," I snap. Then I curse. "Sorry, Chase. Berkeley just got snatched out of here by her dad, and he wasn't gentle about it. I'm worried about her, too. I don't even know how I'm still standing here right now."

"Because you know I'll drag your ass back if you try to go after them," offers Drake. "She said she'd call you."

I pull my phone out of my pocket and stare at it, willing it to ring, knowing she hasn't even had time to get home yet.

"Are you ready?" I ask them both. I can't stay here anymore. Every second the music pounds into my eardrums, I grow a little more anxious and fidgety. I need to get the guys home and be ready to get to Berkeley if she needs me.

They both nod, and we exit the club after Drake picks up our beer tab. The entire drive home, I replay her exit with her father. I definitely didn't win any points with him tonight, but I wasn't trying to. I was trying to keep him from ripping her arm off in order to yank her out of the club. How'd he even find her, anyway? The thought crosses my mind that he probably has a GPS tracker on her phone, or even her car.

The man has some serious control issues.

And I can't stand the thought of Berkeley being caught up in them. The more I question what he's capable of, the more anxious I become.

I can wait only until after I drop off Chase and Drake at home. I'll give her that long. I know I won't be able to stay put if Berkeley hasn't called me by then.

I send a silent prayer up to the giant black expanse above me that she'll call me by then.

20

Berkeley

It's late. The Admiral is usually in bed by nine, unless he's working, so the fact that he'd shown up at Smash to collect me at least two hours after he's usually snoring the night away tells me that he's very serious about the whole "Force Berkeley to Fall in Line" plan. I'm beyond pissed.

As soon as we walk in the front door, I storm for the stairs.

"We're not finished, Berkeley," his stern voice calls behind me.

I whirl around. "No, you know what? We are. This will never happen again. I'm a grown woman with a college degree. I don't have to stay here and tolerate this borderline psychotic behavior! I'm going to pack a bag, and I can stay with Mea until I find my own place. But I'm not doing this anymore, Daddy."

I start up the stairs and don't stop running until I reach my room. Slamming the door behind me, I lean against it, my chest heaving. A million and one emotions are chasing one another through my head, but the one at the front of the pack right now is fury. How could he treat me like a child? What have I done over all of these years to encourage him? He thinks he owns me. He thinks that his job as a father is to *make* me into the person he wants me to become. And my mother? She just repeats whatever he says like it's the Bible.

I take a deep breath, sucking air in through my nose and blowing it out of my mouth. My hair lifts up with the exhaling breath, and when it falls back against my face I think of Dare.

Shit. He's probably one step away from getting into his truck and barreling over here like…well, like an Army Ranger, and attempting to save the day. A war with my father is exactly the last thing he needs in his life right now, or ever.

I pull my phone out of my clutch and punch in his number. I smile wryly, unable to remember the last time I actually called a guy.

"Hey." His voice is low and relieved when he answers. It sends all kinds of tingly feelings shooting through my belly. "Are you okay? Do you want me to come get you?"

I hear his keys jingling on the other end, like he's already walking toward his truck.

"No." I sigh. "I'm packing up, though. I can't stay here, Dare."

"Berkeley." His voice is calm and commanding, and I can tell his training has just kicked into high gear. "I'm already inside my truck. Let me come and get you. Please."

I shake my head as I crouch down beside my bed to pull out my Coach suitcase. "I need my car, Dare. I'm going to go stay at Mea's. Tomorrow, I start applying for jobs with interior design firms anywhere and everywhere. It's time for me to start my life."

"Good for you," he says. The pride seeps out of his voice, making me smile. "Show him exactly who Berkeley is. You're so strong, baby. You can do anything you want to do."

More than anything, at this moment, I wish his strong arms were wrapped around me so I can feel the truth in his words. I'm not nearly as sure as he is. But I can draw from the strength he gives me. The strength he's given me since the first night I spent alone with him.

"I'll text you when I get to Mea's, okay?"

"Okay. Be safe. I…I'm thinking about you."

I smile as I press END, and throw the phone on the nightstand.

It takes me about half an hour to pack my suitcase full of everything I think I need from my room. Mostly clothes, shoes, and toiletries. I'm lucky my bag is humongous. When I wheel it behind me to the landing, ready to lug it down the steps behind me, I hear a snippet of voices coming from the entryway below.

Male voices.

I creep down a step, peeking through the iron railing to see if I can catch sight of the owners of the voices. I can't; they're actually farther into the hallway.

I noiselessly steal down two more steps, listening.

"You haven't fulfilled your end of the bargain, son. I have. What choice do I have now?" The Admiral's voice is unusually quiet, dangerously low.

"What am I supposed to do? Tie her up and make her love me? I can't force emotions on her she doesn't feel! I tried. She's with someone else. And even if she wasn't…I don't think I'd be the guy for her. I have to respect her decision."

I cover my mouth with both hands when I hear Grisham's anguished reply. *Oh, hell no.*

"I thought you were a stronger man than that. Women need to be convinced, pushed. I thought you had it in you to be stronger than my daughter's will. I guess I was wrong. Was I also wrong when I recommended you for the position at NBSD? All it takes is a phone call, Grisham. Your father has clout, but not nearly as much as I do. I got you that job with the promise that you'd be taking my daughter with you and starting the life with her that she needs and deserves. You've failed, it seems."

I stand up, unable to listen to any more of the bullshit spewing out of their mouths. My legs tremble, but I grab the handle of my suitcase and pull it loudly down the steps behind me. When I reach the bottom, I race for the front door, slamming it behind me. I'm in the Escalade and pulling away before anyone follows, and I text Mea on the way to let her know I'll be crashing at her apartment.

Indefinitely.

I wake to the chiming of my phone. I groan, squeezing my eyes shut. When the chiming continues, I peek one eye open and stare around me. Where am I?

Oh, yeah. I'm sleeping on an air mattress on the floor of Mea's room in her three-bedroom apartment. Still lying on my stomach atop the mattress, I look over at her bed. Empty. I wrinkle my nose. Mea is such a morning person.

Next, I reach over and check my phone's busy screen. It's just after nine in the morning, and I have four missed calls and three texts. Scrolling through the texts first, a smile is brought to my lips.

Dare: I know you're not awake yet, and if you are you're really hating life. I'm at the garage, call me or better yet, just come show me your beautiful face.

The second text makes me laugh.

Wake up! I'm coming to jump on you if you aren't out here by ten.

Ugh. She's probably already completed a round of morning yoga. The third text pulls my mouth into a snarl.

Came to check in on you last night and heard you leave. Worried about you, Berk. Call me.

Grisham. *Came to check on me?* Yeah, right, if checking on me involves plotting about me with my father. Just thinking about it sends hot flames of angry confusion skimming through me. I never had to consider Grisham's intentions. I just knew without a doubt that he was on my side. That he understood what it was like having parents like mine, because his were almost as bad.

But he'd been playing by my father's rules all along. For a coveted position in a fantastic location.

I decide to shoot Dare a text before I appease Mea's demand.

Awake and so not loving it. Loving seeing your name on my phone first thing, though. Headed to work in a bit for the lunch shift, but I'm free for dinner!

I literally roll out of the bed, very ungracefully, and crash onto the floor. I'm sure the resounding thud lets Mea know that I'm indeed awake, but I throw on a pair of cutoff sweats and a tank top anyway.

She better have coffee ready.

Before I leave her bedroom, my phone chimes and I glance at Dare's message.

Have Mea drive you to work so I can pick you up after. Missing you.

When I venture into the living room, Mea is upside down. Literally. Her tiny, lithe body is flush against the wall, her pointed toes reaching for the ceiling. She smiles serenely at me, and I turn to her roommate, Greta, who's sitting at the bar with a cup of coffee and a bagel.

"Good morning, Berkeley," says Greta.

We don't know each other very well; she and Mea met in college and moved in together in Lone Sands just after graduation. But from what I know, I like her a lot. She's also from Brunswick County, but a little farther from the beach than Lone Sands. She's sweet to Mea's sassy, and down-to-earth to Mea's flighty. She balances out my friend perfectly. Her long, dark hair almost reaches her waist, and she's much, much taller than both Mea and I. In my head, I call her Greta the Gorgeous.

Her stunning, crystal-blue eyes lock on mine as she takes in my appearance. Crap, I didn't even check myself in the mirror yet. I was too focused on achieving a caffeine high as quickly as possible.

"You look tired," she announces, sliding a mug in my direction. "Mea said you had a rough night. I'm so sorry, Berkeley."

I grab the mug and start pouring. "Thanks, Greta. Parents suck sometimes, you know?"

She nods sympathetically. "I know. Mine are split up, and I could write a book on all the crap they've put me and my little sisters through."

I study her. Her face is drawn at the mention of her parents. I decide there's a darkness there worth pulling out, but today isn't the day. Maybe I'll get to know her better soon.

Mea gracefully lowers her legs from the wall and flips herself upright. Her eyes are alight and her smile is bright as she bounces over to the little kitchen. Kissing me on the cheek, she opens the fridge and grabs a tiny carton of organic soy milk. She stares disapprovingly at our mugs of coffee.

"Don't start," I warn.

"Wasn't going to," she snaps back. "It's your funeral." Then her serene smile is back. "I'm glad you're here, Berk. You needed to cut the cord anyway. How's Dare?"

The question is innocent, too innocent. I narrow my eyes at her. "He's fine. Seeing him for dinner tonight. Why?"

She focuses on an invisible speck of dirt on the countertop, polishing the gleaming surface with her thumb.

"Mea? Why were you so mean to Drake last night?"

"Who's Drake?" asks Greta, her interest piqued.

"Dare's roommate," I tell her. "Mea was a raving—"

"Easy!" Mea glares at me. "He was too pushy."

As long as I've known Mea, she's never had a serious boyfriend. I naturally thought she and Drake would hit it off, but apparently I was so very wrong. However, her reaction to him was extreme, and I'm more than a little confused by it.

She continues under her breath. "Buying me a drink."

"Oh, the horror," says Greta, her face contorting in mock shock. "How dare he!"

She earns Mea's trademark eye daggers. "You weren't there. He's all huge and gorgeous, and then he smiles like he has a secret none of the rest of us know about. And I don't let guys buy me drinks. You know my rules."

Yes, we all know the rules. Mea has a strict no-dating rule. I know she doesn't trust men because of the strained relationship she has with her father. She refuses to link the two, though. She's an expert at closing off the hurt and pain her father's absence and indifference has caused her, and the subject is always off-limits. She's totally put-together and peaceful on the outside, with her yoga and all-natural healthful diet, but I know the issues with her family have eaten up her heart until she had to build a concrete wall around it.

"I've gotta get to work in a bit, Mea, will you drive me?"

She nods.

"Thank you." I slide off the stool and wrap my arms around her thin frame. "And thank you for leaving your door open for me last night."

"I've always got your back," she whispers in my ear. It's so true. She's always been my cheerleader when I didn't think I could stand up to my parents. Anytime I need Mea, she's there.

As I'm passing the closed door of the third bedroom at the front of the hall, I pause. "When's your third roommate moving in?"

Mea sighs dramatically. "She's not. Found out she didn't get the job she thought she had in the bag, so she's staying up north." Her eyes meet mine, and she smiles so big her cheeks crease. "Berkeley!"

"What?"

"*You* can be our third roommate!"

"Oh, my God," exclaims Greta. "That's the best idea ever! Say yes, Berkley!"

I shift, looking from the empty third bedroom to Mea, to Greta. There were so many times in the past that Mea and I talked about living together. Could this really be the time we can make it happen?

"You guys…I don't have the job I want yet, either. I don't make much at See Food. My parents will never support this. I don't give a flying freak about their opinion, but I do need to find a way to support myself. I don't know…"

But suddenly, I *do* know. I know how much I want this, and I know that's all it will take for me to make it happen. Suddenly, the idea of having my own space with two amazing girls pushes aside the hurt and anger I feel about my father and Grisham conspiring to run my life behind my back. I imagine having my own space to bring Dare to, and my face grows warm with want.

I *need* this.

"I know that look." Mea waves a hand dismissively and goes to sit on the couch. "We'll move you in this weekend."

The dark-haired beauty squeals.

I have an apartment of my very own. I fly down the hallway to Mea's room. I have some résumés to e-mail out before I head to See Food.

21

Dare

I have news. Big, big, BIG! news.

The text from Berkeley puts a curious smile on my face. I know she'll be at See Food for the afternoon shift today, and I plan on picking her up after I shower off the oil and grease from the garage.

I, unbeknownst to Berkeley, have big news, too. Or, more like big *plans*.

Making plans with someone else in mind, a mouth-wateringly beautiful someone especially, is becoming a habit. Berkeley's taking my previously ordered, solitary life and turning it upside down. Something like that should be freaking me out, sending me running to build all kinds of walls and steel-reinforced doors around myself to keep her out. All my life, getting close to people has left me in pain. People go away, or they send you away, or they hurt you. It's what I learned growing up, first with the death of my parents and then with every horrible home I was placed in afterward. I never got a break, not until I aged out and took my life into my own hands.

But I haven't been able to keep Berkeley at arm's length. I picture her face in my head and realize I never had a chance.

It's impossible not to…*feel* when I'm around her.

After lunch, I complete two tire rotations and a transmission replacement before cutting out for the day. On the way home, I make a quick phone call to ensure all the arrangements I've made are still firmly in place, and thank a friend for helping me with them.

"Can I talk to you a minute?" asks Chase when I walk in the front door.

I nod, knowing that we haven't discussed how I can help him beyond our last conversation where he told me about Shay. "Yeah."

He waits for me to take a seat on the couch before diving in. "I don't want to take your money, Dare."

I shake my head slowly, focusing on Chase's face. His expression is intense, he's looking me straight in the eye, and I know there's no bullshit in his words. "Come again?"

He stands, pacing toward the massive stone fireplace and spins around to face me. His hands are clasped behind his neck. "I don't, Dare. I don't want to do this to you anymore. I can figure it out. I really just need your brain. Help me figure out how to help her, man."

I nod, slowly. "I'm working on it, Chase. I promise. When you go back to Florida, it will be with a plan to get Shay away from that dickwad Chavez. Okay?"

He closes his eyes and blows out a harsh, anxious breath. "Okay."

"Have you talked to her today? Is she doing okay?"

He shakes his head. "No, I haven't. I think she's hanging in there, but she's cautious. I don't get to talk to her that often. Only when Chavez is out and he hasn't yanked her along with him. Sometimes he has her running errands for him, and it's dangerous. I can't stand the way he uses her. It drive me up the goddamned wall."

I nod sympathetically. I can picture losing my shit if some ruthless criminal had his hands on Berkeley. The thought ignites a fire inside me, sending me to a dark, dark place in my head I haven't been in a long time.

"What other…business ventures is Chavez involved in?" I ask suddenly. I lean forward, elbows on my knees, hands clasped in front of me. Something's struck me about Chase's situation, but I need more information in order to put the pieces together for the plan formulating in my brain.

Chase's hand comes up to scratch his temple thoughtfully. "Uh…other than the gambling? It's mostly that…but I think he also does some smuggling when he can get a big enough cut. It's not his main thing, it's more of a side hustle. Why?"

I nod, rubbing my palms together absently. "Just wondering. What kind of smuggling?"

Chase shrugs, lifting one shoulder into the air before dropping it and folding his arms across his chest. "Drugs. Pills. The high-dollar stuff that suburban housewives trip out on."

"So, it seems like our friend Chavez doesn't like to get his hands too dirty. He deals with pretty light stuff, considering."

Chase snorts. "Considering what?"

"Considering it could be worse. You think he's capable of putting someone in the ground?"

Chase narrowed his eyes. "You think I want to take the chance? Not when Shay's in there with him."

I nod. "Yeah. I get that. I think we can set him up, somehow. Make him an offer that he can't refuse, something that will end up with him a lot richer if he does what we say. We just need to work out the details."

Chase nods slowly, pushing up off the stone behind him and walking to the middle of the room. He stops directly in front of the couch, the beginning of a smile playing on his lips. "Yeah. I think we can do that."

I stand. "I gotta go shower real quick. I'm supposed to pick up Berkeley at work."

Chase nods. "Yeah, man. Thanks for listening. See you."

I clap him on the shoulder as I slide past him on my way to the bathroom. "I've got you, Chase. Don't worry."

After I've showered and dressed in jeans and a white tee, I nod to Chase on my way out the door. In the driveway, Drake is pulling in as I open my truck door.

"All set for tonight?" he asks, smirking.

I've told him some of what I have planned for Berkeley, and the twinkle in his eyes lets me know that I'm going to end up wishing I hadn't said a thing.

"Yeah," I say warily. "Are you jealous? Because if you are, Drake, you can come. I'm sure Berkeley doesn't mind sharing me."

He shakes his head. "I'm good. Get out of here."

He bumps my fist as he walks by my truck door.

The entire drive to get Berkeley from See Food, I'm in my own head. I'm practicing for every scenario. What will I do if my guy didn't set up everything according to my strict instructions? What will I do if Berkeley hates the whole thing? I plan for every contingency. That's who I am. That's who I've been trained to be.

And that's how I keep a chokehold on the control of my life.

Better than anyone, I know that's borderline fucked-up. If I could help it, I would. In this case, I'm hoping it earns me points. Serious, sexy, brownie points with Berkeley.

When I pull up in front of the restaurant, she comes running out the front door. I smile, opening my truck door.

"I was coming in to get you," I point out as I walk toward her.

I grunt as she slams into me, her arms winding around my neck. When I look down at her, her caramel eyes are bright and her dimples are denting her cheeks. Damn. She's pressed against me in every place that matters, and her body is so plush, all I want to do is squeeze. Then I mentally punch myself. Because her lips are moving and I'm not hearing a word.

"I'm so happy to see you." She breathes, her sweet-smelling breath tickling my chin.

Cupping her face, I gaze down at her, a complete and utter goner, and return her smile. "Yeah? I like it when you show me how happy you are by tackling me. Very effective. Genius, even."

She giggles softly, blowing the chunk of hair out of her eye. "Genius? You're admitting that in our little duo, I'm the smart one?"

I nod. "I'm admitting that you are definitely the smart one. And I'm the one who's about to blow your mind in a few minutes."

She pulls back, and I grumble inwardly about the loss of flush body contact. I slide my hands down to her hips and pull her back against me. *Much better.*

"Blow my mind? Are you sure?" Her forehead breaks into those wrinkles I love. "That's placing very high standards on my reaction to whatever surprise you have in store for me this evening, Dare. My mind is not easily blown."

Releasing her hips, I smirk and clasp her hand, pulling her around to the passenger side of my truck. "That sounds suspiciously like a dare."

As I place her on her seat, she reaches for her seat belt. Just before I close the door, she grabs my collar and pulls me until I'm millimeters from her full lips. She brushes them, like the sweetest whisper, against mine. Then she groans softly.

She releases me, and slams the door.

Groaning loudly, I head to my side of the truck.

She just undid me.

I've been trying so hard to tell myself that I'm taking time to get to know Berkeley, to learn about her and spend time with her. I'm not trying to fall in love with her. But then she goes and does something ridiculously sexy and cute, which shouldn't even be a legal combination.

And I slip just a little further off the steep incline that leads to certain doom.

She's wearing a very self-satisfied little smile when I climb in on the driver's side. I remind myself that she can be as righteous as she wants right now. Because wait till she sees what we're doing tonight.

Or rather, what she's doing tonight.

We drive to the trendy, artsy section of town that's just past the cushy boutiques and restaurants and just before you enter the warehouse district. After I park the truck, I lead her into a coffee shop with a CLOSED sign on the door.

Inside, the rich aroma of coffee beans swirls around us. The place has a Bohemian feeling that you can only achieve with a free-spirited approach to décor. It's colorful, with a youthful vibe that sings to people in their early twenties. The chairs and tables are an eclectic mix of iron, colored wood, and wicker.

Contemporary-inspired artwork adorns the walls in a variety of forms, from a dog wearing a straw hat to a coffee mug amid a strikingly colorful background.

Berkeley's gaze swings around, her eyes piquing with interest. "You realize the sign on the door said 'closed,' right?"

I nod, taking her hand tightly in mine and leading her to the iron stairwell. "I know. But I know people that know people. There's a loft space upstairs I want to show you. Come on."

She allows me to tug her up the ultramodern spiral staircase, her eyes soaking in the paintings surrounding us. "My God. These are beautiful."

"Thank you," an answering voice offers when we reach the top. The man standing there is in his mid-thirties, with long, blond hair secured off his face in a ponytail. He's dressed in jeans and a T-shirt splattered with color, and his feet are bare. He holds out a hand to Berkeley after nodding at me.

"I'm Thomas Callo," he introduces himself. "I'm the artist of said 'beautiful' art, and the owner of the coffee shop downstairs."

Berkeley smiles warmly at him. "Berkeley Holtz. It's nice to meet you."

He returns her smile, shaking her hand. "Nice to meet you, Berkeley. Your boyfriend here"—he indicates me with a sweep of his hand, and I quickly glance at Berkeley at the mention of the *B* word—"has arranged an evening here for you." He gestures behind him, and I take Berkeley's hand and lead her around Thomas.

There's a small, round table laden with hors d'oeuvres that I hoped Berkeley would love. Little crepes filled with cream cheese, mini-crab cakes, shrimp on toast. I tried to give her plenty of choices from the sea, because I know that's what she loves. Her eyes widen as she takes in the table of food, and the bottle of white wine breathing right beside the plates. Two glasses stand beside it.

"Holy shit," she gasps, her eyes wide.

I smile. I like that reaction. At lease I think I do, unless I have the meaning of "holy shit" completely wrong. Women are complicated. She could very well be saying "Holy shit, I hate this!" Scowling at the thought, I watch Berkeley's face carefully.

A few feet away from the table stands an easel with a blank canvas. A wooden stool waits for Berkeley to take her seat.

She turns from the food and spots the easel. She stills.

"Dare?" she asks, her voice low and raw as she turns toward me.

Thomas drops a hand on my shoulder as he retreats. "I'll leave you to it. Be downstairs when you're finished."

I nod, keeping my eyes glued to Berkeley's face as I move toward her. "That day at the university...I saw your face when you looked at your paintings. You missed them. You miss"—I gesture toward the easel—"this. I wanted to put it back into your life. So, until we find you your very own place to paint, Thomas says you can paint here. And he'll store them for you, too. He owns the gallery next door."

Her eyes are alight as she stares at me, two big, shining pools of pure happiness. She blinks rapidly once, twice, and then swipes a finger under her eye. "I can't believe you did this for me," she whispers. "No one's ever...I mean, no one understands..."

I reach out and pull her across the remaining distance between us. I look down into her eyes, using my thumb to brush away the line of water cascading from her eyes. "I understand."

"You do, don't you?" Her voice is filled with wonder. "You're amazing, Dare."

I nod. "I know."

She half laughs, half sobs. "Cocky."

"Confident?"

She shakes her head and looks again at the easel. "I wanna paint now."

"You don't want to eat first?" My stomach rumbles as I say it, giving away the selfishness behind my question.

She grins. "You eat. I'll paint, then I'll eat. You can pour me a glass of wine, though."

I nod, liking this plan. "Okay."

Joy radiates through me, starting in my chest, as I watch her settle herself on the stool. Her black shorts barely cover her ass when she sits down, the fabric riding up her thigh. I gulp, and then I look away. I will not distract her while she paints. No matter what kind of fire she sets to my body just by breathing in the same room I'm in.

I bring her the glass of pinot, then hastily retreat. I don't trust myself to stand next to her for too long. But the beaming smile she gives me before I walk away sends my heart thumping in my chest and I can't help but grin as I fix myself a plate.

Then I sit down, facing where she sits behind the easel, and wait for my girl to finish her painting.

Even though to me, the real masterpiece is sitting on the stool, not on the easel.

22

Berkeley

We don't talk while I paint. He eats, and I can feel his eyes burning into my skin, even from the other side of the easel. I sip my wine in between brushstrokes, eyeing the canvas while I add brushes of color here and there. But my mind isn't empty the way it normally is when I paint.

Usually, I paint to escape the pressure. Whatever kind of pressure my parents have placed on me, or the pressure that I've put on myself. Sometimes I feel like I could crumble beneath the weight of it all. And that's when I leave it behind, sit down, and put brush to canvas. My paintings are always full of rich, bold color and texture, reflecting the very heart of me.

What I capture tonight is no different, except for the way my mind feels while I'm doing it. Instead of empty, it's full of whirring, swirling thoughts of the man sitting just behind my canvas.

He did this for me. I'm thinking it over and over again, stunned by the sentiment behind this date. Dare didn't just take me to dinner and a movie, even though I would have been completely fine with it if he had. But this is so much deeper than that. He listens when I talk. He understands what I need. He asks for nothing in return, effectively eliminating the concept of pressure from our relationship. When I told him I wasn't ready to sleep with him yet, he wasn't fazed or disappointed. Most guys would have thrown their hands up then, running away full speed from that kind of effort.

But not Dare.

Maybe I really did put a spell on him. Why else would he stay? Especially after my father made an appearance, pulling me out of the club like a twelve-year-old out past curfew.

I don't get what keeps him with me. Even more, I don't get what makes him do incredibly sweet things like what he's done tonight. But I don't want to lose it. I don't want to lose Dare. My heart flutters around in my chest, a caged bird trying to take flight, at the thought of it.

My heart grows fuller as I think of him, and my skin begins to flush, starting at the tips of my ears, when I imagine how I'm going to thank him for this incredible gift.

Peeking out from behind the canvas, his light-green eyes pierce me, and I lean back quickly behind my barrier. I hear his deep chuckle, and when I peek around again his mouth is tipped up in his crooked smile.

Ducking back behind the easel, I can feel my cheeks blushing a furious scarlet.

"What are you doing, baby?" he asks.

Heat pools in the very center of me as I hear his endearment. Crap on a cracker, that shouldn't make me feel so…hot. God, he turns me into a mess of quivering Jell-O on the inside, just by saying a *word*. His husky voice is like a rough caress on my skin.

"Uh…I'm painting?" I manage to croak.

"Yeah? Am I your subject? Do you need me to lose the clothes?"

Oh, my God. If he does that…there will be no more painting tonight. And the way I'm feeling right now, there may also be no more self-control that keeps me a safe distance away from him. My thighs clench together in response to the rough timbre of his voice, and I curl my toes against the floor.

I'm being absolutely ridiculous right now.

After about ten more minutes, I close my eyes. The electric heat that's building in the room has reached an unbearable temperature, and my body aches from the effort of holding myself together. I haven't peeked at Dare again, but I know he's just on the other side of the easel…

I pick the paintbrush up off the canvas, and tilt my head to the side as I eye what I've done. I'm mostly finished, although I need to go back and add some shadowing.

I'm so engrossed, I haven't heard Dare come up behind me. My nerves are a frayed mess of sensation, so when he places his hands on my shoulders I jump what must be a mile out of my seat. There goes that deep chuckle again, and my insides turn to molten lava. I close my eyes again.

"Berkeley," he murmurs, and I'm trembling. My name is like a luscious piece of candy on his tongue. "Oh, baby…that's beautiful."

My eyes pop open, absorbing the painting in front of me. His hands remain hot on my shoulders. I've painted something impossible, a fiery sunburst in violent shades of red and yellow and orange, slammed against the backdrop of an inky-blue nighttime sky. Glimmering stars dot the scene around the sun, as if they're falling from their heated maker.

I tilt my head again, assessing it. The hair on the back of my neck stands on end as Dare moves in closer. He stands just behind me, and I can feel the pressure of his chest on my back as he leans down and places his lips against my skin. The spot at the apex of my shoulder and my neck catches fire, and the trembling my body is already enduring turns into a violent shiver. I quickly place my paintbrush on the easel before I drop it.

He freezes beside me, and I can feel his breath pulsing against my skin. "Did that feel good?" His whisper is husky and deep, and it does terrible, amazing things to the muscles in my thighs. They clench of their own accord. I say nothing, trying fiercely to stay focused on my painting.

Dare uses a hand to sweep my hair away from my neck, and dips his head low to place another kiss just below my ear. A tiny, traitorous moan escapes me, and my head drops fully to the side as I give him full access to my neck.

"Ah," he whispers. "So you *did* like that, didn't you, Berkeley? What else do you like?"

I press my lips together. If he wants to know, he's going to have to figure it out.

Oh, that's a dangerous thought to be having right now.

His tongue darts out to draw a tiny circle on the sensitive skin beneath my earlobe as his hands trail down my arms. They break free of my palms, which rest atop my bare thighs. Oh, why did I wear shorts this short? I silently curse myself and praise myself.

"You always feel so fucking good under my fingers," whispers Dare the Devil. "So damn good."

His fingers create a hot trail up my thighs as his touch moves upward. When they travel past the hem of my shorts and underneath my shirt, I shudder.

My breath is coming in heavy pants, and I squeeze my eyes shut as I basically sit helpless before him. When his fingers touch me like this, when his lips command me like this, I'm complete dough in his hands.

"Lift your arms, Berkeley." I can hear the command in his tone and automatically want to defy it. But something about being under Dare's command sends sexy shivers of delight through my body, so much stronger than the desire I have to push back against it.

I do as he says.

He pulls my tight T-shirt up over my head and discards it, so that I'm in just my bra from the waist up. His hands continue their path against the soft skin of my stomach stopping just beneath my breasts. I gasp, and lean back against his solid chest. His thumbs rub gentle circles just out of reach from where I want him to be, and I groan in frustration. His breath is against my ear again.

"What, baby? What's wrong?" His thumbs continue their torturous movement while he speaks.

I shake my head, shifting on the stool so that his roaming digits inch higher.

He stills them. Damn. Him.

"What?" he asks again. "Tell me, Berkeley."

"Touch me, Dare," I ask finally. "Your hands…are driving me insane."

"No yet," he promises. "But they will be."

Finally, *finally*, his fingers reach their destination as he palms both my breasts simultaneously, sending my body into a writhing fit and fire and drawing a heavy moan from my mouth. Pushing down the soft cups of my bra, he pinches my nipples with his fingers and pulls, and I cry out.

His body is a solid wall behind me, so when I sag back against it there's no danger of falling off the stool. Thank God. My lips part, and I lick them as he continues to torture my breasts.

Seeing it, he leans forward and takes my mouth with his. His kiss is punishing, his tongue parts my lips and swipes against mine, tangling and teasing. I moan into the kiss, wanting more of everything he's dishing out. He's like a sweet, sinful dessert I can't get enough of.

Then he leaves my tender, aching breasts, and I groan in disappointment. Chuckling, he pulls his lips away from mine.

"Stand up, baby."

I don't hesitate, but my legs are weak as I stand, wobbly. He holds me against him as he climbs astride the stool, pulling me onto his lap.

"That's better," he growls into my ear. The sexy-growly, bossy Dare is turning me into a needy mess. It's so freaking hot.

"Is it?" I whisper.

"Oh, yeah," he answers me roughly. He reaches down and pops the snap on my shorts.

Oh. Now I see why it's better. He slowly undoes the zipper, and as his fingers brush against my panties I jerk back against him. He strokes one finger against the center of me gently, and I buck again. He dips his head, nipping at my earlobe.

"Fuck, Berkeley." He groans. "I can *feel* how wet you are right now. This so wasn't the plan tonight, baby. But I could see you over there, blushing, and I could hear you sighing from my chair. I couldn't stay away from you anymore."

His finger stays busy as he speaks, stroking me up and down, and I keep my eyes closed, barely holding myself above water as his touch and his words threaten to pull me under. His voice is a shiver dancing along my spine. My insides are burning, and the inner siren Dare is convinced lives within me slowly unfurls her wings, ready to begin her song.

"God, Dare," I gasp.

"Yeah, baby?" His fingers still and I groan in dismay. "I touch you on your terms, Berkeley. I only want to do what you're ready for. What are you ready for right now, sweetheart?"

I writhe in his arms, but he holds me steady. I can feel the harness of his very ready erection under my butt, and I grind into it. He freezes.

"Your terms, Berkeley," he says in a strained voice. "But *Jesus*, you're making it hard on me."

"I want you to touch me…under my panties," I whisper urgently. "Just like before. Right the hell now, Dare."

He curses again, making a noise of pure male delight deep in his chest. It's guttural and sexy as hell.

He slips one hand beneath the waistband of my thin, lace panties, and as soon as his fingers graze my slick, wet heat I nearly *let go* right then and there. My eyes roll back in my head and my mouth fills with saliva. My hips are grinding so hard into his lap that he hisses a quick intake of air through his teeth. I swivel my hips, and his answering groan makes me melt.

His other hand slides up my stomach until it's once again cupping my breast, and he gives equal attention to my achiest bits like only Dare can. It's unfair, really, how much of a state he can leave me in. He knew what he was doing to me the moment he leaned down and whispered in my ear.

"Dare." His name is a needy moan torn from my lips, and his finger draws small circles right over the smallest, most tender part of me.

"Berkeley," he whispers, his voice so deep and low in my ear that I shudder yet again. "Come for me. Right the hell now."

And that's all it takes. All the pieces of me fly apart as his words and his touch and his all-male, all-Dare scent surround me, overwhelm me, control me. I quake as I say his name again, and he buries his face in my neck, inhaling.

"Fuck it to hell," he says. "You are fucking amazing, Berkeley. You're the most beautiful, dangerous thing I've ever laid eyes on. What have you done to me? Fuck."

His words are uttered between kisses on my shoulder, nips on my ear, licks on my neck, and I sink into him.

I curl into him, turning to the side and pulling my legs up on his lap right along with the rest of me. I'm languid, sleepy, and I want nothing more than to be totally wrapped around him right now.

He kisses my forehead tenderly, then brushes my hair back out of my face.

"Do you know what you do to me?" he asks, his voice raw.

I shake my head. "Make you really, really horny?"

His rumble of laughter brings a wide smile to my lips.

He uses a finger to turn my face up toward his. "That's a given. Your magic powers guarantee that. But you also make me...want things I've never wanted before. You make me believe that...that goodness is possible for me again. After everything I've done."

I rear back and stare into his eyes. "What you've done?"

He shakes his head. "I mean everything I've been through. I don't know, Berkeley. I just never saw you coming. And you're a very, very pleasant surprise."

I just stare, transfixed in his stunning green eyes. I can't look away. Everything inside me is still trying to recover from what he just did to me. The way he knows my body and how to touch me and talk to me is putting me in serious danger of grabbing him and throwing him down on the floor so that I can finish what he started.

I shake the thought free, and the corner of his lips turn up in a half-grin.

Crap. Damn, damn, damn. I'm in major trouble here. I'm in serious danger of getting in over my head with Dare. He's everything I said I didn't want. He's ex-military, he's stubborn, he's commanding. He's got a lot of darkness in his past, from his childhood demons still chasing him at night and from a faraway combat zone I can't reach him in when he disappears there.

But then, he's also sweet and considerate. He does things for me that no one has ever bothered to do. He protects me and he makes me laugh every single time I'm with him.

And the combination of all of it, not just the good, puts me in danger of falling in love with Dare Conners.

23

Dare

It takes two weeks for me to admit it to myself.

It happens while I'm tying a black bow tie, preparing for a formal event in Berkeley's parents' backyard. I stare at my reflection, my dark hair touching the collar of my tux. I'm shaking with nervousness and anticipation at seeing her in a formal gown. Just the thought of her all dressed up makes something in my chest clench tightly.

I'm falling in love with Berkeley. It's just as unbelievable as it is undeniable.

And with that thought comes a flood of unexpected, un-fucking-welcome questions. Do I tell her? If I do, will she run in the other direction? Does she feel the same way? Do I even understand love well enough to recognize this as real?

Those questions give way to questions from my past that turned my world upside down and inside out more than once. *Did they suffer? Where will I live now? Will they find me if I hide in the closet? Are they all dead? Shouldn't I be?*

I shudder, my fingers trembling as they struggle with the knot at my neck. *Questions about love are not the same as questions about survival.* I repeat the words like a mantra, over and over again inside my head. I picture Berkeley, eyes closed, lips parted. My name a strained whisper tumbling out of her mouth. My pants immediately tighten at the thought of what she looked like when she was vulnerable like that. In my arms.

Shit. She was beautiful.

Attending a black tie event with her parents and all their boring-as-hell, rich friends is the last thing I want to do tonight. I'd rather scoop Berkeley up and take her off somewhere to be alone. But I'm doing this for her. Because she has to be there, and she needs me by her side.

I'm nervous during the entire ten-minute drive to the Holtz home. I'm not nervous to be around people who have more money than me. I could give two shits about that. I'm nervous to be in the same room as Berkeley's father and still keep a handle on my temper.

If he touches her again like he did that night…

I suck in a deep breath as I walk up the paved drive and around the side of the enormous house. There are lighted torches leading the way from the front of the house to the backyard. When I round the back of the home, I'm met with a myriad of black and white.

In the dusky evening light, lit torches are setting an ethereal mood around the grounds. The home isn't located directly on the water, but the smell of the ocean is in the air. The lush green grass lets me know that the Holtzes have laid turf, because the landscape should have been less green and lush, more sandy and scraggly. There are pathways of cobblestones laid out leading to an enormous covered patio and screened-in porch, the pool, and a sun lounge.

A large, white tent is set up in the grass just beyond the patio, and I can see tables covered with black tablecloths inside. Light, classical music is trickling over the approaching night, and I search the faces around me for the only one I'm interested in seeing.

"Dare!"

I turn toward the house, and there she is. She's walking quickly toward me in a long, flowing black dress that gathers just beneath her breasts. The material alludes to the voluptuous curviness that is Berkeley's body, but just barely as it swishes against the ground. Her hair is smooth, free of its normal wild curls, and swept up in an elegant bun on the top of her head. She looks gorgeous, like a fucking angel.

I let out the breath I've been holding and gather her up in my arms as she reaches me. "Hey."

"Hey." She breathes, and I inhale. She smells like roses, as usual, with a hint of something fruity in her shampoo. "I'm so glad you're here."

"I'm wherever you want me," I reply simply. "You look…" I pull back and hold her out at arm's length. "Stunning. Perfect. You're slaying me right now, baby."

Her dimples appear in her cheeks as she smiles at my words. Then she assesses me right back. God, I love that about her. She can give it right back to me, threefold. "You look…dashing. Ridiculously handsome. Good enough to eat."

I raise my eyebrow. "Eat? Do we need to stay at this party? I really like the sound of 'good enough to eat.'"

She giggles, slapping my bicep. "Later. I have to be here."

I nod, holding her gaze with my own. "You just made me a promise, honey." My hand sinks lower on her waist, and she smirks.

"Yes, sir."

I grab her hand before she can salute, and bring her knuckles to rest against my lips.

She nabs a passing waiter and grabs two flutes of champagne off his tray. She hands me one, and takes a large gulp of hers.

"Easy, there," I murmur. "It's going to be a long night."

She sighs. "I know. But just look at this place." She gestures around us, and I look.

It looks beautiful, like a picture in a magazine, but admittedly, it's not Berkeley.

"Black and white everywhere! Classical music! Ugh. It's beyond boring."

I nod, in complete agreement. "How about when we leave we blast Rise Against?"

There are the dimples again, the forehead folds disappearing instantly. "Make that the Eli Young Band and you've got a deal."

I wince. "Ain't gonna happen."

"There you are," a cool female voice greets us.

I look up from Berkeley's face, and her mother stares back at me. Her expression is extremely guarded, and the muscles around her mouth twitch as she purses her lips. She glances from Berkeley to me, and holds out a hand.

"I didn't realize Berkeley had invited a friend," she greets me. Her voice drips with icicles. "I'm her mother, Denise. And you are?"

I shake her hand, gripping her thin fingers tightly in my own before I release it. "I'm Dare Conners. Thank you for having me. Your home is beautiful."

Berkeley glances between us, anxiety written in her features. I place my hand on the small of her back reassuringly. Her mother doesn't miss it, her eyes going straight to the point of contact.

"Dare, would you excuse Berkeley for a moment?" My name leaves her mouth as if it's created a bad taste. "I have some people I need her to speak with."

Berkeley releases an exaggerated huff. "Momma, I—"

I give her a gentle shove in her mother's direction.

"Go," I say with a smile I don't actually feel. In fact, I feel like doing the opposite of smiling, but I don't want to make things any harder for Berkeley than they clearly already are.

She narrows her eyes on me for about two seconds before she's yanked away by her mother's hand. Damn, apparently that thin, frail-looking woman is a hell of a lot stronger than I gave her credit for.

I stare sympathetically after Berkeley for a minute before taking my first sip of champagne. Wow. I'm a beer guy, but this bubbly shit is kind of delicious. I can see how downing that whole glass and then some would work quickly in my system.

I make my way around the outskirts of the party. I just need to be moving. It's hard for me to stay still, to stay in the same spot for too long. I people-watch as I slide through the crowd. Everyone here seems happy to be here, but at the same time they all seem like there's somewhere better they could possibly be. It's so weird I find myself being pulled into listening to conversations and just trying to understand where some of these people are coming from. I fail every single time.

I finish my glass of champagne but opt to wait awhile before I have another. I suspect I need to be ready to shepherd Berkeley out of here at a moment's notice.

As Berkeley takes longer and longer to return, I find myself wishing I had some company. The party sucks, but it would suck less if I had someone to talk to. Or commiserate with. Mea would be perfect.

The thought of Mea brings me back to the night of the loft above the coffee shop. After Berkeley and I were done upstairs, I took her down to speak with Thomas again. He'd explained that he owned the gallery next door and that he displayed his own art there as well as works by up-and-coming artists. He offered to hang her piece of the sunburst, and she'd been over-the-moon excited.

"Like, for people to actually *buy*?" she'd squealed.

Thomas had chuckled. "Yep. I'll price it and hang it, and we'll see what happens." Her piece had sold less than a week later, and I will never forget the look on her face when she found out. She's been back to the loft to paint several times since then.

That same night she told me about the apartment with Mea and Greta. Her eyes shone with excitement, and I was so happy for her it hurt. I wanted her to get out from under her father's thumb, but I had no idea how to go about making it happen. Then it just fell into her lap, and I was more than relieved. Her parents hadn't taken her moving out well, but she hadn't expected them to.

And now she is on her own. I know she'll nail down a job next, because the girl is seriously capable of just about anything.

I'm broken out of my thoughts when a deep voice beside me pulls me back to the present. "I'm surprised you'd show up here."

I look up, straight into the icy blue eyes of Grisham. Fuck. On principle, I want to punch this fucker in his smooth, perfect face. My fist curls just looking at him. I force myself to relax, uncurling my fingers.

Berkeley isn't with him.

She's with me.

"Yeah, well, I'd go wherever Berkeley asks me." That's the only answer his ass needs.

He keeps staring forward, a frown marring his features. "That's…good. I'm glad to hear it. She deserves someone who will put her first. She's never had that in her life. I hope you can give it to her."

I glance at him, somehow keeping my tone even. "Why, because you'll be waiting in the wings if I don't?"

He shakes his head, finally meeting my gaze. "She's made it clear she doesn't want me. Losing her cost me a lot. But I never really had her to begin with." He nods toward the house. "You know she told her parents about you. Not sure if they're gonna approve. I hope for your sake they take it easy on her."

I nod coolly, taking in the action of the party once more.

"Do you surf?" he asks suddenly.

Where's he going with this?

"I'm from Florida," I answer warily. "Of course I surf."

He nods, chucking. "Don't ever take Berkeley. She hates it."

Something in my memory clicks into place, shifting, forming a picture in my mind. "Wait. She said she was surfing a few weeks ago. Was she with *you*?" Unease roils my gut, and I try to force it away.

He nods. "Yeah. I've taken her lots of times. She does it for me, but she really can't stand it. Athletic activities aren't Berkeley's strong suit."

Fuck. She didn't tell me she'd been surfing with *Grisham*. And I knew she didn't like to do athletic stuff, which is why up to this point I hadn't taken her.

Fuck.

Inside me, jealousy rears its big, green, ugly head. It coils in my stomach like a snake, poised to attack. It's a brand-spanking-new emotion for me, and I have to say it sucks. It really, really sucks.

Grisham is watching me carefully. "She didn't tell you I took her surfing."

It wasn't a question, more of a statement. So I don't bother answering him. We just stand there, watching the crowd swirl around us.

"She's been gone a long time," I muse, finally. "I think I'll go see if I can find her."

He nods, and I leave him standing there. If I'd stood next to him any longer, I'm pretty sure I wouldn't have been able to keep ignoring my hand-to-hand combat training impulse lighting a fire inside my stomach. It wasn't *his* fault she hadn't told me who she'd been surfing with. And she and Grisham are friends, so she hadn't done anything wrong.

But the idea that she hung out with him, without letting me know about it, feeds a nasty suspicion that maybe she did more things with Grisham she hadn't bothered to tell me about. Maybe every second she isn't with me, she's with him. The thought eats me up from the inside out, and I can feel my body coiling tighter and tighter with every step I take.

I scan the patio and grassy area as I walk, not spying the coiffed blond hair and curvy figure I'm searching for. I know she isn't in the tent, because the fancy dinner has yet to be served. As I walk closer to the house, a waiter comes strolling out of the kitchen door carrying a tray of shrimp cocktail. I catch the heavy wooden door with my hand and push inside.

Hearing voices coming from the dining room just past the

kitchen, I inch forward. I don't want to be seen, I just want to see if any of the voices is Berkeley's. As I get closer, I can begin to make out the conversation unfolding before me.

"God, Daddy, I'm so sick of going over this with you! I don't want to talk about it again!"

That's Berkeley, and she is obviously talking to the Admiral. Does she need me? Should I bust in and pull her out of there?

"You brought that trash to our house tonight, Berkeley. That doesn't sit well with me. These people are my friends and my colleagues, what will they think? And Grisham's parents are here. Do you really want to throw the fact that you ditched their son for someone who is so far beneath him into their faces? Didn't I raise you better than that?"

She sounds so angry, I still at the tone in her voice. Feistiness in full force. "No, Daddy, that isn't my fault. Grisham and I have always been great friends. You pushed him on me, trying to turn it into more than I ever wanted. It's your fault if anyone thinks we're supposed to be together, not mine."

"And so what? Now you're going to end up with army trash?" He barks out an ugly laugh. "That's just perfect, Berkeley."

She sighs, sounding beyond exasperated. "Are you really going to cut me off because I didn't choose the man you wanted? That's so petty, Daddy."

"How badly do you want to stay in that stupid little apartment of yours? Badly enough to take out the trash?"

She groans in clear frustration. "Daddy! It's not like I'm going to marry the guy. Shit! He's just someone I hang out with. It's not worth losing our entire relationship for!"

I stumble back a step like I've been punched in the gut. I grab my stomach. Shit, *have* I been punched in the gut? It hurts like I have.

I turn and walk as quietly as I can back out of the kitchen.

I've admitted to myself today that I've started falling in love with Berkeley. It is something I am terrified to admit, because anyone I've loved, I've lost. And I was right to worry about that, wasn't I?

What a fucking mistake. She thinks of me as little more than a "for right now" kind of thing. Falling in love? Laughable. No wonder she hasn't given herself to me. She just isn't that into me. Where I thought we were heading down a path to what could have been perfection, she just thought we were heading down a temporary road. Well, lesson learned.

I walk past Grisham on my way toward the front of the house without really seeing him.

"Hey," he says loudly, startling me out of my own head. "Where are you going? Where's Berkeley?"

He blanches when he gets a good look at my face. I don't blame him; my expression probably tells him I could kill someone with my bare hands. And I can. I've been expressly trained to do so, and the disgusting feeling snaking around my heart right now has definitely made it possible. Grisham's perfectly controlled academy training, even navy, can't possibly compare with that.

"You're leaving?" he asks quietly. "You're leaving *her*?"

I bark out a laugh, running a hand through my hair. "You can have her, man. Congratulations. I'm done."

And then I walk away.

24

Berkeley

I gawk at Grisham like he is speaking to me in Chinese. We're standing outside, my eyes roving around the party as I search for Dare. *Shit. Where could he be?* I'm still fuming from my conversation with my father moments ago. I snatch a glass of champagne off a passing waiter's tray.

"What do you mean, he left?"

Grisham comes closer, so that he's standing inches away from me. He looks at me strangely. "What happened? What did you two talk about?"

I shake my head impatiently. "Grisham, I have no idea what you're saying right now. I haven't seen Dare since my mother dragged me away half an hour ago. What, you saw him? Where'd he go?"

I try to walk around Grisham, but he stops me with a gentle-yet-firm hand on my wrist. "Berk—"

"What?" I snap. I never snap at Grish, but I'm agitated and anxious. *Where's Dare?*

Without another word, Grisham begins towing me toward the front of the house. His vise-like grip on my hand is infuriating. "Grisham! I'm so not in the mood for this shit. I need to find Dare, and I just had an awful fight with the Admiral. What the hell are you *doing*?"

I haven't really spoken to Grisham since I overheard him and my father's little arrangement. He's been trying to get in touch, but I've ignored every single one of his texts and phone calls. He knows I moved out of my parents' house, but he hasn't been to my new apartment. I'm actually wondering why he isn't in San Diego right now, but I don't have time to wonder long.

There's other things on my mind that take precedence right now.

"Stop struggling, Berk," he says through his teeth. "Just trust me. Hold on a second."

We reach the driveway. Most of the cars have been valeted to a lot a little ways away, but I knew for a fact that Dare had parked his truck in the driveway. But it isn't there now.

I turn to Grisham, frowning. "Where is he?"

Grisham lets go of my hand and throws his up into the air. "That's what I've been trying to tell you! He left, Berkeley."

He watches my face carefully, like he's waiting for some reaction. I stare back blandly. "He left? Why?"

We haven't even had dinner yet.

"I was hoping you could tell me that, sweetheart," says Grisham gently.

Oh, shit. Why is he calling me sweetheart? Opposite of my father, he only does that when he's trying to comfort me, when he's being extra sweet if I'm upset about something. Do I have something to be upset about?

"Give me your phone, Grisham," I demand suddenly.

Shaking his head, he pulls the thing out of his pocket and hands it over. I punch in Dare's number by memory and hold the phone to my ear.

Voice mail. His phone goes straight to voice mail.

"What the *fuck* happened? Did you say something to him?"

Grisham's eyes widen in shock. "Shit, no, Berkeley! I didn't, I swear. He…left on his own. I thought you two had a fight."

"I told you I haven't seen him in a half hour!" I scream. I'm nearly hysterical. My insides are sinking, plummeting really, and I'm having trouble catching breaths. I gulp down some more champagne in the flute still clutched in my hand.

"Okay, okay," says Grisham, coming toward me with outstretched hands.

I bat them away. "Don't touch me!"

I turn and run back around the house, into the kitchen door. I slam it with a satisfying *bang* and lean against it. Then I sprint up to my old room so that I can call Dare on my own goddamn phone.

Straight to voice mail again. I'm tempted to just jump in my car and track him down, but I'm already swaying on my feet from the champagne I just chugged. Then I remember that I have roommates. And isn't it a roommate's duty to double as personal chauffer when her fellow roomie is having a crisis? I dial Mea. No answer. I dial Greta next.

No. Fucking. Answer.

What the crap? Where is everyone? Am I in an alternate universe right now?

"I can take you," says Grisham quietly from the door.

I look up, startled, and then narrow my eyes on his expressionless face. "No, thanks."

"Berkeley," he says, venturing farther into my room. He spreads his hands out in front of him, gesturing openly toward me. "I understand you're pissed at me. I would be, too. Know that I refused to try and push you into doing something you didn't want to do. I lost the position in San Diego because of it, but I don't give a shit. You're my best friend. You always have been. You can forgive me later, but right now, let me drive you where you need to go. Okay?"

I take a deep, rattling breath as I assess him. He's right. I *am* still pissed at him, he *has* always been my best friend, and I *will* forgive him later. I nod. "Okay."

It's been a little over a week since my mother's garden party. That means I got to enjoy an amazing June and three-quarters of July blissfully happy with Dare Conners. And now?

Nothing.

I texted him. I called him. Grisham took me by the beach house right after we left my parents' house that night. He hasn't responded to a single call, message, or visit.

And now I'm done.

I'm not one of those stupid girls who continues to throw themselves at a guy who, clearly, is no longer interested.

I am, however, one of those girls who eats a ridiculous amount of ice cream, gains five pounds, and sits around in her sweats after a breakup.

Nothing Mea or Greta do convinces me to leave the house. I called in sick at See Food for a week, and I know I'm super lucky that Lenny loves and understands me, because my ass would have been canned at any other job. I just can't seem to motivate myself to do anything.

I'm not pining away for Dare. Okay, maybe I'm pining just a tad bit. But I'm just completely at a loss for *what the hell happened.* One minute, he's right there with me, understanding what's in my heart as if he shares the same beating organ, and I'm falling in love with the guy. In a way I've never fallen in my life. And the next, he's gone.

Without a single word.

What happened? All I can think of is that at that damn party, my mother got to him. It couldn't have been the Admiral, because he was with me. But is Dare the kind of man who can't take a harsh word from my mother? I didn't think so before.

I've wracked my brain, and I can't come up with a better explanation.

So ice cream and sweats it is.

It's on the next Saturday night, a week and one day later, that I'm sitting on my couch, alone, doing exactly that. My hair is atop my head in a messy, curly bun, and I'm wearing a white tank top and light gray sweats. My feet are bare and I'm in danger of going up yet another jeans size. I'm even thinking of giving my ass its own area code.

There's a knock at the front door.

I stare at it, wondering if Mea and Greta are too drunk to remember that they live here and don't have to knock. They attempted to convince me to go out to a bar with them tonight by telling me how pretty I looked. I laughed right in their faces.

The knock sounds again, pounding and insistent. I sigh, pausing my DVR'd episode of *Teen Wolf* and drag myself off the couch.

When I pull open the door I'm staring into the hard chest of

Grisham. I sigh heavily, moving away from the door and going to plop back on the couch.

"Seriously, Berk?" he says, screwing up his face and closing the door behind him. He indicates the coffee table. "An entire carton of Ben & Jerry's?"

I glance at the tub, shrug, and pick up the remote. Hitting PLAY, I don't look at him. "You can sit, Grish."

He perches on the edge of the couch, staring at me. "You've been like this for an entire week, Berk."

"I have? Shit." I eye him with an exaggerated look of pure shock, and he scowls.

"Get up," he orders.

I stare. "Excuse me?"

"You heard me. I'm not letting you do this anymore. Get up and get dressed. We're getting a drink. We'll meet up with Mea and Greta."

I fold my arms and remain seated. I turn my focus back to Scott and Stiles.

Suddenly, Grisham yanks the remote from my hand and flicks off the television.

"What the f—" My shrill protest is cut off as Grisham scoops me off the couch and carries me, fireman-style, to my bedroom. He thrusts me unceremoniously on the bed and proceeds to open my closet door.

"If you get up, you will get thrown right back on that bed, and I will use my body weight to restrain you. Does that sound fun, Berkeley?"

"No." I pout, pushing up on my elbows.

"Have you showered today?" He tosses clothing at me and turns.

I set my lips in a stubborn line. Maybe he can force me to comply, but he cannot force me to speak.

He sighs and jerks his thumb toward the doorway. "Shower, Berkeley. Now."

I rise from the bed and storm past him on the way to the bathroom. "I like reserved Grisham so much better than bossy Grisham!"

All that follows me into the bathroom is his chuckle.

So I shower, and I dress in the flowered, short skirt and V-necked tank top Grisham has set out for me. And every second I'm doing it, my body is aching. It radiates out of my chest and settles into my limbs as if I've recently completed a very rigorous workout. Too bad I haven't burned any calories lately, unless you count crying into my pillow at night an exercise.

As I pull a brush through my wet curls, I hear a knock at the front door.

"Why am I so popular tonight?" I mutter as I enter the hallway.

I walk into the living room just as Grisham pulls the front door open.

And reveals Dare, standing there on the mat with a serious expression on his face.

Oh, God.

I haven't seen him in a week, and he looks…delicious. Seriously, good enough to eat. His dark hair touches the collar on his crewneck shirt, and his jeans hug the muscular legs I know for a fact are hidden beneath them. I unconsciously lean forward, because if I can get close enough, I know I can smell him. And he always smells so good.

"Dare?" I croak.

His gaze crashes into mine, and I'm lost in a wave of stormy sea green. The words I may have uttered get stuck in my throat, and a huge lump forms above them, making it impossible for me to speak again.

Dare's eyes flicker from my face to Grisham, who's standing at the door glaring at him. Then they move back to me.

"I need to talk to you," he says carefully. Some sort of shutter closes over those eyes, and his expression is completely unreadable. Guarded, even.

"I don't think so," growls Grisham. "She's been trying to talk to you for a freaking week. You—"

"Grish."

His eyebrows shoot upward and he swings his gaze around to mine.

"Let him in."

I can see a tiny muscle pulsing in Grisham's jaw, and when I look at Dare I see an identical one pulsing in his.

"Can you give us a few minutes?" I ask Grisham quietly.

He opens his mouth, and then snaps it shut when I shoot him a pleading glance. He nods, exiting the front door and closing it behind him.

I know he won't go far.

Dare stands just inside the doorway, and his gaze sweeps over my body, a long, slow perusal that takes him from my bare feet and legs over my skirt and top, past my ample, exposed cleavage and then back up to my eyes. He leaves a flush on my skin every place his eyes touch, and then he closes his eyes briefly.

When he opens them again, he gestures toward the couch. "Sit with me?"

I proceed forward without a word, perching on the end of the cushion.

I stare down at my hands, which are folded in my lap. If I don't keep them folded, they'll tremble.

"I needed to come by and see you," he begins, sinking down on the opposite end of the couch. He leans forward, his elbows resting on his thighs and his hands clasped under his chin. "I know you've been trying to get in touch with me. I wasn't ready to talk to you yet."

Anger flares through me, erupting in my belly like a volcano. "You weren't ready to talk to me? What the fuck did I *do*?"

My words hit him like a slap; he flinches. He lowers his gaze, and continues. "You know what? You didn't do anything. I was just at that party, and I realized…I realized I don't fit into that world. I won't fit into *your* world."

My mouth drops open, and the shock frees my hands from their death clasp on one another. My fingers spread over my thighs. "Dare! I don't even fit into that world! It's not my world, it's my parents'! You know that."

He shakes his head. "I can't do this with you."

His voice is so low, I almost can't understand him. I stare at his hands, now rubbing the fabric of his jeans. Back and forth, back and forth.

"You mean…you don't want to."

His eyes dart to mine and hold them. I can't help falling into the abyss of his eyes. No matter how deep and dark the depths take me. "If that's what you want to think to help you sleep at night."

"Help me sleep at night? How do you think I've been sleeping at night without you next to me, Dare?"

He barks out a dry laugh. "I think you've been sleeping just fine, Berkeley."

Berkeley. Not baby, not honey. I'm back to just being Berkeley to him.

"Why?" The word falls out of my mouth as a whisper.

He shakes his head slowly. "Because we're not right for each other. I always knew it, deep down. I hoped I could be good enough for you…and I thought maybe I could be. But I was wrong. That night, at the party…that proved it."

"Did someone say something to you?" I ask him. Because I will literally wring my mother's neck.

He stares at me, his eyes searching and sad. What is he searching for? I will give him absolutely anything he needs. Anything. "No, Berkeley. No one said anything to me that night. I didn't hear anything that I didn't already know."

Now it's my turn to search. His words are full of a meaning I don't understand. His eyes are so dismal, I can't see anything more than what he gives me. What is he trying to tell me?

"Dare—"

He stands. "I should go. I'm sure Grisham is waiting for me to get out of here."

I stand quickly, too. "You can stay. We can talk about this."

He reaches out, and I feel the touch of his cool fingers against my hot cheek. He strokes my skin gently, so gently it makes my eyes shine with unshed tears. *Please don't leave.* I want to say those words aloud, but I don't.

"There's nothing else to say."

And then his hand is gone from my cheek and the front door is opening. I take a step toward it, but he's gone.

I crumple onto the couch, and I almost wish he hadn't come. Everyone who says closure heals wounds can take a trip straight to hell, courtesy of my foot, because they're wrong. Seeing him again broke me into pieces, sharp, jagged pieces that are going to be impossible to put back together.

My face is wet and my body is shaking when Grisham walks back in.

"Oh, Berk." He breathes, almost too softly for me to hear him through my tears.

He picks me up, cradling me to his chest, and sits on the couch with me in his lap. The last thing I remember before I pass out from pure exhaustion is him placing me in my bed and covering me with my blanket.

"Sleep, Berkeley," he whispers just before he leaves. "Tomorrow is a new day."

25

Dare

"I'm fine," I snap. I don't even need to glance behind me to know that Drake's beefy presence has approached.

"Right," he scoffs, sitting in the sand beside me. He draws khaki shorts-covered legs to his chest and rests his forearms on his knees. I remain stony and silent, staring out into the crashing waves. Leaning back on my hands, I wait.

Drake says nothing.

Finally irritated, I ask, "What do you want? Don't you have a party to host?"

He shrugs. "It ain't much of a party when my battle buddy bails."

I close my eyes. The very last thing in the entire fucking world that I want to do right now is entertain people in my own home. It's bad enough Drake's been trying to get me out of the house since my breakup with Berkeley, but when I refused? He decided to bring the fun home to me.

Not cool. Not even a little bit.

He sighs. "Look, I'm sorry, man. I just thought…shit, it doesn't matter. I'll go up and kick their asses out."

He starts to heft himself out of the sand, but I stop him with a shake of my head. "Don't bother. I like it out here. It clears my head."

He settles back in. "Yeah? Because it doesn't seem clear. It seems to be pretty damn full of a hot-as-hell blond chick named B—"

"Don't." I cut him off. "Don't even fucking say her name or I swear to God I'll lose my shit on this beach."

Usually we'd banter around, and he'd have some witty response for me threatening to lose my shit. But tonight, Drake seems to sense that I'm in the anti-mood for bullshit jokes.

"Exactly." Drake hesitates before he continues, digging his feet deeper into the sand beneath us. "So you're not fine. Look, Dare…are you sure you did the right thing? I mean you basically let her dad run you out of there, tail between your legs. That ain't the Dare Conners I know. Fuck no."

I shake my head. "You don't get it. I was never good enough for her, you know? Hearing her dad say the shit he did just confirmed what I was already thinking. She belongs with someone…I don't know, someone better or something like that."

He doesn't answer, just keeps on staring at the waves. Drake can stretch out a silence if he needs to, and apparently he doesn't have a response for me just now. I can think of times in a sandy desert or a wild jungle where we would just walk for hours, not needing to say a word. Being stuck on patrol with Drake was always easy.

So we just sit for a bit, while the gathering at our house carries on without us.

Finally, he pipes up. "I don't know exactly what he said, but I got the gist of it. And he doesn't know you, man. He doesn't know shit about you or he wouldn't have said it. And if he really cared about his daughter the way he should, he'd get to know the man she loves."

"She doesn't lo—"

He waves me off. "Whatever. Semantics and shit. All he had to do was make a phone call and he could have found out what kind of hero his daughter was dating. That's all I'm saying. And Berkeley didn't even admit to the conversation…so this may have all been a misunderstanding on her part. You didn't give her any kind of lee-way or chance to explain herself."

My heart, traitor that it is, clenches somewhere deep in my chest. I haven't felt it in so long, I wasn't sure it still beat steadily until this moment. "I heard her, Drake. That's all the confirmation I need. I know a failed mission when I see one."

Standing, he nods and dusts the sand off his hands. "All right. I trust your judgment. I just hope you're not making the biggest mis-take of your life."

As he walks away, I turn to stone. I don't move, I don't think, I don't feel. I just sit, watching the waves do what waves do. One rolls in, another washes out. It's comforting to know that some part of the universe is working exactly the way it's supposed to.

Almost two weeks to the day after that last night in Berkeley's apart-ment, Chase drops a bomb on me.

"Say that again, Chase. One more fucking time, just to make sure I heard you right."

Chase crouches down next to the car I'm currently sitting next to, wiping my hands on a towel. At least he isn't making the "this is no big deal" face. He actually looks concerned about something for once in his life.

"Look, a buddy of mine back in Florida told me that Chavez has been looking for me, and that he got wind of me being in Carolina. So he may or may not have figured out where I am."

I sit up suddenly, throwing my wrench aside. It clatters on the concrete floor. "Then you need to not be in Carolina anymore, Chase."

He sits back, his mouth falling open as he stares at me in shock. "Nice, Dare. Real fucking nice. What am I supposed to do? Be on the run the rest of my life?"

I shake my head slowly, realizing that I just don't have the patience for Chase's shit anymore. "I don't know, Chase. At this point, even if you give him his money is he just gonna roll over and forget about the drama? I doubt it. You don't have many options here."

He stands. "Thanks, bro. That's all you got for me? 'I don't have many options'?"

I stand, too. "I'm always gonna be here for you, Chase, but—"

He holds up a hand, taking a step back. "Yeah, I got it. Your priorities have been real different Dare. First the army, and now all you can think about is this girl. I'm your brother, and you're just leaving me hanging."

My fist slams into a cart of tools unlucky enough to be next to me. "Goddamn it, Chase! I don't know what else to do here. This is your mess. You need to man up and deal with it. Yourself. You can stay until you figure out where you're going next. But I have a life here, and I'm not dragging Drake into this. Not on our turf."

He takes one more long look at me before turning around and heading out. He has nothing else to say, which is good because I don't think I do either.

26

Berkeley

July rolls into August, and the few months I spent with Dare in my life are beginning to feel like they never really happened. I can go to sleep at night without feeling like a piece of me has cracked off and been lost. When I wake up in the morning, I don't automatically reach for his huge body in the empty space beside me. When I'm driving somewhere, I don't continually check my phone to see if I've missed a text or a call from *him*. And I don't constantly evaluate what the hell happened between us. Because, the truth of the matter is, we were fine. We were absolutely freaking perfect, and then all of a sudden we weren't.

And he left.

It was easy for him. And reliving that and evaluating it over and over again just about killed me.

So I had to stop. I'm stronger than my last relationship. I have to be.

Living with the girls has been a complete godsend. They're two little opposite balls of sunshine, lighting up my day from the second

I wake up in the morning until I lay my head on my pillow every night. If I were still living with my parents, I may not have survived this.

I have a job. Grisham was so right when he said "Tomorrow is a new day." Because the very next day, I received a call from the interior design firm where I interned. The owner, Beth Eisengard of Beth Eisengard Interiors, was on the end of the line, offering me more saving graces.

"I was so thrilled to see your résumé!" she'd exclaimed from her end. "Come in tomorrow for an interview, but it's just a formality, hon. Of course I want you on my staff!"

Just like that, I was a design assistant for Beth. And working for her has been filling my days like nothing else would be able to. I don't have time to think about you-know-who, between taking room measurements and photos, matching paint color wheels to fabric swatches, and practically stalking potential clients.

And then there's Grisham. Thanks to my father, he lost the job in San Diego. He's now stationed at the same navy base as both of our fathers in Brunswick County, and he's paying dearly for his "disobedience." He's an officer, but he's really starting on the low end of the pole when he could have been handling a lot more responsibility in California. I feel sorry for him. Grisham was being my friend, and he's paying for it.

I see him nearly every day.

At first, I didn't want to do anything. I would sit on the couch after work and turn on a movie, zoning out while Greta and Mea cooked dinner and opened a bottle of wine. They would flutter around me, clucking over me like old mother hens, and then Grisham would show up.

Without saying a word, he would sit next to me on the couch and watch whatever stupid girly movie was running across the screen. We'd sit in silence while the girls served us a meal and continued with their evenings. Then, at around ten, he'd kiss me on the cheek and say good night.

That continued for days until one day I asked him if he'd like to watch anything else. He'd sent me a shocked, small smile, and turned the channel to SportsCenter. I caught Mea and Greta exchanging a look, but they'd said nothing in response to our changeup.

Today, a blistering hot, mid-August Saturday, Grisham has convinced me to go surfing. I hear the knock on the front door to the apartment while I'm pulling on my tankini, and I know he's here to pick me up. I grab my wet suit and head to the hallway, stopping short at the door to my room.

"Shit, Grisham," grumbles Mea. "She's actually leaving the house with you to do something *fun*. This is kind of huge? Why the hell can't you take her to do something she actually *likes* to do?"

Her grumbly voice is so freaking cute; I bite the inside of my cheek to keep from giggling. She's totally fussing him out, but it's reminiscent of what a baby cheetah might sound like when it's mad. Shaking my head, I start through the doorway but pause when I hear his quiet answer.

"She likes surfing, she just doesn't know it yet."

I can only imagine Mea's dubious expression. She's perfected her "what-the-fuck" face over the years.

"I'm serious. She needs this. She needs to do something active and just let go for a while. This is the best way I know to get her to do that."

I ponder this for a minute, standing in the doorway in my

bathing suit and bare feet. Surfing is definitely an adrenaline rush, if you're actually doing it right. When you stand on your board, your stomach begins to drop out from under you, and when the wave takes ahold of you and pulls you into the shore you get kind of lost in the roar of the wind and the spray of salty sea in your face.

Normally, just after that is when I bust my ass and crack an elbow or a knee on my board. And I completely forget about the feeling I just had right before I crashed and burned.

Hmmm. Maybe Grish is right. Maybe I need to embrace the sport a little more.

"She hasn't been the same since Dare," warns Mea. "You know that. She needs a great day today, because…" Her voice cracks a little, and I feel my throat closing up.

She said his name. Fuck, she said his name and now I can't really breathe. I've avoided saying it, even in my head, even in my *dreams*. I suck in a gulp of air, and then another, as I process the rest of her sentence.

"Because she doesn't laugh anymore, Grisham. I haven't seen Berkeley's dimples in I don't know how long. Actually, I do know *exactly* how long. I want to see her happy again. This Berkeley hasn't been happy. Not since…"

"I know," snaps Grisham. He sounds really irritated. "I fucking know, okay? She'll be fine. She doesn't need him."

I can't listen to this anymore. I pull myself together, tying up the invisible laces that hold in my insides, and walk down the hallway.

"Hey, Grish," I say with tons of cheery, false enthusiasm. "I'm ready to hit the waves."

He stares at me, his plush bottom lip hanging open a little. "What…you are?"

I nod, pulling my board shorts off the back of the couch and shimmying into them. "Yeah. So let's go."

I smile cheerily at Mea, who narrows her eyes at me, and walk out of the apartment. I pause on the landing, waiting on Grisham to step out after me. He does, closing the door behind him, and I continue down the two flights of steps that lead to the parking lot of our complex.

If they think I'm falling apart, well then it looks like I have some convincing to do. Whatever is happening on the inside of me is my business, not theirs. I have a right to my emotions, without everyone around me evaluating them and picking them apart like I'm some kind of psychiatric specimen for study.

Grisham is quiet on the five-minute ride to his favorite surf spot, glancing over at me occasionally. He'll open his mouth as if to say something, and then snap it shut again. I ride silently, my right foot hitched up on the dashboard and hanging out the open window.

"Since when do you paint your toenails black?"

I look at him sharply, and he's glancing pointedly at my exposed toes. I look down at them, and then sigh.

"They're not black," I inform him. "They're Wild Cherry Nights, and I love this color."

Grisham raises two dark-blond eyebrows in response, but says nothing. He pulls into the sand-covered lot and exits the Audi. He busies himself removing our boards from the rack on the top, and I stare out over the cliff we're parking atop of. The ocean is crashing roughly against the shore and into the craggy rocks right beside it. It's a very windy day down here at the beach, and I suddenly can't wait to be in the water.

When Grisham hands me my board, I place it over my head and

begin picking my way down the hill toward the beach. I can hear him behind me, and as we reach the bottom I suddenly turn to face him.

"Stop worrying about me, Grisham," I order. "I'm fine, okay? You don't have to walk on eggshells. I just want to surf."

His eyes widen in surprise. "You *want* to surf?"

I smile at him. "See? Fine. Now let's do this."

We take the rest of the rocky path down, and then I strip off my shorts to pull on my yellow and black wet suit. While Grisham is still tugging on his solid black one, I grab my board and take off for the water. I hear him chuckle behind me, and blow out a sigh of relief. Maybe now he'll stop looking at me like I'm going to break into tiny little pieces right in front of him.

The water is cool despite the summer's heat, and I relish the feel of it as it covers my ankles, my knees, my thighs, and my hips. When I finally get to the point where I can climb atop my board, I sit serenely, surveying the scene around me. I'm surrounded by solid blue in almost every direction. The gray-blue water meets the turquoise sky in a collision of hue, and I close my eyes, breathing in the salt. For the first time in a month, I feel…peaceful. Calm. Steady. I pull in a breath and let it out again, and as I do I feel the swell of a building wave.

"Do it, Berk!"

Grisham is next to me; I never saw him ride out, but I do as he says and begin paddling. He's next to me stroke for stroke, and when I see him start to stand up a few feet away, I scramble lithely to my feet. I swear it's the smoothest transition I've ever completed, and then I'm soaring.

I hold my hands out to either side of me and bend my knees, reacting to the movement of the water beneath me as I ride the wave into shore. When I reach the sand, I hop off and throw my hands into the air, curling my fingers into jubilant fists.

Grisham is right behind me, and he tosses his board to the ground and sprints over to where I stand. He scoops me into his arms, and I'm suddenly laughing my ever-loving head off.

"Oh, my God!" he shouts happily. "That was amazing, Berk! That's the best one you've ever done. You rode the shit out of that wave!"

"Holy fuck, I did, didn't I?" I ask in wonder. His arms tighten around me, and I throw my head back. My heavy, wet curls slap us both in the face, and Grisham bursts into laughter beside me.

When he pulls back, his face is shining and bright with elation. "You want to do that again?"

"Hell. Yes."

It's nearly dark when we finally pack it up and head home. Grisham has a perma-smile on his face, and I'm pretty sure I do, too. Only, as soon as we get in the car, the bubble of happiness the day has created begins to fade and ebb.

He reaches over and clasps my hand in his across the center console. "You laughed today," he says fiercely. "You laughed, dammit. Don't pull back into your shell now. Stay with me, Berk."

"I'm right here," I whisper.

I glance at him quickly, and then look out at the dark forms the trees take as they fly by outside the car. "I'm hungry."

"Yeah? You should be. You killed it today, Berkeley. I've never seen you like that...you were amazing. Do you get it now? Why I like to surf?"

He guides the car off the road and into the parking lot at See Food.

"Yeah, Grish. I do. That was…it was freeing. I don't know. That sounds weird, right?" I clasp my hands together in my lap, toying with the tie on my board shorts. I feel my face heating as a blush creeps up from my neck.

He squeezes my hand. "It's not weird. That's exactly how I feel when I'm doing it. Want me to grab some food to go?"

I nod, and he walks up to the restaurant. Just as Grisham reaches for the door, it opens, and Drake walks out with a to-go container in his hands.

He freezes when he sees me, glancing from me to Grisham and back again. His eyes are warm when he settles them on me and he wallops me with his killer grin.

I unfold myself from the car, leaning awkwardly against the door. "Drake…" Just seeing him fills me with nostalgia, and the pain that simmers beneath the surface rises, ready to slice me open.

"Hey, Berkeley," he says gently. "You been doing okay? I miss you, girl."

I nod numbly, and swallow so that I don't look like a mute. "I'm doing fine, Drake. How are you?"

He nods, glancing at Grisham again. Grisham is watching us warily. I realize he never met Drake. "I'm doing really good. This is still my favorite restaurant."

I nod. "Drake, this is my friend Grisham. Grish, this is Drake. He's…" I trail off, at a loss. How am I supposed to get this out? It ain't gonna happen.

Drake shifts his food, and holds out a hand to Grisham. "I'm Dare's roommate."

And there it is. Shit! The pain rips through me, and I bite the shit out of my lip to stop it from trembling. Grisham shakes Drake's hand quickly and then lays a steadying hand on my lower back.

He knows. Damn.

"Good seeing you, Berkeley." Drake frowns at me, as if he's trying to figure out what just happened.

Dare's not with him. Where is he? Maybe he's seeing someone. Maybe he has a date. Oh, God in heaven. What if he's inside with said date right now? If I see that, I'm going to hurl right on the hardwood floor at See Food. Lenny and Boozer will kill me.

"Where's your roommate tonight?" The question is casual, but I can hear the slight edge to Grisham's tone when he asks it.

Drake hesitates, staring at me cautiously. "He's been helping his brother out with something. Been pretty tied up with that."

Grisham nods, visibly relieved.

"It was good seeing you, Drake."

"You too, Berkeley. Don't be a stranger."

He walks away, and Grisham guides me into the restaurant.

Lenny rushes over, happy to see me, asking questions about the new job. I'm swept up in her excitement, and it allows me to push all thoughts of Dare way down deep and focus on telling her all about being a design assistant. Grisham leans back in the front booth and watches, a small smile etched on his sun-bronzed face.

"What?" I demand, once Lenny is gone to get our order.

He tenses his jaw, keeping his eyes on me. "I like seeing you talk about your job. It's something you're happy about."

I mull that over, and his smile grows. "Yeah, I guess it is."

He's quiet for a few minutes, alternating between staring at me and strumming his fingertips on the table. I just wait. Finally, he asks. "Are you okay? After seeing Drake?"

Ah. It all comes flooding back. The pain, the anxiety, the whirlpool of emotions that leave me hanging on for dear life. I'm teetering on the brink of a tearful, embarrassing breakdown, and I suddenly feel like if I start I may never be able to stop.

"I'm tired," I choke out, pushing away from the booth. Grisham stands, too, his features full of concern. "I'll be in the car."

He nods. "Berk—"

I throw a hand up at him, because I know one more understanding word from him may break me.

Then, just before the tears begin to fall and my heart starts to constrict, I turn and flee the restaurant.

I'm not over Dare Conners, my ex-Army Ranger. I might never be over him.

Grisham knows me well enough by now to realize I'm not up for company tonight. So he takes his dinner and makes it an early evening.

A minute or two after he leaves, there's a soft rap on the door, and I smile wryly as I pad over to open it.

"Grish, what'd you forget?" The words fade off my lips as I open the door.

I don't recognize the girl standing there. She's short, like me, with black spiky hair cut in a crazy-cute style and amber eyes. She stares at me, and I stare back.

"Um, hi? Can I help you?" I ask tentatively.

She shakes her head, as if shaking herself back into the moment. "Yes, I'm sorry to bother you. Can I use your cell phone? Mine died, and so did my car. I'm doing a walk of shame, and this is so embarrassing."

The words tumble out of her mouth at a quick clip, and I smile sympathetically. Walk of shame, huh? Sucks to be her right now. I gesture inside the apartment. "Come on in."

She takes a few steps over the threshold and stops. Huh. I guess we're not doing the warm and fuzzy thing. Okay, then. I head for the counter where my purse is lying, half of its contents scattered over the granite. Rooting through the mess until I find my phone, I turn.

Oh, this chick is stealthy. She's *right there* when I turn around. Weird. Smiling uncertainly, I hand her the phone. "Here you go. Can I get you—"

She cuts me off when her hand jerks into the air and I see the syringe. What the hell? My initial reaction is to open my mouth and ask a question.

I wish I had better reactions.

"I'm sorry, Berkeley," she whispers, just before plunging the needle deep into my neck.

The point of contact feels immediately cold, and then the coldness spreads through my body faster than I would have thought possible. My last thought, before the floor rises up to meet me, is that I really wish Dare were here.

27

Dare

Chase looks up as I pull the truck into the parking lot of the Brunswick County Sheriff's Department. "What the fuck is this, Dare? I thought you were done with me."

I turn off the ignition and sit back against my seat, glancing at him. I was done. But he's the only brother I have, and it was damn near impossible for me to send him packing without trying one more thing. I'm attempting to get him to do the right thing.

"This is the plan. I waited for you to come up with one, you didn't. So we're going in there, and you're going to tell them everything. Then we're going to get an order of protection against Chavez, because it's smart to have a paper trail where shit like this is concerned. You're in my town now, Chase. I love you, but I can't protect you by myself."

Chase's face reddens. "I'm not asking for protection, Dare! I asked for your help. All I need is the money."

I shake my head. "That's not gonna do it, Chase, and you know it. The guy you described…just handing over some cash isn't going to get rid of him. Trust me. I want to help you, and this is the first step."

He sighs and leans his head back against the seat. "Shit. I don't want to do this."

I clap a hand on his shoulder and open the truck door. "I know. But sometimes we all gotta do shit we don't wanna do."

Just as I'm preparing to step out of the truck, my phone rings. Distracted, I pull it out of my pocket and answer.

"Hello?"

Mea's voice on the other end of the line borders on frantic, and I'm immediately alert. "Dare!"

The rest of the words out of her mouth are a jumble of incoherence, and I bark into the phone. "Mea! Slow down. What happened? Is it Berkeley?"

My pulse races in my veins. Because, *Christ*, of course it's Berkeley. Why else would Mea be calling me?

"You need to come to our apartment right now, Dare. Berkeley's been—taken—and there's a note for you."

My stomach sinks like I just swallowed a ton of stones. I can't remember a time in my life that I've ever felt this terrified. Dread is building up in my body, and my palms begin to sweat. *This isn't happening.*

Not to her.

"I'm on my way," I growl into the phone before tossing it onto the console and slamming the truck door closed again. I glance at Chase, whose mouth is set in a firm line as he stares at me. "Change of plans."

"What happened?"

"We'll find out when we get there." My foot stomps down heavily on the floor as I sweep my arm across the top. Someone grunts.

The drive to Berkeley's apartment is a blur in my memory. I can't remember if I stopped for a single red light. Probably not. And by the time I'm finally running up the stairs of the building, the sweat is pouring down the back of my neck.

Someone took her. Whoever had Berkeley wouldn't be breathing much longer.

As I burst through the door, Mea's tear-stained face is the first thing I see. I storm over to her. "Where's the note?"

"Easy, Dare." Greta places a hand on my shoulder. "We called Drake. He should be here any minute, too. Do you want to wait for him?"

Mea whirls on her. "We don't have time to wait for anything! They have my best friend. We need to find her!"

"Have you called the police?" Chase sidles up beside me, placing his hand on my other shoulder. It's like everyone thinks I'm about to blow a fuse. Which could definitely fucking happen.

Mea, maybe reading my mind, hands over a folded piece of paper. Damn, she handled it. "Anyone else touch it?"

She shakes her head, sniffing. "No...just me."

I grab a pen from the counter and gesture for her to drop the note on the shiny surface. Then I use the pen to slide the note in front of me. "Good."

I scan the note.

As long as you're helping your brother get me my money, I thought I'd give you some incentive to move more quickly. Meet me at the address below in 24 hours. If you're late, your Berkeley will bleed.

The growl begins in my chest, and becomes a roar when it bursts from my throat. "Son of a *bitch*!"

The contents of the counter, including the note, go crashing to the floor as I sweep my arm across the top. Someone grips me from behind, but then I hear Drake's voice from the doorway.

"Let him go. He has a right to be pissed."

I ignore Drake's voice as he enters and turn on my brother. "How does he know about me, Chase?"

Chase hangs his head. "I dropped a line to a friend back home, letting him know my brother was helping me out with the Chavez problem. I wanted Chavez to know I didn't just flake out on him."

Drake slams the door behind him as he strides quickly over to where I'm standing, now quaking with unbridled fury. "What's the situation, Dare?"

I gesture blankly toward the note now lying on the floor. I'm inhaling deep breaths through my nose, and the room in front of me is taking on a red tinge.

Drake crouches, reads the note, and stands again. He glances at Chase. "Cops?"

Chase shakes his head. "We just got here. We haven't decided…what to do." He turns to me, and there's real pain and regret in his eyes. "I'm so sorry, man. I fucked up."

I can't look at Chase right now, can't deal with his apologies. So I turn to Drake. "We have to get her back, Drake. The asshole could hurt her. I can't…"

Trailing off, my legs give out and I crouch to the floor beside the note. I read it again and again. He didn't say anything about watching us, about knowing if we contact the cops. So maybe we can gather reinforcements. All I know for sure is that I'm going to that address tomorrow, and I'm walking out of there with Berkeley in my arms. It's up to Chavez whether he's alive when I'm done.

"Dare?" says Greta tentatively, somewhere behind me. "I think we should call my dad."

The tension in the room is so thick it nearly chokes me. We're sitting in Greta's father's office. Greta informed us that her father owns a private security company and has many connections with the local law enforcement. He has a nondescript building overlooking the ocean, and his office contains one large wall of windows. He's sitting at his desk, appraising Drake, Chase, and I. We sit on a leather couch directly across from Police Detective Lawrence Henderson. Greta's father, Jacob Owen, studies us all with serious interest.

"So, Lawrence, you can see why I called you in on this. We need to be discreet. I'm sure if they smell cops, they'll kill Berkeley."

I stiffen. "That's not going to happen, dammit."

Detective Henderson shakes his head. "No, son, we're going to try to make sure it doesn't. You need to leave this to us. I can get a team—"

I interrupt him. "If you want a rogue ex-soldier out there, doing whatever the fuck I see fit, you go ahead and leave me out of this operation. Otherwise, I suggest you tell me exactly what's going to happen, and then I'll be the one going in to get my girl. The note was addressed to me. I'm not sitting on my hands on this, Detective."

Drake nods, seconding my statement.

Detective Henderson sighs, scowling at me. Then, leaning forward on his elbows, he turns to Chase. "So you owe this Chavez money? That's why he's in my town?"

Chase, looking extremely uncomfortable, nods.

It's been about three hours since Berkeley was taken, and I still haven't been able to bring myself to say more than two words to

Chase. He's my brother, sure, but it's his damn fault that the girl I gave my heart to is in danger. Everything I went through with Berkeley now seems like a distant, painful memory. All that matters now is that I get the chance to tell her that I love her. Because, *dammit*...I do.

"That, and I made a move on his girl." Chase has been totally honest with both Jacob and Detective Henderson, which is good, because I would have beaten his ass if he left anything out.

Detective Henderson abruptly stands. "This can be our home base. I'm going to make a call, and get a team working on this. We'll get her back." He pats my shoulder kindly on his way to the door.

I lean back on the leather and scrub my hands over my face. My chest gets tighter with every hour that passes and I don't have eyes on her. I'm used to missions being planned out perfectly, and then planned out again. Right now, I feel so fucking blind I want to yell, or hit something. Or both.

"We'll get Berkeley back, Dare," says Drake quietly. "I'm with you, man."

Chase nods. "Me, too."

I look at my brother for the first time in hours. "You better be right."

Pacing and thinking, I pass the half hour until Henderson returns. Neither of which are helping Berkeley right now. But at the moment, everything else is out of my hands.

It's been a long time since I felt this helpless. I became a soldier so I'd never have to feel that way again.

The door silently swings open and in walks Henderson with two guys I recognize instantly as brothers.

Henderson nods in my direction first. "Teague, Shaw, this is Dare

Conners. He's ex-army, like you guys. Conners, these guys are with me. Jeremy Teague and Ronin Shaw are plainclothes detectives with our department. They've been briefed on the situation, and we have some men out scouting the location now."

I nod at the two newcomers, but my ears prick at the words Henderson just uttered. "They're being discreet, right? I don't want Chavez sniffing them out. If he suspects anything..."

I don't want to finish that sentence. I just want reassurances that Henderson and his team know their shit, and then I want to get my hands dirty. If I have to spend another minute sitting and waiting, I'll lose my goddamn mind.

Henderson nods. "We're discreet. We wanted to know the lay of the land. Everybody listen up, I have some intel for you."

We all take seats and lean in, Jacob, leaning over his desk steeples his fingers as he takes in Henderson's words.

"The address is a bar/restaurant in a seedy area near downtown Wilmington. The place can gather a crowd late at night, and he asked for you to show up in the evening. I'm not liking the odds that civilians will be present."

I nod, my forehead creasing as my concentration level rises. He's speaking to me in a language I understand fully. I want to talk strategies and tactics, and I want to know as much information as I can about the place where Berkeley is being held. It's all I can do not to walk out and show up at the address myself, early, but I know that's not in Berkeley's best interests.

"We won't send you in blind," continues Henderson. "We'll make sure we can hear everything that's going on, and if we can get eyes in there we will."

"What about me?" asks Chase. He leans forward, meeting first my eyes, then Henderson's. "I'm the one who got him and Berkeley into this mess. I want to go in there with him."

Drake snorts under his breath, and I glance his way before leveling my gaze at Chase. "What can you tell us about how Chavez usually operates?"

"He's known in my area as being ruthless. That's how he got to the status he's at. He's no dummy, and he doesn't care about shit except the money someone owes him."

"From what we've gathered in our research," Jacob breaks in, "he has one prior conviction, about nine years ago. He spent six years in prison, but since then he's kept his nose squeaky clean. On the outside."

"What was his conviction for?" For me, information is like a lifeline. I grab ahold of it and soak it up. Being briefed keeps me from focusing on the emotion side of this situation. It keeps the worry for what Berkeley's going through right now from creeping in. And it keeps the rage boiling inside me at bay. As long as I think of this situation like any other rescue I've attempted, I can bring Berkeley home safely.

But there are no promises guaranteed to the people who took her that they'll come out of this unscathed.

"Drug trafficking, resisting arrest, and conspiracy to commit murder." Henderson's answer isn't exactly music to my ears.

I turn to Chase. "I think if Chavez sees you, it'll wind him up. I don't want that. Not with Berkeley in the potential crossfire."

Chase frowns. "You don't want me with you?"

Rubbing a hand through my hair, I shrug. "It's not a matter of what I want, Chase. It's a matter of procedure, and the best way to go about getting her out of there alive. And unhurt. And I need training and experience on my side. That's not you. What about Shay?"

His eyes shutter. "I haven't been able to get ahold of her. I need to find out whether Chavez brought her with him, or whether he left her in Florida."

I nod. "You work on that."

I turn my eyes to first Jacob, and then Henderson. "Drake goes in with me, because he has the same skills that I do. I trust him. And I want your best by my side as well." My gaze darts over to Teague and Shaw. They both nod in return.

Henderson rubs his hands together and leans forward. "Okay, then. We'll have a map of the interior shortly, and within the next couple of hours we'll find out how many men are inside, and try to pinpoint the exact area of the building they've got Berkeley. The plan will depend on that intel. Get some rest until then, boys."

We all nod, but I know I'll never rest until I have the girl I love in my arms again.

28

Berkeley

I start awake. Staring around the room, my brain feels fuzzy around the edges, like I'm only seeing my surroundings through a tunnel deep under the ocean. I shake my head, but it doesn't clear. I sit up on the twin cot beneath me, the thin mattress shifting as I move.

"Oh, my God." I breathe. "What the hell happened? Where am I?"

I try hard to think, but my head just won't cooperate. I was in my apartment, with Grisham…no, wait, Grisham left with his dinner. Then what? My face scrunches up as I try to remember.

The room I'm in is small, and it's clearly an office space. It reminds me of the office at See Food, only much grungier. Other than the cot I'm sitting on, there's a battered wooden desk cluttered with papers and used mugs. Apart from a dented filing cabinet and a calendar hanging on the wall, and—oh, my God, so gross—some dead roaches on the floor, the room is pretty bare.

My eyes are still focused on the roaches when the door opens. My muscles immediately tense as a feeling of foreboding creeps over me. Whoever may set foot into this room isn't my friend.

A man in his early thirties emerges around the door, and behind him stride two men in black jeans and sweaters. Their heavy black boots indicate that they mean business, and that's before I get to the hard expressions on their faces.

The first man, obviously in charge, curls his lips into a mean grin. "Berkeley. How are you feeling? I'm sorry I had to take you out of your home, but I have business to settle here and I needed you with me in order to do that."

Feeling like I'm the leading actress in a feature film, I gape at him. "You needed *me*? Does this have something to do with my father?"

Confusion flashes in his eyes for just a moment before he smoothes out his expression. The man speaking to me is tall and broad, with thick, black hair that curls over his forehead. He's wearing fitted jeans and a thermal shirt, and his shoes are—is that *alligator*?—expensive-looking. I can detect a slight Latino accent when he speaks. His eyes are basically dead. Like the eyes of a shark circling a tasty assortment of chum.

"I do not know your father. This is business with your boyfriend, Dare, and his brother. Chase owes me money, and he will give me what he owes one way or another."

One way or another. The words chill me to the bone, and I'm not even sure exactly what they mean. It can't be good, that's for sure. But if this is about Chase…

"Does Dare know I'm here?" I try to keep my voice even, because the thought of Dare knowing I've been taken means he will probably move mountains in order to get me back. Not to mention if the

Admiral's been alerted. This man has no idea the hell that's about to rain down around him.

My thoughts must have made me smirk, because the man's eyes narrow.

"Who are you?" I ask quickly to distract him. They won't hurt me, at least not until they get what they want. But that thought doesn't keep my palms from turning sweaty or my heart from attempting to thump right out of my chest. I feel a bead of moisture drip down the back of my neck, where my hair is sticking uncomfortably.

"I'm Javier Chavez. And, Berkeley? I'm the best friend you have right now, so you should stay on my good side."

With that, he nods to one of his goons, and all three men walk out of the room.

I sit back on the bed and let out a breath I didn't even know I'd been holding. Then I proceed to freak out.

OhmyGodohmyGodohmyGodohmyGod.

I try to breathe deep to keep my breath from totally running away from me but it's difficult. I've been freaking kidnapped. Like in the movies. And the guy…Chavez? He's freaking scary. Maybe even legitimately evil. And I'm here all by myself.

What am I supposed to do in this situation? I scan the room again, searching for an exit that doesn't involve going out that door. Because I doubt that's a possibility. The room has no windows. There's an air vent in the ceiling, but I'm not a freaking ninja.

Biting my lip, I sink back down on the cot. My head is searing, and I've found myself in the most dangerous scenario I could have imagined. I need help.

I need Dare.

29

Dare

Drake's tone is incredulous. "I can't believe you called him."

We watch Berkeley's father, the Admiral, as he paces back and forth in front of the wall of windows and barks orders into his phone.

"It had to be done." My tone is cool and functional, and I notice Drake eyeing me from the corner of my vision.

The absolute last thing I wanted to do was call Berkeley's father and tell him I'd let his baby girl be taken away from us. I made it clear to him that I wasn't going to stop until I had her back. He had insisted on joining our ranks, and now was determinedly attempting a takeover of the team, getting his word in wherever possible. I can see the irritation on Jacob's face growing as his jaw clenches tighter and a vein begins to bulge on his temple. I wish I hadn't had to make the call.

I can only imagine what he's going through. The loss of Berkeley, no matter how temporary—because it *is* temporary—is tearing me apart inside. To know your only child has been kidnapped, and you have the skills and connections to help bring her home? I had to make the call.

Drake studies me. "It's nice to have Cujo back in the building."

The old nickname causes a twitch of my lips and nothing more.

In my Ranger days, the men in my unit called me Cujo whenever we were preparing or embarking on a mission. They said it was because I was like a rabid dog with a prey in its sights when I was on the front lines. I feel that way right now more than ever, the nickname settling comfortably into my whole body once again.

"Everyone needs to get your asses over here and lean in." Jacob raises his voice to be heard over the din surrounding us. "Conners here is going in without wearing devices, so it's our job to make sure we have ears and eyes in the place."

I didn't know I'd be going in blind, but I know what I need to do, and nothing and no one will stop me from doing it.

As an elite soldier, everything was done to make sure we had the most intel possible before entering any situation. We received information, we assessed the need, and we trained until any possibility of failure was eliminated. Didn't matter how prepared we were though, there was always a chance for something to go wrong. Always a slight element of the unknown involved.

Berkeley's rescue? No different. The unthinkable has already happened. Now it's my job to go in and kick ass until the danger is maintained and the target is eliminated. Without innocent casualties. And Berkeley is beyond innocent in this scenario.

Henderson leans over the table we've gathered around and points to a small listening device I recognize from my time as a Ranger. "Shaw and Teague will enter the dive about forty-five minutes before Conners, as patrons. Stupid idiots are leaving the place open, so it won't look suspicious if they're dressed like punks. Make sure these are in your ears, men."

Both Teague and Shaw nod their understanding. They've both dressed down for this evening's operation in jeans and long-sleeved T-shirts. Their feet are clad in boots, and with their shaved heads and tats, they look badass. I nod to them.

"You two," Jacob says as he gestures to Drake and me, "will carry in the briefcase containing the cash Chavez has asked for. In a perfect world, you hand over the money and he hands over Berkeley. Then Five-O can storm in when you're clear and arrest the bastard. But we don't live in a perfect world, do we?"

Better than anyone in this room, I know we don't. I can hope and wish and pray that this goes down without bloodshed, but I'd be dreaming if I did. I know better, and based on what Chase told us about Chavez, I don't think he'll be playing fair.

Jacob and Henderson run through a few more notes and then run it all down one more time just to make sure everyone's got their head on straight. I successfully push all thoughts of whether or not Berkeley's unharmed, whether or not she's scared and asking for me, out of my mind. If I let myself go there, I'll crumble.

And I will never crumble when there's a job to do.

Drake bumps my knuckles. "Shoot, man. I swear to God I never thought I'd be doing this shit again. You ready?"

I nod. "I've been ready since the first phone call, Drake. Do me a favor and go call the girls. I don't want them to worry. Tell them we'll bring Berkeley home tonight."

He hesitates, and then leaves the room to make the call. I turn to the windows and stare out at the darkening sky above a rolling sea. I close my eyes, trying like hell to send a message to her.

I'm coming for you, baby. Be strong. Stay safe.

I feel movement next to me, and see the Admiral standing there, also staring out. I wonder if his thoughts are similar to mine. I'd be willing to bet they are.

"This is all your fault, you son of a bitch," he growls.

I turn to look at him, but I try and keep any hint of anger I'm feeling out of my voice. This isn't the time to get into it with Berkeley's father. I look him straight in the eye.

"I know."

"I chose the right man for her a long time ago. I knew what was best for her. I'm her father. Maybe I shouldn't have demanded that of her…taken away her choice. But dammit, look at what's happened now!"

My blood rushes to my ears, pounding a deep rhythm. He's talking about the conversation that changed everything between Berkeley and me.

"We're not together anymore, sir, so you don't have to worry about it." I clench my teeth together and hope he's done talking. All I want to do is find her. Thinking back to that night just long enough to send shards of pain slicing through my chest, I can only nod. "She made her own choice, sir."

The Admiral sighs wearily, clasping his hands behind his back. "She made the choice because I was threatening to pull everything away from her. My money, my support…even my love."

I stare at him. What kind of father does that to his daughter? I can only imagine the kind of pressure she was under, hearing that from him. I can only imagine the things she might say in order to…oh, shit.

"Whatever she said that night," he continues, "she said under duress. She was very upset, Conners, about what I said to her. I can't stand the thought that wherever she is right now, she's angry with me. I don't like you for her now any more than I did before. If it weren't for you…but it looks like you might be the only one who can make sure my daughter comes back to me."

If I'm understanding the context of what she said that night…about not planning a future with me, about me not being worth ending her relationship with her father over…damn. Maybe she hadn't meant it.

The night on her couch flashes into my mind. How hurt her eyes were, how evident it was that she'd been crying. Over me.

A wall of pain slams into me. I hurt her…I hurt her because instead of letting her explain the conversation with her father and what she meant, I just dropped her out of my life.

Fuck. I'm an asshole.

My hands ball into fists at my sides. I was going to save her before, but now I'm in beast mode. I want to get to her, and I want to get her out of Chavez's dirty grasp. I want to bring her home, and I want to make her *mine.*

I offer the Admiral my hand, and he shakes it.

"Bring my daughter home, Conners."

Nodding, I take his words and stake my life on them. "I'll die before I let anything happen to her, sir. I'm not coming home without her."

They weren't lying when they said the restaurant/bar was seedy. The area is just north of downtown Wilmington, and I'm being nice when I say the place is run-down. There are sketchy characters hanging around smoking out front, under a holey, striped awning, and

on the adjacent corner are girls in short skirts calling out at any male
who passes by. Speaking out of the side of my mouth to Drake, I
comment on the trashiness of the place.

He nods. "I'm really missing my Kevlar and my M16 right now,
dude. And I want commo in my ear, giving me a play-by-play."

I nod my agreement. In the field, we were always able to commu-
nicate with our Signal Corps, and right now I feel very naked. But
there was a time while I was in the field that I was more alone than I
am right now…so I can deal with it more easily than Drake can.

There's no line at the door, but as we enter the dark establishment
we can see that the place is plenty crowded. There's a girl in a short
black skirt and a skimpy tank top wobbling on thick high heels at
the platform near the door.

Stepping up in front of her, she shoots me a flirty smile. "Well, hi
there. Can I get y'all a table for two? Or do you want to go sit at the
bar?"

She leans over her podium, allowing her breasts to squeeze together and nearly spill over the front of her top. Refraining from
rolling my eyes, I smile at her.

"We have an appointment. Is there someone here named Javier
Chavez?"

The smile disappears from her face, and fear lurks in her eyes as
she nods. "You're supposed to follow me."

She turns and begins walking toward the bar, and we follow suit.
I scan the restaurant as we move, spotting Teague and Shaw perched
on stools at the bar. I don't nod to them, but it's evident they both
notice Drake and me as we walk past them.

Carrying the briefcase at my side, we follow the hostess past the
bar and down a dim, narrow hallway. The walls are dingy and the

carpet beneath our feet is filthy. Rage that Berkeley's been forced to stay in a place like this for an entire twenty-four hours threatens to consume me, but I swallow it down and relax my features.

"Atta boy, Cujo," mutters Drake beside me.

As we file past a closed door with brass letterings reading OFFICE hanging on the front, my legs grind to a halt.

Fuck me. I don't know where it's coming from, but every fiber of my being is telling me that Berkeley is behind that door. I could bust in right now and grab her. My fingers twitch, itching to grab the doorknob and turn.

Drake pauses, turning his head and speaking through clenched teeth. "Don't do it, brother. Let's follow the plan."

"Excuse me?" says the hostess, turning around to stare at us.

"Nothing." I force my feet to keep moving, and my heart to slow its frantic pounding.

Finally, we're led through a back door and out onto the loading dock for the restaurant. Empty pallets and cardboard boxes are strewn about the concrete surface, and the dark blue night sky smiles down on us.

The girl turns around and hurries back into the building, letting the door slam shut behind her. We're left facing a small group of men.

One, obviously the leader, steps forward. His hair is thick and shiny on his head. He's young, maybe early thirties, and he's dressed to the nines with alligator shoes gleaming under the light of the lamp on the wall beside us.

He speaks with a slight accent. "Dare Conners, I presume?"

I nod, my eyes narrowing on him as I take in every single detail of him and our environment as I can.

"Chase couldn't accompany you tonight, Mr. Conners?"

"My brother is no longer a part of this equation, Chavez. You made this very personal to me when you took my girl. Where is she?"

His cold, calculating eyes lighten as he smiles. "Oh, Berkeley? She's inside. An associate of mine will bring her out as soon as I get my money. She's really been a delight, Mr. Conners. That body...a man could get used to —"

"I wouldn't do that, asshole." Drake interrupts Chavez, which is good because I'm starting to shake with anger. Any second, if he kept talking, I was going to have to shut him up.

"I won't be handing over shit, until you show me that she's not harmed."

Chavez studies me closely, my tone telling him I mean what I say, and so he nods to the two men behind him. "First, I want you to show Mr. Conners here why he's not in charge."

One of the men walks over to me, frisking first me, and then Drake. After he's sure we're weaponless, he turns back to Chavez and nods. Then he lifts the hem of his shirt to show us the heat he's packing. The comrade still standing beside Chavez does the same.

"Now that that's settled, you may go and fetch the girl, Montanero."

The man beside Chavez moves, walking past us and disappearing inside the restaurant.

"He'll bring her. Now, let's see what's in that briefcase, shall we?"

My grip tightens on the case, and Drake tenses beside me. I'm sizing up both Chavez and his entourage. He should have brought more men. Even when we aren't armed, Drake and I are lethal.

I smile. "Come and get it."

Just then, the back door opens once more, and my whole world is dragged out.

The breath leaves my body when I see Berkeley. She's rumpled, and she looks exhausted, but otherwise unhurt.

"Dare!" she screams.

The man who has her—Montanero—yanks hard on her arm to pull her over toward Chavez, and I almost lose it right there.

Clenching my teeth tightly, I thrust the briefcase out in front of me.

"Place it on the ground about ten feet away from you." Chavez's voice is almost gleeful as he gives the command.

I glance at Drake, who shrugs. Then I slowly walk forward, depositing the briefcase on the ground. Movement catches my eye in the alleyway beyond where Chavez and Montanero are standing with Berkeley. I purposely avoid letting my gaze wander in that direction.

"There," I say, keeping my voice level. "Your money is all there. Come here, baby."

I gesture to Berkeley, and she yanks herself loose from Montanero's grasp.

"No!" shouts Chavez. Montanero dives to grab ahold of Berkeley again, and her fingers graze mine right before she's jerked back into the asshole's arms.

I can't contain my rage this time. "Get your fucking hands off her. Now. Or you're all dead."

Chavez tsks. "Chase didn't tell me his brother was such a hot-head. Patience, Mr. Conners. I'll just check my money first."

He flicks his wrist toward the goon still standing beside Drake and me, and the man lumbers forward and crouches down in front of the case.

It's at that moment that I can no longer keep Cujo penned. Something tells me, and I just *know*, that Chavez isn't going to turn Berkeley over to me unharmed with no strings attached. I can't let anything happen to her. I won't.

My foot rockets forward and catches the man squarely in the back of the head. As he goes down like a sack of potatoes, both Drake and I lunge forward.

30

Berkeley

D_{are!"}

I didn't mean for my voice to sound so desperately relieved when I screamed it. But at the sight of him, his name just hurtled free, and it was completely out of my control.

I am so happy to see him.

He's going to bring me home. And then I was shoved directly next to the devil-man, Chavez, and a cold shiver ran the length of my body. So this wasn't going to be as easy as falling into Dare's arms and getting the hell out of here.

His face is deadly serious; it's a mask I've never, ever seen on him before. Stupidly, in that moment I remember that I haven't seen him in weeks. And that we aren't together anymore. And that he broke up with me. Maybe he hates me. Maybe he's pissed that he has to rescue me from this psychopath.

And then, as I'm having all of these thoughts, all hell breaks loose.

Dare kicks one of the guys hard in the head. All the background noise drops away, and I hear the *crack*, the sound that his boot makes when it connects with the man's skull. The man goes down, hard.

And then both Drake—Drake?—and Dare are flying toward me and Dare is yelling at me to get on the ground. As I'm dropping, the man with a vise-like grip on my wrist jerks it back, and I can distinctly hear the *snap* amid all the other melee going on.

I scream as a gunshot slices open the night. A heavy weight falls on top of me, and the rest of the sounds are muffled.

It feels like forever when Dare's voice finally reaches me, but he's closer than I expect. He groans as he rolls over and off of me.

The weight covering me was Dare.

"Berkeley, talk to me. Everything okay?"

I wince as I try to move my wrist, and then nod my head. Opening my eyes, I stare up at the velvety sky. "Dare? What happened?"

Sitting up, I look over to my left and see him sitting beside me. He reaches a hand out to cup my face. "Are you sure you're okay?"

I nod. And then my eyes flick down to his chest, and I see the hole in the front of his shirt. "Oh, God…Dare, are you shot?"

He fingers the hole, and then smiles wryly at me. "My vest is shot. But other than a bitch of a bruise, I'll be fine."

I lean back in relief, and my wrist doesn't hold my weight. Crying out, I cradle it against my chest. Dare's eyes cloud over as the hand on my face drops down to support my arm.

"Everybody okay over here?"

I don't recognize the man asking, but Dare calls him Henderson. He tells Henderson that we need an ambulance, and I start to protest.

Dare silences me with a hard look. "Don't, Berkeley. Just let the paramedics take you to the hospital. Your wrist is probably broken. Okay?"

My eyes fill with stupid tears as I nod. Dammit! *Now* I'm crying?

"Oh, baby," murmurs Dare. "I won't leave you. Never again."

We watch as the police crawl over the scene. Chavez and his henchmen are gone. There's yellow crime scene tape going up around us, and uniformed officers are taking the statements of everyone involved. I see Dare nod to two tough-looking guys discussing something with Henderson. They both grin in return.

"Friends of yours?" I ask. I need him to talk to me as a distraction from the pain in my wrist.

He meets my eyes, and I'm home again in his light-green gaze. His stare is intense; it causes butterflies to take flight in my stomach.

He quickly fills me in on what's been happening since I was taken. All I can feel is relief at the fact I have someone like Dare in my life.

"Dare…" I begin. His eyes are aflame. "What?"

"I missed hearing you say my name." *Oh, heaven help me.* "Why did you break up with me?" Against my will, my voice breaks on the last word.

Dare leans forward, and I close my eyes as his fingers tuck a strand of my hair behind my ear.

"I…I heard you. That night at the garden party, when you were inside with your dad. I heard what you said about me being nothing to you." The pain in his eyes breaks my heart again in two clean pieces.

I swallow, and the vision of his face in front of me sways a bit. Well, damn. I wasn't expecting that at all.

"Those were just words to shut the Admiral up, Dare! I swear to you, I meant none of that. You *are* worth it. God, you are so worth it! I haven't spoken to my dad since that night, anyway, and I haven't needed his money. I don't want it. I want *you*. Only you."

I'm crying quietly now. The thought that he heard those words I never even meant is tearing me up from the inside out.

"Please forgive me, Dare. Please come back to me. If you do, I swear I will stand up to my father and tell him exactly where he can shove his money and his opinion of you. I've been going insane without you, Dare. I miss you so much—"

"Stop." He cuts me off, and both hands gently encase my face.

"You didn't mean what you said to him?" he asks. "You promise me you didn't mean that shit?" His fingers are firm on my face, his lips only inches from mine.

"I didn't mean any of it. Dare, I want you with me. So much."

"Oh, baby."

And that's all he gets out before his lips crash into mine.

"Excuse me?"

We break apart, and there's a paramedic standing there smiling amusedly at us. "Are you the girl with the broken wrist?"

A little dazed, I nod. "Yep. That's me."

I can feel his eyes on me as the paramedic gingerly turns my wrist this way and that, and then she declares that it's indeed broken and I need to head to the hospital to have it set.

"Dare will take me," I announce.

He smiles. "Damn straight. I'm not letting you out of my sight anymore."

We're preparing to leave the loading dock when a black-haired woman is led past us in handcuffs.

"Oh, my God." I breathe, and the officer walking with her stops.

"It was you. You came to my apartment, and you...you drugged me! Why? Why'd you do it?"

The petite woman lifts her chin. "I didn't want to hurt you. But Chavez threatened my son. His son. So I did what I had to do."

The officer nudges her, and they continue walking while I stare after her.

Dare is shaking beside me, and I reach out to grasp his hand in my good one.

"It's okay, Dare. She can't hurt me anymore."

He meets my eyes, a determined gleam in his gaze. "No, she can't. And neither can Chavez. He's going back to prison for a long time, Berkeley."

I lean against him as we begin walking toward the front of the building. "I know, Dare. And I have you."

He kisses the top of my head. "Always. You'll always have me."

31

Dare

Berkeley is the proud new owner of a hot pink cast. I laughed so hard I almost choked when she picked out the color. But was I actually surprised?

Hell, no.

Since I still wasn't able to let her out of my sight, we said good-bye to her parents at the hospital. Her mother and father were actually cordial toward me, and the Admiral shook my hand and told me he'd be proud to have me in Berkeley's life.

I feel like I'm living in an alternate universe right now.

Mea and Greta greet us at the door of the apartment, and both girls sweep Berkeley up into a gentle hug, cautious of her arm.

"I was so scared, Berk-baby!" Mea's tearful gaze is locked on her friend. "Are you okay?"

Berkeley holds up her casted wrist. "Other than this, I'm good you guys. Thanks for worrying about me. Dare was my hero."

Greta cheers. "Yay for Dare!"

I smirk and sit down on the couch, watching their reunion. "It was nothing."

"So, what now?" asks Greta. "What happened to the people who took you?"

Berkeley sighs, sinking down next to me on the couch. I put a reassuring arm around her shoulder. "They were arrested. I'm sure it will be a long road, but I'll cooperate with their prosecution as much as I can. And that's all I can do."

I'm still so fucking angry that she has to deal with any of this. I'm going to eventually have to sit down with Chase and have it all out. I'm trying not to feel resentful of him for bringing Chavez into Berkeley's world, but it's hard. Really damn hard.

Thinking about Chase is souring my mood, and I excuse myself to go in the bathroom and rinse my face.

Sitting on Berkeley's bed a few minutes later, my heartbeat begins to race. We haven't talked about what we expect from each other, now that we're back in each other's orbit. I'm not sure how far to push things with her tonight, and I don't have to push them at all if she's not ready. I just want her in my arms, where I know she's safe.

I'm leaning back on my elbows, just waiting for Berkeley, when the door opens and my girl is standing there to greet me.

I just sit still, drinking her up with thirsty eyes. She's wearing a long, ribbed tank top that stretches snugly over her breasts and tight, gray leggings. Her hair is exactly the way I like it best, wild and loose, like it's attempting a grand getaway. I notice now that it's a little lighter than the last time I saw her. Must be the summer sun adding those bleached streaks. She's staring right back at me, a slow fire burning in her eyes that's been lit just for me.

Fuck. Me. Slowly.

"Dare." It's a whispered statement full of so much meaning that my throat instantly clogs. I open my mouth to respond, but I don't have time to get the words out before she rocket-launches herself into my arms.

I rise to catch her and hold on tight, because whether I want to admit it to myself or not, I *need* this girl. I need every part of her to collide with every part of me right now, and then I need to put it on repeat. Her beautiful scent washes over me, and I'm completely lost, or I'm completely found again.

"Hey, baby," I whisper into her ear, and her whole body lifts and falls in a sigh that reverberates deep in my soul.

She's wrapped completely around me, legs circling my waist and arms clasped around my neck, so I shuffle backward against the bed. The feeling of her body fused to mine this way is something I'm probably going to patent, so I'll never lose it again.

I feel a searing kiss as her lips burn into my skin. My knees buckle slightly, but I manage to back up until my legs hit the bed and I collapse onto it with Berkley sitting astride me.

We stare into each other's eyes, not saying a word.

Finally, I can't take it anymore. I need those plump lips to be touching mine. I know that there's talking to be done, but I'm reading every word she's writing with her eyes, and right now we both agree that we can save that shit for later.

Keeping her gaze locked in mine, I reach out and grasp the wisp of hair I love, that hangs over one eye, between my fingers, tucking it behind her ear.

Then, moving as slowly as I can, I lean forward to take her lips.

Heat surges between us instantly, a heat that's always been there but we've never fully explored. Our tongues tangle furiously, her hands are up and buried in my hair and I groan my pleasure into her ready and willing mouth.

Damn. I thought that having her limber limbs wrapped around me like she'd never let go was my new favorite state of being, but now I know that having her lips fused to mine, her tongue teasing the inside of my mouth, is something I can't ever give up again.

I want—no, I *need*—to feel her skin against mine. In the next second, I'm yanking the pink tank up and over her head. She raises her arms to oblige me, then returns her lips to mine and her hands cup my face. The tenderness in her touch makes my chest hurt. It also sends my dick into overdrive, and I push my hips against hers. She moans into my mouth, and I allow my hands to roam freely over her skin.

Running my palms up her bare back, I bring them up to her shoulders, sliding my fingers under the straps of her white, lacy bra. I slowly slide them down her shoulders and leave her mouth to trail kisses down the side of her neck. She tilts it to give me better access, and I gladly take it, sucking my way to the crook of her shoulder. Now it's her turn to rock her hips against my growing erection, and I *groan.*

Gingerly, I flip her so that she's flat on her back in the middle of the bed. I pull the cotton fabric over my head and my shirt disappears, landing somewhere unseen on her bedroom floor. I stalk her as she leans back on her elbows, smiling coyly at me.

"You know exactly what you do to me, don't you?"

Her dimples appear as she feigns confusion. I kiss the wrinkles created by her raised brows, and she giggles.

Giggles.

"That's funny?" I whisper as I lean forward. Her giggle stops abruptly, turning to a gasp as my teeth graze the fabric covering one perfectly round breast. Her nipples are quickly hardening through the fabric, forming two delicious peaks there for the taking.

She drops her head back as her hips move restlessly underneath me. "No, not funny."

"No," I agree. "It's not funny." I reach around her to unclasp the barrier between us, and the bra falls away. I toss it aside and pull one nipple fully into my mouth, sucking hard.

Holy mother...she tastes like every kind of fruity, succulent candy I wasn't allowed to eat as a kid. And the way her body jerks under mine, just because of how my tongue caresses her...it's enough to send me spinning toward the edge of pleasure.

Rearing back, I reach down to the waistband of her leggings and tug. I tug, and with each pull of the fabric I lay a chaste kiss on another exposed patch of her silky skin. When her pants are tossed in a heap on the floor, I go back to make quick—and I mean really fucking quick—work of her panties.

Now every single dream a man can possibly have is coming to life, right in front of me. Berkeley is completely bared to me, lying back on her bed like the sexy vixen she's always been, her eyes dark and smoldering, her hair wild and free. And she's looking at me like...like she wants me.

Something somewhere deep inside me speaks then, telling me that I want to open up to this girl in a way I've never opened up before. I never even told the VA therapists everything that happened in Africa. Not everything. But for this girl? For this girl I want to pour out my soul right in front of her and lay it on a platter. Just for her.

I love this girl.

32

Berkeley

$D$are's lips are scorching me. His fingers are lighting me on fire. His words are turning my insides to molten lava. His eyes are leaving me breathless, electrified.

My senses are all tangled up, and every time I try to catch my frenzied breath, I just breathe him in even deeper. He's completely consuming me, and I freaking *love it.*

As his burning lips travel south, tracing a fiery line along the side of my belly, I arch up toward him, wanting more. More of him. More of this. More of us. But instead, I blurt out something that I haven't forgotten, something I can't forget even right now at this pivotal moment.

"Secrets," I gasp.

He stills, frozen above me. He looks up, his clear, bewitching eyes meeting mine, his lips still touching my hip bone. Keeping me locked in his gaze, he drops one more soft kiss on my burning skin and then departs, moving up adjacent to me until he's lying on his side right beside me.

He trails light fingers between my breasts, down to my belly, back and forth, and I shiver in response. Damn my fucking mouth.

"I'm sorry." A lump forms in my throat, because I think I've ruined the moment.

No, I'm pretty *sure* I've ruined the moment. Maybe the night. My life?

"Don't," he says quietly. "Don't apologize. You deserve to know me. All of me. Before we…before this happens."

"You're not mad?"

He sighs. Then he pushes himself up in one fluid movement until he's hovering over me once again. His eyes hold that familiar, intense expression that is so totally Dare, and his dark chocolate hair falls over his forehead and around his face. It's a little longer since the last time I saw him, I realize suddenly. It's curling toward the bottom of his neck.

"Understand me right now, Berkeley. I am not mad at you. I'm worked up right now because you're lying in a naked heap underneath me and my body is screaming at me to take you. I want to worship you with my lips. I want to fucking devour you right now. Because, whether you know it or not, you already own me in every way that means shit. But I'm not mad. I'm just ridiculously hot for you."

Heat pools in the very center of me and speeds to the throbbing spot between my thighs. He can do that to me with *words alone*. I seriously can't decide if this man is angel or devil.

Feebly, I nod as I squirm a little under his hard body. So hard.

He rolls off of me again, returning to his spot beside me.

And then Dare tells me his story.

"I enlisted in the army when I was eighteen. I'd been shuffled throughout foster homes for years, and none of them were good. I saw way more pain than any kid should have to see, and I was empty inside because of it. I barely graduated high school because of all the days I missed. Some days I just didn't go, others I was suspended for fighting. I was an angry kid, Berkeley, and there wasn't any hope for me.

"I was damn lucky the army found me. I talked to a recruiter one day at a mall, and that was all I needed. When I enlisted and started out in infantry, I learned a discipline I never had in my life before then. I learned how to answer to somebody, and I learned how to trust other people. I had to trust the guys in my unit because all of our lives depended on it. For the first time in my life, I began to thrive.

"I was good at this job. I was strong. I loved the workouts and the training that went along with being a soldier. I rose through the ranks pretty quickly, because I deposited everything I had into it. I had nothing else, no one else. Army was my life. I lived it and breathed it. I loved it.

"When I made Ranger, I was stoked. I relished the opportunity to plunge into enemy territory with my brothers, scoping dangerous places out for our Airborne friends to demolish, or for our marine friends to storm. It was what I was good at. I could plan and execute better than anyone else."

He pauses, his fingers still trailing along my belly, and looks up into my face. I'm riveted by his story, but one hand is stroking his hair as I stare back. I'm holding my breath, waiting for the rest of his tale.

He bends and softly kisses my shoulder before he continues. "One night, we're on a mission to clear an airfield in the C.A.R. That's the Central African Republic. Rebel forces in the country used this particular airfield to distribute illegal weapons throughout the nation. It was our job to go in, make sure the place was clear for our other forces to land and take over.

"It was pretty routine. We dropped in from the air, which we'd all done a hundred times before. But somehow, there were rebels waiting for us when we arrived, and an ambush ensued."

His body begins to tremble slightly, as if he's sitting outside without a coat in the dead of winter. I run my hands through his hair, over the side of his body, and caress his face, trying to comfort him. But he's telling his story now as if he's somewhere far, far away. Maybe he's still in that hellhole he's describing. Snaking fingers of dread are beginning to climb up my spine.

"It's pitch-black out there. My buddies are screaming instructions around me, trying to get the upper hand on the situation. I'm holding my sidearm, but my night vision is busted and I can't see well enough to know whether I'm shooting friendly or enemy. So I don't shoot. I can't.

"Then my guys' voices weren't screaming orders anymore, they were just screaming. And something exploded around us. After that I couldn't hear anything but the ringing in my ears. Everything else went quiet. Something hot sliced through the side of my fatigues, right here." He runs a hand along his left side, where I know his scar lies.

There's a thin sheen of sweat covering his exposed skin. I can feel his growing agitation, but don't know what to do to calm him. So I just keep my hands on him, continuing to run them across his bare skin.

I place my hand directly over his sternum and squeeze my eyes shut when I feel how his heart is racing beneath my hand.

My Daredevil isn't scared of anything.

But it seems he's very, very afraid of this memory.

"You can stop if you want to, Dare." My whisper is scratchy and urgent. I don't want him to feel like this. "You don't have to tell me."

He grunts, giving a quick shake of his head.

"I want you to know," he whispers raggedly. "I just want to get this out there between us. Because if you don't know all of me, of what I've done to be here with you right now…then you don't know me at all."

I nod, and hot tears spring to my eyes.

"Okay, Dare. Tell me. I'm right here, and I'm not going anywhere."

He sucks in a shuddering breath before he continues.

"When I woke up, I was somewhere stifling hot, and dark. I was on the floor, but my hands were chained above my head, cuffed at the wrists. My left side felt like it was on fire, and when I looked down I almost lost it. My side was sliced open, and there was a bandage covering it that was soaked in blood. I was woozy, I was aching. I knew right away that I wasn't going to make it. Not imprisoned the way I was. I just started praying, and I'd never done that before."

The tears spill over, cascading down my cheeks. I love this man. I truly do, and everything he's telling me is just making my love grow. The fact that he's been through something like this is breaking me apart. I've only ever seen Dare as this strong, confident guy. The guy who makes me laugh. The guy who sweeps me off my feet. The guy who's made me fall in love with him. The little boy who endured so much heartache and pain is somehow a dark part of who makes him the man he is today. But this? This is something else altogether.

"I kept phasing in and out of consciousness, and I have no idea how much time passed. But after a while, the rebels came into the room in the hut where they were keeping me. I couldn't understand what they were saying. There were three of them. They were just screaming at me. I couldn't answer them. Finally, they got so pissed that they knocked me unconscious with the butt of one of their rifles."

I jerk involuntarily. He strokes my hair again, trying to calm me. *He's* trying to calm *me*?

"Eventually, one of their leaders came in to talk to me. He was...a monster. The coldest man I've ever been in contact with, ever. He just sat across from me and stared for a long time. And then he would ask me a question in English. He'd ask about our military forces, about strategies that we used, about our plans for their rebel forces."

He looks down at me, and his pupils are so wide they're swallowing his irises. It's a vast difference from the normally light green they usually are. It's startling. "And every time I refused to answer, he would hurt me."

He must have read the look of horror on my face, because he shook his head. "It was always something minimal. He would break bones in my fingers or cut me somewhere on my body. Once time he broke my jaw. I've had so many surgeries to fix everything broken, I've lost count."

The last remark is wry, and his lips twist in a humorless smile. "I never told him a damn thing."

Finally, I can't contain myself anymore. "Dare...how long did they keep you there?"

He sits up, agitatedly running his hands through his hair and sighing. It takes him a long moment before he answers me.

Finally, he replies, "They intended to keep me there until they killed me, Berkeley. But I escaped before they had the chance."

My mouth goes slack. I sit up beside him, and he leans back against the ivory upholstered headboard of my queen-size bed. "You escaped?"

He nods, weary now. "It was an act of God. I can't call it anything else. I should have died there in that hut. Hell, I should have died at the airfield like the rest of my guys. They uncuffed me when they tortured me. It was after one of our interview sessions that I was lying on the ground, beaten and broken...so they thought. I slipped into an unconscious state, and I guess they just left me that way because they thought that if I wasn't dead, I was close enough to it that I wouldn't be able to move, even if I did wake up. I shouldn't have been able to. But when I woke, I realized that I wasn't chained. My body was heavy and in really horrible pain, and I was bleeding from a head wound. My ribs were cracked. But somehow, I got to my feet. I could hobble pretty well, and that's what I did. They were gone. Must have been doing a raid on women and children."

He sounds bitter, angry. And rightfully so. I can't believe what he's telling me is true. He should be wearing so many medals of valor he can barely stand up from the weight of them all. He should be commanding some humongous unit of men, even helping command a base. What the hell happened when he got back?

"As soon as I left my prison, I realized I wasn't alone after all. They'd left a guard just outside the hut. Just one guy."

He takes a deep, shuddering breath, and looks me straight in the eye. His gaze is tortured. I gulp, terrified of what he's about to tell me.

"It was my only chance to escape, Berkeley, and I wasn't losing it. He wasn't expecting to see me there. I caught him by surprise, and...I killed him." His eyes close briefly, and when he opens them again I see the bleak emotion filling them up. "I killed him with my bare hands."

Tears stream silently down my face, and I can feel my body going numb as I listen to the rest of his story.

"It took me days of just surviving in the jungle to make it to the nearest village. I dragged myself forward, I ate what I could find, I drank rainwater. When I finally crossed into that village, into safety, I fucking cried. And then I passed out."

I can't take my eyes off of him. "What happened? They contacted the army?"

He nods. "They did, with a short-wave radio. And the PJs were there within hours. I was a mess. I was in the hospital for a month after that. But when I finally got out, I wanted to go back to duty. I had to go through all the standard testing for that. Physical and emotional. I was cleared emotionally, somehow. But physically...I was done. I couldn't serve anymore, unless I wanted to be behind a desk. I'm not a desk kind of guy. So I took the discharge."

My eyes widen in disbelief. I know, I can hear by the way he talks about his time serving, that he loved it. That it is in his blood and he's made to protect people. My heart cracks for him, right there on my bed.

"I'm so sorry, Dare. I don't even know what to say. The fact that you survived something like that...no wonder you still have nightmares. I hate that it even happened to you. I hate you can't do what you love anymore. I hate—"

"Berkeley." He interrupts me, his voice so quiet I have to lean toward his face. "Did you miss the part where I just told you I killed someone with my bare hands?"

I shake my head quickly. "Do you think I'd judge you for that? My God, Dare. You're a soldier. It was your life, or his. I would never—"

He stops me with his lips. They're upon mine, and it's...different. It's tender, more loving than any kiss Dare has ever given me. His lips devour mine, as usual, but in a slow, agonizing way. When he pulls back, his eyes are fierce.

"Thank you," he says.

My head is spinning, and I grip his shoulders to keep myself upright. He pulls me astride him, into his lap. We face each other, staring. "For being Berkeley. The only person on the planet that I could share that with in detail. I'll never tell you about everything that happened to me in that hut. But the fact that I could share that story at all...it's everything, Berkeley. It's *everything*."

I reach up, tangling my fingers in his hair and pulling him toward me. My voice is just as fierce as his expression. "That part of you? The part of you who fought against the odds of being a product of the foster care system? The you who clawed your way back from hell out there in the jungle? The part of you that did whatever you had to do in every dangerous situation you've ever been in? I love that part of you just as much as all the other softer, sweeter parts, Dare. I love you for every facet you have. To me, *you're* everything."

He stares at me, eyes wide. I realize belatedly that this is the first time I've ever told him I love him. His face changes with a myriad of emotions. Finally, he settles on deep, hungry desire. My body turns liquid, just waiting for him to strike.

He does. He grabs my face and melds his lips to mine. The gentle caresses of his lips and tongue from a moment ago are gone, and my fierce, ferocious soldier is back. He kisses me like he wants a piece of me.

And God, I hope that he does.

33

Dare

Thank God the girl's already naked, because with the way I'm feeling, her clothes would have been ripped to shreds. I need her under me, and I need it *now*.

She loves me. I know how I feel about her, and I know how I hoped she felt about me. But now I know.

She fucking loves me.

I try, and fail, to remember the last time anyone uttered those words to me. It hasn't happened since I lost my parents. So many families I belonged to since then. No one ever, ever loved me. I didn't realize how starved I was for it until that very moment.

When those words fell out of her mouth, she put a cast on all the pieces of me that were broken. She healed me in ways the doctors never could.

Now I'm starved in a whole new, dangerous way. I'm starved for her.

My body is reacting of its own accord. All of her naked, smooth skin slides underneath me as I lean over her. Her soft curves, so sensual and hot, curl around me in exactly the right places. I couldn't have fantasized this better, and I fantasize about naked Berkeley a whole hell of a lot.

She whimpers as my hand grips her good wrist and holds it above her head. I don't want the distraction of her hands right now. I just want to appreciate this goddess-like body that's been placed in front of me on a platter.

I trail my lips down her neck, forging a moist trail down until I reach the round curve of her breast. Remembering the feel of it in my mouth a while ago, I reinvest in this activity full-force. Her answering cry of encouragement is like the universal thumbs-up letting me know that what I'm doing is invariably awesome.

"Baby, if you're going to stop me…now's the time to do it," I growl. Shit, I don't mean to sound so gruff, but I really don't want her to ask me to stop. I actually might cease breathing if she does.

"Don't stop." She breathes. "Like, ever."

I grin against her sweet skin as my hand strokes her stomach.

Berkeley's body is something men like Homer and Virgil wrote about ages ago. It's not like any other girl's I've dated. She respects it in a way that I've never seen. She doesn't starve it; she doesn't abuse it. She takes pride in it and refuses to hide it. It's elegant and erotic at the same time, with all her soft, plump curves and lean, strong limbs. I'll gladly worship this body, as often as she'll let me. It's the kind of body men *really* want to see in magazines, and yet she's here lying naked in this bed with me.

My hand reaches the junction between her thighs, and the skin there is stripped bare. I almost convulse right there, and I'm really regretting the fact that I'm still wearing my jeans.

Bare.

My finger easily finds the sweetest spot on her body, and as I draw tiny circles she begins to unravel beneath me.

Holy fuck, she's beautiful. She's writhing and tugging her hand, trying to yank it away from my pinning hold. I lean over and whisper in her ear. "Tell me, Berkeley. Tell me what this does to you."

Her eyes slowly open, dark and wanting, sending an intense need straight to my manhood. I fight the urge to reach down and adjust everything that's going on down there.

"It's…it's driving me insane," she whispers. "Your touch, Dare…it's freaking, God, it's gonna…"

Ah, there it is. My Berkeley's nothing if not vocal. I circle my finger a little bit faster, watching her face closely as her lips part and a moan escapes. Fuck, just watching her is going to make me lose it. "It's gonna what?"

She squirms as I draw my finger through her wetness and back to stroke her most tender spot once more. Her legs wrap around my waist, clenching in a death grip I think leaves dents in my sides. "Oh, God, Dare…please!"

I don't want her to beg. She doesn't have to. I'm right the fuck here. I move away from her to stand, and she groans softly.

"Don't, baby. Look at me." She responds to my order and looks up, watching me as I unclasp the button on my jeans and pull them down. The wrinkle in her forehead appears as she bites her lip, and I step out of my boxer briefs. Reaching down to my jeans, I grab a square foil packet and tear it open. Holding it up to her, I raise a brow.

"This?"

She nods emphatically. "That, and then *you*."

I roll on the hardware and then take my place on top of her once more. Spreading her legs wider with my knee, she gladly opens them for me and we're closer than we've ever been before. Closer than I've ever been to anyone, because it's so much more than just my body that's involved here.

She reaches down and grasps the length of me, running her hand down my shaft and back up again. I freeze, closing my eyes and trying desperately to control my urge to slip inside her and just start thrusting wildly.

I take my hand and run it across her cheek, staring into her eyes with the now-familiar ardor I always feel when I look at Berkeley. "Let's take this slow, okay? I want this to be perfect for you."

"It's already perfect for me," she whispers as her fingers take root in my hair. I fucking love it when her hands are in my hair. I close my eyes and she guides me toward her. I can feel her before I get there, she's hot and ready. "It's been perfect for me since that first night on the beach, Dare. We don't have to take it slow, I just want you. I want my no-holds-barred soldier. Nothing less."

Growling, I rock my hips into her and she cries out from the force of the impact. It's...*Jesus*.

It's bliss.

I can't take it slow if I tried, now that I've started. I pull back out and then thrust back inside of her with abandon. My mind travels to a place where it's only me and my sexy, evil vixen siren. Acute ripples of pleasure pulsed through my entire body, focusing on the very center of me, at the place where our bodies are joined together. It's unrivaled; nothing I've ever experienced can ever compare to this. Nothing I ever experience from this point forward *will* ever compare to this. Being inside of Berkeley is the key to what I've been searching for since my parents died.

I'm home.

She cries out beneath me. "Dare!"

The way her body is arching beneath mine, the way her muscles are clenching and unclenching around me, I know she's close and I want more than anything to push her over the edge and watch her break in my hands before I follow her into the abyss. I pull out slowly, agonizingly slowly, and reach a hand down between us.

"Berkeley." My voice is rough, strained with all of the heat and passion she's stirred up inside of me. "Let me see you, baby."

She lifts hooded eyes to mine, and I use a finger to circle her once more. God, she's soaking wet and pulsing gently beneath my finger. Oh, God, I can't hold out.

As if in answer to my silent thought, she stiffens, her whole body quivering with impending release.

I circle my finger faster and keep my gaze focused on her beautiful face. Her lips part as she screams my name. "Let go, Berkeley. I protect what's mine, remember? Let go for me, honey."

"Dare!" she screams, and her body relaxes. Her chest heaves as she stares up at me.

"I love you," she whispers.

I'm not a fucking superhero. With those words, I can't hold on any longer. I bury my face in her sweet-smelling neck, bathed in the scent of roses, and groan into her skin. My release overcomes me, and I think I actually black out for a few seconds. When I come to, soft fingers are trailing along my back, my side where my scar usually lies hidden, and my neck.

Once again, I have the immensely comforting thought that I've finally made it home.

"I love you, too," I whisper against her skin.

* * *

I wake up to the sunlight streaming in through Berkeley's window. The gauzy curtains on either side of the opening do little to suppress the light, and I groan before reaching out for her. I instantly remember every single detail about the previous night, and I want her close to my side.

When I realize she's already lying on her side, I open my eyes and find her amber ones burning into mine.

"Hey." I smile sleepily. "You're staring at me. Did you write on my face?"

"No." She giggles. "Your face first thing in the morning is something I thought I'd never get to see again. So, yeah, I'm staring. Can't blame a girl."

I pull her closer. "I'm not going anywhere, ever again. So you can stare all you want."

She nods. I see the hesitation in her eyes, and I reach out to smooth the wrinkle on her forehead.

"What?"

"You didn't have a nightmare?"

Oh. Huh. "Uh, I guess not. The last thing I thought about before I fell asleep was about how I finally made it home. Meaning, you. You're my home."

Her lips turn up in a smile that brings her dimples front and center. Every soft part I have inside melts at the sight of that smile. She's reduced me to sappy-ass inner monologues. It gets better and better.

She snuggles into my side. "I'm glad you're back. I don't care what my parents say. I don't care what anyone says, Dare. I want you, and I'll fight for us if I have to."

"Me, too." I kiss the top of her wild, curly head. "You just made it to the very tip-top of my list of Top Five mornings ever."

She laughs. "I still want to hear that list."

"I bet you do. Breakfast?"

"Oh, Dare," she says breezily. "You'll learn. I *always* want breakfast."

I smile at the repetition of the phrase she used the first time she spent the night with me.

She jumps out of bed and heads for her bedroom door. I almost choke at the sight of her. Her bare ass waves at me as she walks.

"Get dressed, Berkeley," I growl.

She looks back and smirks. She heads back toward her closet. "Gotcha."

There's nothing shameful about this walk. When I enter the living room a few minutes after Berkeley, the gigantic grin on my face fades when I get a look at Grisham sitting on the couch, a mug of steaming coffee in his hands. He looks perfectly comfortable.

Here, in my girl's apartment on a Sunday morning at around—I check my cell phone—9:00 a.m.

What the fuck is he doing here on a Sunday morning at 9:00 a.m.?

"Good morning, Dare," says Mea. She's bright and chipper in the mornings, but I think that's her normal state of being. "Coffee?"

I nod. "Please."

Grisham keeps his eyes locked on me, a slight frown etched in his features. I don't see Berkeley.

"She went out to grab some breakfast," explains Mea. "We didn't have any eggs in the house."

Shit. I wish she'd let me go with her. After her kidnapping and being with her last night, I'm a changed man. I don't want to let her out of my sight.

I sit on the couch next to Grisham, wondering how to best pose my question. *"What the fuck are you doing here?"* seems rude.

Mea perches on the edge of a barstool, eyeing us warily, like she's waiting for an explosion to erupt. She might not have to wait long.

I focus on Grisham, whose expression is calm. But I can see that under the surface of that placid expression, anger is simmering just below.

"You want to know why I'm here?" he asks quietly, his jaw clenched.

Leaning back against the cushions and propping my right foot over my left knee, I stare at him.

He leans forward and sets his mug down on the dark wood coffee table. Just as he's sitting back, Greta emerges into the kitchen. She stops cold when she sees the two of us sitting on the couch. Assessing us, she continues her trajectory into the kitchen, raising her eyebrows at Mea speculatively.

"Everything okay?" She keeps her tone casual, but her gaze is locked on the two of us while she pours herself some coffee.

I nod, trying to put the girls at ease. "Fine. I'm just waiting for Grisham here to tell me what he's doing in my girlfriend's apartment at nine in the morning on a Sunday, that's all."

My voice is light, with an edge that lets Grisham know I want the answer, and I want it now.

"I'm here because I've been here every single day you haven't." The anger in his voice is palpable now, traveling around the room like a comet that won't be slowing down anytime soon.

Feeling like I've been punched in the gut, I wince. Mea's eyes are suddenly downcast, and Greta clears her throat loudly.

"You weren't here two days ago," I shoot back. "You know, when she was kidnapped? Where were you then?"

I can see the same injured look on his face that I probably just had on mine. Taking a deep breath, he continues.

"And since when is Berkeley your girlfriend? Didn't you just dump her and run last month? What the hell are you doing, man?"

The hostility in his voice is muted, but the dude is clearly pissed. I take a deep breath, because shit…he's got a point.

I haven't been here.

And it was entirely my own fault that I wasn't here. The fact that he has been…it stings. I allow my mind to wander back to the fact that maybe he hasn't just been here as Berkeley's friend. But then her voice telling me she loves me echoes through my head, and every jealous thought I have is stamped out.

"Look," I begin. I see both Mea and Greta subtly lean forward, because they want to hear what I have to say just as much as Grisham does.

"I fucked up. I left before I had the whole story, but in my defense I thought Berkeley was just screwing with my head. I fell in love with that girl a long time ago, and it hurt to think she didn't return those feelings."

Grisham's brows arch toward the ceiling and he barks out a laugh. He runs a hand through his hair and rolls his eyes. Everything about his body language says he doesn't believe a word out of my mouth.

"But everything is different now." Berkeley shuts the front door behind her as she enters the living room, carrying a grocery bag.

Grisham and I both stand, but I reach her first and grab the bags from her hand. I carry them into the kitchen while she turns and faces Grisham.

"He explained everything, Grish. He overheard something really awful I said about us to my dad. It was my fault."

"Berkeley—" I break in. I don't want her blaming herself. That's not what this is supposed to be about. I never should have walked away without talking to her first.

She walks toward him and reaches up, placing her hands on his shoulders. I stiffen, staring at them from my spot in the kitchen. Greta reaches over and pats my shoulder reassuringly, but my eyes are riveted on Berkeley and Grisham.

"Thank you for being here for me. You always have been, and I will always be here for you, too. Trust my decision here, Grisham. Dare is the guy I always thought he was. Oh, and also? He saved my life yesterday."

He sighs, looking down into her eyes. The defeat on his face is clear. "You sure?"

She nods.

His frown turns into a genuine grin. "You sure you don't want to surf on it?"

Now it's my turn to frown. I thought she didn't like surfing.

She turns to me immediately, once again seeming to read the thoughts floating silently through my head.

"I've picked up surfing over the past month or so," she admits with a smile. "It's been helping me…clear my head."

Huh. Surfing? With Grisham. *Will she surf one day with me?* The thought fills me with heat, imagining her sexy body filling out a wet suit and standing up on a surfboard.

"We'll go sometime," she assures me.

The smile I send her hurts my face. I walk over to stand beside them, wrapping an arm tightly around Berkeley's waist. I hold out a hand, hoping Grisham will accept it for what it is. An apology for hurting her.

"We good?" I ask.

He eyes my hand, and then reluctantly grabs my palm and shakes it. I nod at him.

"I swear to you, I will take care of her. It's my new life's mission."

He looks me straight in the eye, his light blue locking on my light green, and says, "It better be. And thank you for getting her back."

"Good," says Berkeley. "Grish, you staying for breakfast?"

He shakes his head. "That's okay."

Greta walks around the island and into the living room. "Come on, Grisham. You gotta be hungry. Just stay and eat."

He swipes a hand across his forehead, glancing over at her. Something changes in his eyes as he takes her in. I follow his gaze and note that Greta is wearing what, apparently, she sleeps in. Tiny, and when I say tiny, I mean the material can barely count as an article of clothing, shorts and a thin black tank top. Miles of creamy skin are on display for Grisham's apparent viewing pleasure. And I can tell by his darkening eyes and vacant expression that he is definitely enjoying the view.

As Berkeley heads into the kitchen with Mea to begin preparing a major breakfast, I settle onto a barstool and try like hell to keep the gigantic grin off my face.

Everything is right in my world. Chavez is gone from both mine and Chase's lives. I have Berkeley back. And I'm never letting her go again.

34

Berkeley

The same day that Grisham and Dare found common ground, Dare and I are sitting on the couch, with me in his lap. He hasn't let me more than five feet away from him all morning, and I'm secretly loving it. I don't want to be farther than five feet away from him, either, and I think he knows it. He rubs a firm hand up and down my arm reassuringly as I lay my head against his chest. I want to feel his heart beating. The strong, steady thump reassures me, because I'm a pathetic, love-drunk idiot.

"So, what are you going to do about Chase?"

Dare hasn't said it, but I know he blames his brother for what happened. I don't want them to be at odds because of me. That's the last thing I want for Dare.

He looks down with a sigh. "I'm not really sure. I need to talk to him, I know that. Want to come with me to my house?"

He's happy. I can hear it emanating from his voice, can feel it rolling off of him in waves. I smile a small, secret smile, blissed out that I have something to do with his joy.

Shaking my head, I rub my nose against his. "I think you should go talk to him on your own. I've got some design ideas I need to sketch out for a new client I'm seeing this week, anyway. Want to meet back up this evening? Maybe we can all go to dinner together?"

He frowns, staring at me. "I don't really want to leave you here alone."

I slap his chest playfully. "What, like I need a chaperone at all times? I'll be fine."

He stares, doubt evident in his eyes.

"Dare, listen…nothing happened between me and Grisham while we weren't together. You know that, right? He's been an awesome friend to me and nothing more. He hasn't even tried to be anything more."

He nods slowly, and I can see that he believes it's true. He still looks troubled, though. "I trust you, Berkeley. And if you had…well, I couldn't be mad about it." His thick brow furrows. "I just…I don't know…want you with me."

He bends his head and kisses me, softly and slowly. I melt into the kiss, returning it with every ounce of love I feel for him. When we pull apart, his eyes are glittering dangerously. "I don't have to go."

Oh, no. "Yes, you do!" I hop off his lap and stand, scooting away so he can't grab me again. "Go. I'll be here. Text me what time I should be ready for dinner."

"I'll be back before dinner, Berkeley. I'm not staying away all day." He moves toward the door.

It's a little past noon now. "Don't rush on my account. I love you."

He throws me a sexy, toe-curling smile before he walks out the front door. "Love you, Berkeley."

Grinning, I retrieve my laptop and some fabric samples from my bedroom and settle on the couch to work. I'm thankful my dominant hand is still functional. Mea and Greta are having a day out at the beach, but I text Mea and let her know about the dinner plan for later, in case they want to join us. She lets me know that they'll be home well before dinner so that we can get ready together, and I'm suddenly very excited about tonight. I miss Dare already, and he's been gone less than an hour. The thought brings an embarrassed smile to my face. I can feel the flush forming, and I know it's because I'm being so ridiculous. But that's what happens to a girl in love, right?

As soon as I begin to sketch, the front door opens and Mea strolls in.

"Hey," I say, my tone surprised. "I thought you were beaching it today."

Mea smiles. "I was, but then your boyfriend texted me."

Groaning, I push my sketch pad aside and stretch. "Oh, man! Sorry, Mea. I don't need a babysitter."

Mea plops down beside me. "Until further notice, I think you do. I mean, who gets kidnapped, Berk?"

We both crack up, because it's crazy and we both know it.

"Only me," I croak, gasping for breath.

Mea's expression turns serious. "I'm so sorry I wasn't here with you when it happened."

I wave off her apology. "That's ridiculous. They would have gotten me eventually. Chavez was insane. He wanted to have me so he could get to Chase and Dare. There was nothing you could have done."

"Did he…hurt you?" Mea's voice is hesitant.

Shaking my head, I shudder. "No, thank God. He was a monster, but he didn't lay a hand on me. It was all about the money."

Nodding, she wraps an arm around me. "We've been friends for a long time, Berk. I would have been lost if anything happened to you."

I know how she feels. Even though Mea and I had time apart while I was away at school, she was always in my heart and in my thoughts. Whenever I needed rescuing in my life, she was there for me. She knew how I felt about my parents, and the way they planned my life out for me, and she backed me up wherever and whenever she could. I can never thank her enough for that.

"Ditto," I say simply.

35

Dare

Chase isn't at the beach house when I get there, so Drake and I open a beer together while I wait.

"How's Berkeley?" asks Drake as he takes a sip.

"She's doing okay, considering. Her wrist is broken, but her spirits are up and I think she'll be fine." The relief is evident in my voice.

"You two back together?"

Grinning, I nod again. "Yup."

He returns my grin tenfold. "I'm happy for you, brother."

I'm happy for me, too. "Thanks, man. You want to come with us to dinner tonight?"

He props his feet up on the coffee table and grabs the remote. "Who else is going?"

"Just me and Berkeley, maybe Chase, and I'm sure Berkeley will invite her roommates."

Drake frowns, a dark look crossing his face. I have to ask.

"Okay, what's up with you and Mea? Every time I mention her you look like you swallowed something sour. And when you two are together you act like you've been fighting the same battle for years. What gives?"

He shakes his head. "I don't know what you're talking about. I'm cool with Mea. Just don't know if I feel like hanging out tonight. What, you'll miss me if I don't come?"

He scoots closer and puts his arm over my shoulder, which lets me know he's avoiding the subject. He always shoves me off him when I tease like that. I frown at him. "Yeah, right. You're coming."

Rolling his eyes, he scoots back over and flips through the channels until he reaches ESPN. "Yes, sir." He salutes.

"That's more like it. Why don't we make that a regular thing? You can call me sir every time I give an order, and then follow it."

He shoves me, and I go slamming into the other side of the couch. "Not on your life."

The front door swings open and Chase walks in. He pauses when he sees me, and then walks into the room.

"Hey," he says.

Standing, I gesture toward the back of the house. "Let's go out back."

We walk to the deck and have a seat. Neither of us speaks for a few minutes, just listening to the sound of ocean crashing against sand.

"Chase—"

"I'm not staying, Dare."

We speak at the same time, and then we both pause and look at each other.

"You're leaving?" I finally ask.

"Yeah. I want to go check on Shay. I've got to give it a shot with her. I also...I need to get out of your hair. I really fucked up here,

Dare. I'm sorry. I can only hope I can make shit up to you one day."

Nodding, I absorb the information he's just given me. Chase will always be my brother, and I'll keep hoping he grows up one day soon. Maybe a relationship with Shay can help him out with that.

I reach over and hold out my hand. When he takes it, I pull him into a hug.

"Call me when you get to Florida."

He nods. "Will do."

I rise from my seat and head inside to take a shower. I have to get ready to take my girl to dinner.

We pull up to the restaurant, just Berkeley and me in my truck. Everyone decided to drive separately and meet up around seven o'clock. Berkeley and I are right on time. She's forgone her seat belt and is snuggled up next to me on the wide bench seat. As I look down at her where she's tucked beneath my right arm, I just sigh with contentment. She's absolutely beautiful. She's dressed up; a dark purple dress hugs her curves. A thin black belt wraps around her waist, and I know that when she steps out of the car she'll be taller than usual in her wedged black heels.

She's taking my breath away, and that's no easy feat. I can't get enough of her, and now I just embrace that fact instead of wanting to slap myself for acting like a bitch.

Smiling at her, I brush the hair out of her eyes. I let my eyes rove, scanning down her body toward her long, lean legs, and all the way back up again. I appreciate the generous curve of her breasts at the top of her strapless neckline. "Huh."

Curiosity peaks her features. Her brow creases as she inspects herself doubtfully. "What?"

I shake my head, pretending to be lost in thought. "It's just that…I thought I saw you at your most beautiful the first night I kissed you, in this very truck. You were soaking wet from the rain, and you were laughing because of the sudden downpour. Your whole face was glowing."

I take her hand and toy with her fingers, bringing them up to my lips and kissing the back of her hand. "And then I thought you couldn't be more beautiful than the morning after the night you showed up at my house in a cab. That morning, you sat on top of me to shake me out of a nightmare. You were so fierce, and loving at the same time. I think that's when I fell in love with you."

Now she's smiling, her dimples denting her cheeks. She squeezes my hand. "But then I saw you at that garden party. That long black dress, tight in all the right places, but so fucking elegant at the same time. I almost lost my shit when I laid eyes on you. You should have been in a magazine, telling every other woman in the world why they should buy that same dress."

I push her gently toward her seat before sliding out of the car and striding around to open her door for her. Reaching up, I place my hands on her waist, pulling her down to stand directly in front of me. Sliding my hands along her body, I grab her hands and step back, eyeing her again. "But now, tonight? This dress is amazing, honey. *You* are amazing. You have this new job that you love, and you're standing on your own without the help of the Admiral. And…you're *mine*. That makes you the most stunning woman I've ever seen."

She sucks in a breath, then stands up on her toes so that she can meet my lips. Hers brush mine softly, and then she pulls back.

"I love you, Dare Conners."

I take her hand lightly and pull her along toward the restaurant entrance. We've decided to forgo See Food tonight, in honor of wanting to dress up a little and celebrate. I'm wearing dark jeans and a dark gray cotton blazer, black Chucks on my feet. Berkeley shoots me an approving glance as we enter the restaurant, smiling slightly.

Leaning up to whisper in my ear, her voice sends a shudder through to my core, and I suddenly can't fucking wait to get her home. "You're not so bad yourself, soldier. I'm role-playing in my head right now."

Holy…

Then she nods toward my shoes. "Those a nod for me?"

Smirking, I just take her hand.

"Hey, guys," says Greta's bright voice from beside the hostess stand.

We greet Mea and Greta, but Drake is still on his way, I'm guessing.

The hostess seats us in the back of the restaurant, at a table big enough for all of us to stretch out. The restaurant is located just off the small, oceanfront boardwalk. Beside our table, a wall of windows displays the brilliant expanse of ocean. The waves crash into the glittering sand, and the boardwalk and beach beyond are dotted with people walking, talking, or canoodling in front of the crashing waves. The sky is purple with the just-set sun, and with all of the places I've been, it's the most beautiful view I've ever laid eyes on.

Sitting here beside the tranquil bliss beyond the windows, I compare myself to each wave as it connects with the waiting shore. I've always been on my way to this town, to this time, with this girl. Along the way, I had no clue this is where I'd end up. But now that I'm here, I'm happy just letting the new me evaporate into Berkeley and a life with her, while the old me washes back into the ocean I came from.

Drake shows up just as the white-shirted waiter comes to gather our drink orders. He settles into a seat between Greta and me, directly across from Mea, while the waiter scurries off to grab our beers and mixed drinks.

"Greta," Mea begins. She points out one of the giant windows, her finger stretching toward a gigantic, gorgeously ornate beach house perched on stilts about two hundred yards away in the sand. "Didn't you say your dad has just landed a new contract with the new owner of that house over there?"

Drake whistles. "That place is massive. Must be a lucrative contract. Does he only do work in the private sector?"

Greta furrows her brow. "Actually, Dare, he wants to talk to you about maybe taking a position with his company. And no, Drake, I think that they often take on government Special Ops contracts as well. My father is ex-army."

I glance up at her in surprise. "Wow. No wonder we related to each other so well during…" I glance at Berkeley. "The situation."

She snuggles closer into my side. The waiter returns with our drinks, and Mea rolls her eyes. "Greta's family is loaded, thanks to Daddy dearest."

Greta shrugs. "I'm an adult now, Mea. I don't get to go running to Daddy for money anymore."

Mea just shakes her head, her dark curls bouncing with the movement, as if she doesn't believe a word of it.

Leaning to the side, I bend so that I can lean into Berkeley. Her rosy scent captures my complete attention, and I nuzzle my nose into the luscious curve of her neck.

Damn, she smells delicious. How much longer before I can sweep her out of here and back to my house or her apartment? I scowl into her skin, knowing I at least have to make it through dinner.

Berkeley giggles, and the sound echoes through my body, bringing *all* of me to attention. She clears her throat to cover her giggle, and then leans away from me. At the same time, her hand reaches over and grips my thigh. Her fingers trail upward, and I choke on my beer.

Everyone at the table is busy relaying their orders to the waiter. When the man's eyes stop on me, Berkeley speaks up. "He'll probably want one of everything."

I smirk at her, remembering, and then give the waiter my real order.

Leaning over to her, I whisper into her ear, "Eat fast, baby. I've been waiting to get you home since I saw you in that dress."

She shares my smile, and I know that once we finally do make it home, that dress won't stay on her for very long.

Epilogue

Dare

Moving to Lone Sands has changed my life a million times over.

First change: Berkeley fucking Holtz. That girl came in like a freaking missile, blowing shit up and taking names. I really want her to take *my* name, but I have to ask her first. And that day will come. Soon.

Then, my brother moved to town. He and Shay are one blissfully happy couple. So blissfully happy in fact, that in the four months they've lived here, they've created another life. Shay just found out she's pregnant, and I'm going to be an uncle. I've never seen Chase this happy. And seeing him happy makes me happy.

Lastly, I had a meeting with Greta's dad, Jacob. Who offered me a full-time job as a security specialist with his firm. Which I accepted.

It's this brand-new job that the alarm on my phone is currently waking me up for.

"Mmmm," murmurs Berkeley as she wraps the leg slung over the top of me even tighter. Not the greatest idea, since the morning hard-on is raging, and painfully aware of her closeness.

No nightmare. They're pretty much gone these days. I give all the credit to the evil vixen siren with the heavenly body currently wrapped tightly around mine.

"Time to get ready for work, baby," I whisper in her ear.

She moans. My Berkeley is still definitely not a morning person. I stare at her, her hair a glorious, wild mess of curls all around her head as she snuggles closer to me. Her mouth is still slightly parted in her half-sleep, and her lashes are long enough to touch her cheeks.

Fucking gorgeous.

"*You* have to get ready to work," she murmurs sleepily. "I still have half an hour to sleep."

I innocently run my hand from where it's resting against her plump, round ass, along her thigh until it's resting on the underside of her knee. Her leg, where it's slung over my middle, tenses.

She's not a morning person, but it doesn't stop me from trying to turn her into one.

She exhales as my fingers begin tracing tiny circles on her skin. My other hand joins the party, edging from her tangled curls, down the curve of her neck, over her delicate shoulder. I drop down from where her arm hugs my middle, and suddenly I cup her breast fully in my hand.

Shit. I just turned myself on, probably more than I did her. Groaning, I carry the weight of her in my hand, kneading the soft, supple skin. My fingers act of their own accord, circling the tip of her before grasping her taut nipple between two fingers and giving it a tight pinch.

Her eyes fly open, and she immediately grinds against me. Her quiet, answering moan tells me everything I need to know.

"Good morning," I whisper, pulling her on top of me.

"I hate mornings." Her voice is husky and so damn sexy as she leans forward to tease my ear with her tongue. Fuck me, she knows how one lick in that spot drives me utterly wild.

"But I love you," I point out sweetly as I rock my hips into her. There's no fabric hindering our pleasure; she catches her breath as all my hardness melts into all her softness.

She reaches her hand down, amber eyes blazing, and swiftly guides the length of me to her entrance. She's ready for me, so I'm calling her bluff on her hatred of mornings, after all. The heat of her envelops me, and my lips part in anticipation. I want this. I want it before breakfast, and I want it on my lunch break. And then I want it twice when I come home from work.

All Berkeley, all the time.

She raises her hips up, and then slams down on top of me. I roar, and she smiles seductively. "Prove it."

Oh, I'll prove it. I plan on spending the rest of my life proving to her how much I love her. And one day soon, I'll put a ring on her finger that will prove it to the rest of the world.

When I arrived in Lone Sands last spring, the sign told me that my lonely heart was welcome here. Now my heart is no longer lonely, but I still feel more welcome than I've felt in a very, very long time. Maybe ever.

I don't know if Berkeley's parents have completely accepted us as a couple. They had plans for her that changed forever when she made the decision to be with me and not with Grisham. But I hope that one day, they can embrace it. Because I will do whatever it takes to make their daughter happy.

And one day, Berkeley is going to want her parents at our wedding.

Turn the page for the next book in the series,

Saved by the SEAL!

Grisham

The cool blue Atlantic sprays my face as I sit in the sand. My eyes are fixated on the breaking waves. My good buddies—my brothers—are taking advantage of the larger-than-normal swells while they cut in and out of the waves on their boards. I lay back on my elbows and watch…the same way I've been watching for the past month and a half—the time it took for me to muster up the courage and the strength to get back to the beach.

I glance at the board lying beside me. If I can do it, today will be my first time back in the ocean. It's *supposed* to be my first day back. I just haven't been able to get off my ass and into the water just yet.

It's early; the sun just broke over the horizon about half an hour ago and the morning is flawless. I take a deep breath and close my eyes, letting the morning's rays touch my face.

I'm utterly relaxed on the beach, but I'm also at home when I'm working; when I'm strategizing, planning, or embarking on a mission with my team. Working out in the mission field is about as far from the dream my father laid out for me as possible, and this is one of the reasons I love it so damn much. He pulled all the strings he could so that, as an officer graduating from Navy a couple of years ago I'd be placed behind a desk and rise quickly through the ranks without ever touching a battlefield.

He didn't anticipate the fact that I had my own plans for my life, my own goals and ambitions. I wasn't going to be just a douche in a uniform telling other guys what to do, never having lived it myself. If I was going to order other men around, it was going to be while I was risking my life right there beside them.

And my father, Admiral Michael Abbot, would just have to deal with it.

Lawson Snyder disturbs the sand beside me as he dives into place and sprawls out. He places his hands behind his head and closes his eyes. His wet suit is hanging out down around his waist, and his tattoo-covered torso is on display.

"Dude," I slap him on the chest. "That was awesome out there. You've been practicing."

He chuckles. "Thanks, man. That's high praise coming from a beachcomber like you. Us corn-fed Nebraskan boys don't grow up riding the waves. Took me a while to learn."

True. But now that Lawson has found surfing, he'll never quit. There's something about getting lost in the sea and letting the waves guide you back to shore that's addictive.

We sit quietly while Lawson catches his breath, and before long our other surfing buddy and team member, Ben McBride, joins us. We don't call him Ben, though.

"Get your ass up, Abbot!" yells Ben as he runs out of the waves. "You said today was the day!"

I watch him approach. "Did I say that, Cowboy? I meant today was the day I'm keeping my ass planted in the sand. Tomorrow's the day I get back on the board."

"Bullshit!" Ben runs at me, feinting like he's going to tackle me into the sand. I dodge left, laughing as he ends up on his face.

"Still too fast for your ass," I gloat. Grinning at Lawson, we high-five.

"Too slow, Cowboy." Lawson sounds ashamed of Ben as he shakes his head. "Even missing a limb, Abbot's got you beat every single time."

"That's why he's team leader. I don't give a shit. Can we go grab some waffles now if you ain't surfing today?"

I nod, dusting off my hands. "I'll be there in a minute."

They grab their boards and take off toward the steps that lead to the parking lot. I have my own car; I'll meet them at the Waffle King in a few minutes. They'll probably be scarfing down their piles of food by then. I just need another minute with the ocean.

Just months ago, I was still stuck in a place with no ocean. I was in that faraway desert for four months before I was flown to a naval hospital in Germany, only two weeks shy of my assigned homecoming. I let my mind temporarily drift back to that last fateful day in Syria. The things I remember the most vividly are the smells.

The smell of gasoline. The smell of burning rubber and plastic. The smell of dry, desert air as the darkness exploded with orange light. The smell of blood. Your own blood smells really fucking distinct. It's a scent you can never erase from your memory.

Yeah, the smells are still with me every single day.

I'm torn from my thoughts when I hear the scream. It was short and staccato, possibly cut off by the waves.

I sit up straight, my eyes searching the ocean for the source of the scream. Without even realizing it's happening, adrenaline is surging through my body in a way I haven't felt in months. My muscles are taut, alert. My senses are kicking into overdrive as my eyes search the blue-green sea and my ears strain for foreign sounds.

This is a private spot on the beach, usually only occupied by surfers. At seven-fifteen on a Wednesday morning, it's nearly deserted. I scan the sand and notice there's a beach bag and towel about twenty feet to my left and behind me. I'm not sure when that person got into the water, maybe when my eyes were closed. Maybe when I was thinking about the desert.

When I turn my eyes back toward the ocean, I see it. There's an orange and pink surfboard drifting in the waves, minus its rider. I'm up from the sand in seconds, raising a hand to my eyes to scan the water for the missing surfer. I don't need to search the small stretch of beach behind me to see there's no lifeguard stand here. There's a sign on the old, twisty steps leading down to the shore that this is a private stretch and there's no lifeguard on duty.

I step forward, and the foamy sea rolls over my foot. I stare down at it. It's been so long since I've felt it; I'm having a weird reaction. My blood is pumping in my ears and I can feel a thin sheen of sweat breaking out all over my skin that has nothing to do with the sun and the heat.

Then, out past the breaking point, a small figure surfaces, floating on top of the rising and falling swells. I watch for movement and don't see any.

I don't think. I just react.

Taking two running steps, I rush into the waves and dive headfirst into the ocean. I use my arms to pull my body through the rolling waves, kicking out hard behind me. I'm a skilled swimmer; it's kind of mandatory in my job description, but I've been a good swimmer for my entire life. Even though this is my first time in the ocean since the accident, it doesn't take long at all for me to reach the girl floating unconscious in the water. Her raven-colored hair floats around her. Without a second look I flip her on her back, pulling her under one of my arms. Then I use the other to cut through the salt water once more, this time with the beach set in my sights.

I'm winded when I reach the sand, but I stumble up onto the beach carrying the still girl in my arms. I fall to my knees, laying her gently on the sand. Then, still running on autopilot, I brush her hair from her face so that I can assess her situation.

As soon as her face is clear of her long, dark mane, I suck in a breath as recognition slams into me like a truck.

"Holy shit," I murmur. "Greta? Come on, girl, you gotta wake up for me."

She doesn't move.

Breathe for her. Her gorgeous face is turning blue. I use my fingers to tilt her chin back and then I lean in and breathe life into her mouth twice.

Chest compressions. My hands are centered on her chest and I watch her face carefully as I press down repeatedly, counting aloud each time I pump. After thirty compressions, I return to her mouth, pinching her nose closed and breathing in twice.

Repeat. I repeat the process, pushing all fear out of my head. "Come on, Greta! Berkeley will kill me if I let you die. Wake up, dammit!"

Suddenly, she splutters, taking a huge, gasping breath and ocean water pours out of her mouth. I quickly turn her on her side and she retches, coughing again and again. When she's finished, I gently help her sit up on the sand, and I brush her hair out of her face as her crystal blue eyes finally focus on me.

"There you are," I breathe. "Hey, beautiful. You're okay. You're okay."

I repeat the phrase again and again, rubbing her back with one hand while she gains her bearings. She blinks rapidly a few times, and then croaks out in a hoarse voice.

"Grisham? Grisham Abbot?"

I smile, grateful to hear my name falling from her mouth right now. "It's me. Been awhile, huh?"

She nods, coughing again. She raises a hand to her head and winces. That's when I see the blood, nearly hidden in her hair at the top of her forehead.

"Damn. That's a nasty cut. That probably happened when you fell off your board. Let me take you to the hospital, okay?"

She shakes her head. "I hate hospitals. I was just there with my little sister a few days ago. I'll go to urgent care."

I shake my head. "Not by yourself. I'll take you."

She looks reluctant, but nods her head. "Okay."

I stand, holding out my hand to her. "Do you think you can stand and walk? If not, I'll carry you."

She allows me to help her up. She's a little unsteady on her feet, but she seems like she'll be able to make it up the steps and to my four-door Jeep Wrangler.

"Wait!" she cries, turning toward the ocean. "My board!"

"Shhh, I got it," I reply, pointing to where it's laying on the beach. She nods in relief.

"Let me get you to the car, and then I'll come back for our boards. Okay?"

I've almost forgotten about it. It usually doesn't take people this long, but I'm going to give Greta credit because she was unconscious for part of the time we've been together today. Her eyes stray down to my leg, following the metal trail to my prosthetic foot.

"Oh, Grisham," she whispers. Her eyes fill with tears.

"Hush," I admonish her. "I'm used to it by now. Hey, I'm good as new, Greta. I got out there to pull you in, didn't I?"

She nods and rewards me with a small smile. My heart stutters, remembering what it was like when I really saw that smile for the first time.

I met Greta a year ago when she became my best friend's roommate. The best friend I'd secretly been in love with since we were kids. When Berkeley moved in with Greta I didn't pay her much attention. But after Berkeley got together with her boyfriend Dare, my heart took a beating. There was one morning when I was at their apartment, giving Dare the business, when Greta walked into the room wearing really tiny pajamas.

Really. Fucking. Tiny.

I couldn't help but follow the trail of her long legs, past her little shorts, pausing at the small patch of skin exposed on her stomach. Then, when I made eye contact and saw those baby blues, clear as the fucking sky above and filled with desire, I almost lost my mind.

I left, because my head wasn't in a place to deal with feelings for another girl.

But right now, connecting with her again like this…something inside of me is pulling me toward her like a magnet. I can get lost in eyes as big and as blue as hers.

I think I might even want to.

"I'm sorry, Grisham," she says sincerely as she blinks slowly. I'm distracted as she pulls her soft, plump bottom lip into her mouth and bites down. I'm mesmerized as the skin around her teeth turns pale.

"What?"

"I said I'm sorry? About the explosion that caused you to lose part of your leg. I heard about it…" She trails off, her eyes closing briefly as if she's in pain.

I reach out and grab her chin, causing her eyes to fly open and lock with mine once more. A stirring in my shorts grabs my attention, but I push my physical reaction to this girl out of my head so I can finish this conversation. Her eyes stay locked on mine, instead of straying back down to my foot.

This surprises the shit out of me, because usually I can't keep anyone's attention for more than a few seconds before they're looking at it again.

"I can do everything I did before," I tell her softly. "Except lead my boys out into the damn desert again, that is. My career focus has shifted a bit, that's all. But I'm okay, Greta. Thanks for worrying about me."

She nods, giving me a real smile for the first time.

Good Lord.

I'm floored. Two rows of perfect white teeth, perfect full lips forming a smile that's just slightly crooked. She's like seeing the sun again after months in the dark. Holy shit. I'm toast. I'm not ready for this right now. I'm in no better state of mind than I was a year ago. In some ways, I'm worse. So I'm going to chalk whatever I'm feeling right now up to residual attraction from a year ago and from the high I get from saving someone's life.

"Let's get you to the car." I take her elbow and steer her toward the steps.

It's slow going, but we make it to the little parking lot. Her forehead wrinkles in confusion as we approach my Jeep.

"Where's your little sports car? The Audi?"

"Kind of hard to haul my board and my bikes around on that thing. I like to do shit outside…a lot. My Jeep is better for that type of stuff."

And my father bought me that Audi. After I graduated from school, I decided there was no way I was going to let him keep paying my way.

But I kept that thought to myself.

She pulls her pink and black wet suit off her shoulders, and my eyes move to that spot like I've spotted a shiny object. She wiggles, shimmying out of the suit revealing a tiny black bikini underneath. Coupled with miles and fucking miles of milky skin, she's an incredible sight. I let my gaze sweep up and down her frame just once before finding her face again. She didn't seem to notice my gawking, squeezing out her suit and placing it on the floor in the back of the Jeep.

She nibbles her lip again, and I groan inwardly.

"My towel is in my bag, down there." She points toward the beach.

"I'll get it when I get your board. Anything else, ma'am?"

I exaggerate my southern accent on the last line, making her giggle.

"Nope, I think that's it, *sir*." She picks up my game, exaggerating hers and I feel warmth spread through my body starting in the very center of me.

"Funny girl."

After I help her into the Jeep—ignoring her protests about her being wet—and turn on the engine so that the air conditioning is blasting, I turn and jog back down to the beach. I grab my surfboard and hers under one arm and load her bag onto the other.

Even though I'm only taking her to the doctor, and it's been months since I've seen her, I can't stop the feeling of giddy anticipation overwhelming me at the thought of seeing her sitting there in my car.

After Berkeley, I changed a lot about my life. I stopped answering to my asshole father. I gave my mother an ultimatum. I changed my job trajectory in the navy, entering the SEALs training program against my father's wishes. I sold the Audi and bought a Jeep. I also bought a small house in Lone Sands; close to the beach I'd always loved so much instead of living on base.

The one thing I hadn't changed was my relationship status. I was definitely in the *single* category. My parents and I had basically planned my life around their goal for me to marry Berkeley one day. And I'd stupidly bought into it; because she and I were so close there wasn't anyone else I could imagine spending my life with. Any girl I dated before then was just a distraction.

And now any girl I dated was the same thing. A distraction. A way to pass the time. I chose girls who knew the score, girls who typically dated guys in the navy because they weren't going to be around for long. Nothing serious, no strings attached.

But as I climb into my Jeep and glance over at Greta sitting there with a genuine, sweet-and-sexy smile on her face, with that body that could cause men to jump off of bridges, something inside me stirs and stretches. Something that had been dormant for a long time. Something that tells me Greta Owen isn't going to be like other girls. I'm not going to be able to love her body one night and then walk away the next day.

Without even saying a word, she demands to be more than that.

I look down at my left leg. I'm not even a whole man anymore. I'd been through some shit in the last year that had changed me fundamentally, both inside and out. There's no way I can be everything to someone else.

I know it in my gut.

I'm going to drive Greta to the doctor and make sure she's okay. And then I'm going to walk away.

Because at this point in my life, that's the best possible thing I can do for a woman like this.

Just walk away.

About the Author

Diana Gardin is a wife of one and a mom of two. Writing is her second full-time job to that, and she loves it! Diana writes contemporary romance in the Young Adult and New Adult categories. She's also a former elementary school teacher. She loves steak, sugar cookies, and Coke and hates working out.

   Learn more at:

DianaGardin.com

Twitter: @ DianalynnGardin

Facebook.com/AuthorDianaGardin